PAM'S PARADISE RANCH

PAM'S
PARADISE RANCH

A Story of Hawaii

By ARMINE VON TEMPSKI

Illustrated by PAUL BROWN

OX BOW PRESS
WOODBRIDGE, CONNECTICUT

Cover painting by Cecelia Rodriguez

1993 reprint by
Ox Bow Press
P.O. Box 4045
Woodbridge, CT 06525

Library of Congress Cataloging-in-Publication Data
Von Tempski, Armine, 1892–1943.
Pam's Paradise Ranch : a story of Hawaii / by Armine Von Tempski ;
illustrated by Paul Brown.
p.   cm.
Summary: Pam experiences life on a huge cattle ranch in the
Hawaiian islands.
ISBN 0-918024-96-X (pbk. : alk. paper)
[1. Hawaii—Fiction.   2. Ranch life—Fiction.]   I. Brown, Paul,
1893–1958, ill.   II. Title.
PZ7.V9385Pam   1992
[Fic]—dc20   92-24538

The paper used in this book meets the guidelines for permanence
and durability of the Committee on Production Guidelines for
Book Longevity of the Council on Library Resources.

Printed in the United States of America

To
"Lamie" Lucas, and the *paniolos*
of
Puuwaawaa
and to
my god-child,
Pamela Armine Derby

CONTENTS

CHAPTER I

FROM A FAR-OFF LAND

PAMELA GARLAND SOOTHED HER RESTLESS HORSE, THEN watched the speck of the approaching mail truck lurching along the highway that twisted and wound around the island. Below the road, the huge mass of Hawaii sloped with leisurely magnificence to the sea—a sea bluer than the bluest cornflower that ever grew. Inland, three mighty mountains lifted solemn domes to the sky. Their slopes were covered with green pastures and forests and marred here and there by the long, dark stains of black lava flows that had poured down their sides during past ages. Sunlight rained its gold on the earth, which sent up rich, spicy smells, and the light wind, flowing out of the east, whispered about stirring things.

Pamela's horse stamped and shook his head impatiently. Reaching down, she stroked his glossy, arching neck with her small tanned hand, then unbuckled the flat leather bag fastened to the pommel of her saddle. The black letters painted upon it, KILOHANA RANCH, had been shiny and new the first time she had been allowed to take it down to the highway. That had been almost five years ago, on her sixth birthday. Now the letters had faded to dull brown, but still the old sense of importance when she rode home with the mail never dimmed.

You never knew what might be inside the bag. Mostly it was local correspondence, and newspapers from Honolulu and the other outlying islands. Then again there might be letters from Boston, where Aunt Dode and Cousin Emily Price lived. Two or three times a year she and Emily wrote to each other. She told Emily exciting ranch news—what new colts, calves and puppies had been born; about Ah Sam, the Chinese cook; about the Japanese yardboys and Hawaiian cowboys; or what races the ranch thoroughbreds had won on the Fourth of July. Emily wrote about what marks she had made at school, of concerts, and of occasional shopping expeditions with Aunt Dode.

Pam was glad she lived on a ranch in Hawaii and not in Boston. . . .

The truck was getting closer. Dust smoked out behind it. Pili, the Hawaiian mailman, always drove furiously, trying to make up the time he had lost chatting with friends on the way. Pam waited eagerly. Her bronze bobbed curls looked so alive that even when the air was motionless it seemed as though invisible winds were always streaming through them. Thick, short lashes shaded her rosy cheeks and her glowing skin had the bloom of a ripe apricot. She looked as if she had been born at high noon in a golden summer-time and had never known what it was to be poor, sad, lonely or ill.

As the truck came roaring over the rise she waved gaily to Pili, and the mailman brandished his strong brown arm in return, then came to a screeching stop. Pam's horse gave a buck and kicked up his heels, adding to the fun.

"*Aloha*, Pam, you wait a long time?" Pili asked, pawing through tied-up packages of letters and papers stacked on the seat beside him.

"Only an hour today!" she said, laughing. "Is there lots of mail for us?"

Pili nodded and his merry brown eyes grew secret and eager. "And I got some other-kind for you," he announced.

"What have you brought me?" Pam asked excitedly.

"Wait one minute and I show you."

Getting out of the truck, he walked to the rear-end and, after fishing among miscellaneous packages and bundles, he drew out a sack with a squirming object inside it. "Somebody throw away. I find on the road," he said, holding the bag out to Pam.

Spilling off her horse, she dropped the reins on the ground and rushed over. "What is it, Pili?" she cried. He grinned, then drew out a half-grown yellow kitten with scared eyes. Pam pounced upon it and held it to her face, making soft, loving noises until it stopped struggling.

"Poor little kitty," she murmured. "Hold it, Pili, while I mount."

The snorty young horse backed away, but she hoisted herself quickly into the saddle and settled herself. Pili handed her the mail bag, which she strapped into place. "Now give me the kitty," she directed.

After some trouble, Pili managed to get near enough and Pam snatched the cat from him. "Good-bye, Pili, *mahalo nui loa*—thanks a lot! I'll see you tomorrow."

"Sure—and I no be late next time!" he promised stoutly.

Pam's white teeth flashed into a quick smile, because she knew he would be. The truck went roaring off to other distant ranches, hidden behind the long slopes of the island, and clutching the kitten in the crook of her arm, Pam turned her horse toward the nearest of the three big mountains.

Ragged *lehua* trees, growing on crumbling lava flows flanking the road, fluttered leaves like golden-green pennies in the wind. Ahead, a great green hill, with fluted sides like a monster plum pudding, stood out boldly above the lava-stained land. To the right, Hualalai tossed its violent, cindery summit into the cloudless sky, and stretching peacefully away in front were pastures dotted with feeding cattle and horses.

Pam galloped along happily, watching her horse's mane tossing in the wind, but as the road began climbing the lower slopes of the green hill she pulled her horse down to a walk. Drooping pepper trees and dark cherimoyas cast a pleasant green gloom over the road, flanked by moss-grown stone walls. Around the bend of the road, masses of buildings and corrals, set back in gracious gardens, dotted the steep side of the hill.

Pam glanced at the kitten in her arm. "Like your first ride, kitty?" she asked, as her horse walked swiftly forward. The kitten yawned and winked one eye and Pam's laughter spun into the air like the whirr of a bird's wings. She glanced at her wristwatch. It was noon. Her mother would be in the Office, waiting for the mail. As she turned into the garden she called out to two Japanese boys raking up the lawns and they called out to her in return.

"Look!" she cried, holding up the kitten. "Pili gave it to me."

The older of the two men began chuckling. "What-for you like one more cat?" he asked. "Already I tink you got more than two dozen."

Pam stopped her horse. "Pili found it in the lava flows. If he had left it there, it would have died," she retorted indignantly. The yardboys grinned and resumed their work and she started on for the Office, set back among tall trees.

Dismounting, she fastened her horse to the hitching rail, took off the mail bag and ascended the porch of the Office, with the kitten still clutched in the crook of her arm. At the sound of Pam's footsteps, a fat old cream-colored dog woke from his doze and began thumping the floor with a happy tail.

"Hello, Poi," she said fondly, patting his head. The kitten began scratching and spitting. "Poi won't hurt you," she said, holding the little creature down for the old dog to smell. The kitten flattened its ears and kept on spitting. "Silly," Pam scolded. "You'll find out in time that Poi likes cats!"

Poi had been Pam's first dog and she had loved him through all his changes from a roly-poly pup, always in mischief, to an old gentleman, with grizzled muzzle and ears. He still followed her when she rode about the nearer pastures, but never when she set off for the day, and she wondered how he could tell which she intended to do. "You're just an old dog-magician, now that you're full of years and wisdom!" she said, giving his head a parting pat as she started for the door leading into the lofty "Office"!

Pam loved the Office. It wasn't just a place where bookkeeping was done—it was the cornerstone of the 200,000 acre ranch which her widowed mother managed as ably as a man. Each morning, before daylight, the forty-odd men working on the place collected under the big roof to take orders from Mrs. Garland. At sunset they returned to get supplies, for the far end of the room was a sort of careless store. Long shelves with canned goods lined the wall behind the counter. Sacks of flour, coffee, and horse feed were stacked on the floor. Another wall was filled with medicines for men and animals, and from the third the ranch branding irons hung in neat rows.

On Saturdays, when the men were paid off, the room echoed with jingling spurs and laughter. Japanese, Hawaiians, and Chinese joked together, while Pam's mother counted out stacks of shining dollars and put them into outstretched brown and yellow hands.

Pam was sure that her mother was the most wonderful person on earth. Like most Island-born Americans, she had been given a Hawaiian name, *Kulani*, which meant, roughly translated, From Heaven. She was all that it signified; kind, beautiful, courageous, and gay. She kept the books, arranged meat contracts with Honolulu markets, knew every animal in the herd of five thousand registered Herefords, Holsteins and Golden Guernsey cattle. She supervised the training of racehorses and polo-ponies, roped wild bulls. . . . When people were in trouble, they rushed to her for advice and assistance; when nice things happened they hurried to her first to tell their glad news. If anyone was sick, no matter how busy she was, Kulani always had time to go and help them, and comfort them. . . .

At the sound of Pam's footfall her mother looked around from the open ledger on the desk before her. Her brown eyes were kind and a little mischievous, and her dark hair, parted in the middle and drawn into a knot on her neck, suggested a bird's folded wings framing the beauty of her face.

"Late as usual, Pam dear—"

"I know, Mother." Pam swung the mail bag at her, which from long practice she caught deftly. "But Pili brought me this little cat!"

"Another pet. Oh, Pam!"

"But Mother—" Pam told its history.

"Of course it couldn't be left to starve," Kulani agreed

quickly. "Let's see it."

Pam handed the kitten to her.

"Poor little thing, its ribs are showing. Open a can of milk and we'll feed it. It can be the Office cat and keep down the mice."

"Oh, Mother, I love you!" Pam cried, flinging her arms about her and hugging her.

While Pam fetched the canned milk and opened it, Kulani spilled the contents of the mail bag on her desk and began going through the letters and papers. She always read business letters first, in case they must be answered immediately and taken back to the highway before Pili's truck passed at sunset, homeward bound. A husky young Hawaiian came in and went to the medicine shelves. After going through the bottles and cartons, he turned around and looked at Pam. "I no can find the creolin!" he said accusingly. "I tink you no put back, Pam, after you wash the cut in the cow's leg yesterday."

"Of course I put it back," Pam retorted indignantly. "It's behind the picric acid."

Nuhi gave a grunt, picked up the bottle and went out. Pam seated herself on a grain bag, watching the kitten lap milk. After Kulani had scanned the business letters, she picked up a fat envelope and ripped it open. When she finished reading the closely-written pages, she glanced over her shoulder.

"I've a surprise for you, dear," she announced.

"What is it?" Pam crossed the room and perched herself on the arm of her mother's swivel chair.

"Your Aunt Dode and Cousin Emily will be here tomorrow

to stay with us for a year."

"W-h-a-t!" Pam gasped. Pam knew some white children, for occasionally she and her mother visited relatives living in distant sections of the island, but she was always glad to get back to the ranch and be with the people she loved and felt close to—Hawaiians, Japanese, and Chinese.

Kulani's eyes grew thoughtful. "As you know, dear, Aunt Dode has been Emily's guardian ever since her parents were killed in an automobile accident when she was two. Things have been hard for them. They're terribly poor. For the past year Emily has had sinus trouble. Aunt Dode was afraid that the trip might be too hard on her but the Doctor said a change would be beneficial—"

Pam swung her booted leg back and forth. It was odd. . . . Until this moment Emily had just been a name on paper. Tomorrow she would be a little girl of about her own age.

"Aren't you looking forward to the thought of having a white girl to chum with?" Kulani asked, after a moment.

"I'm not sure," Pam confessed honestly. "If she's a good rider and swimmer maybe we'll—"

"I doubt if Emily can do either," Kulani interrupted. "People living in cities, who aren't rich, don't have opportunities to swim and ride."

Pam sighed gustily. "Then she'll be no fun and probably she'll be a sissy and scared of cattle," she added, tossing her bronze curls contemptuously.

Kulani knew that her daughter had a quick, warm heart and tried a new tack. "Try dear," she suggested gently, "to imagine living in a small house with no servants to wait on you and laugh with you, with no horses to ride or puppies to play with, with no mother to love you and only an aunt to care for you. Wouldn't you like to come and stay in a place like Kilohana?"

"Oh, Mother, yes!" Pam said with a rush. "Poor Emily. I'll lend her Forty Dollars to learn to ride on. He's safe and slow. And I'll shine up one of my old saddles for her to use. What room will she have?"

"We'll put her and Aunt Dode in the blue guest-room with twin beds until Emily is well. Later, maybe, if you want it, she can move into the room next to yours."

"Can I sort of fix up the one they're going to use, so Emily'll know we're glad she's coming to stay with us?" Pam asked.

"Of course, dear, do anything you want to it. There's the lunch gong. After we've eaten, I have to go and select steers to ship to Honolulu the day after tomorrow. Tatsu can help you—"

Pam placed her hands on her mother's arms. "Kulani From Heaven," she said, looking into her mother's dark eyes. "You're such fun! I'll make Emily's room so beautiful it'll knock your eyes out!"

Kulani rose, tousled her daughter's bright hair and started for the house.

Pam could hardly wait until sunset, when her mother came in, to show her what she and her old nurse Tatsu had done. When she heard hoofs coming up the tree-shaded road, she dashed out of doors. "Oh, Mother, Tatsu and I have worked all afternoon!" she said excitedly. "Come and see how pretty everything looks."

Kulani dismounted, spoke to the man who took her horse, then started with Pam for the big house which sprawled contentedly among trees and flowers which were settling themselves to sleep. Long rays of bronze sunlight slanted through the garden and evening was creeping across the sea, changing its fierce blue to a smoky purple.

Pam scurried importantly ahead, skipped down the wide, cool hall and seizing the handle of a closed door, flung it open dramatically. Kulani stood in silence on the threshold, then remarked with a rich, low laugh, "It does knock my eye out!"

Pam glowed. A gray-haired kind-faced Japanese woman in a clean blue and white cotton kimono was standing in the middle of the room, critically surveying the arrangement of some flowers in a tall vase in one corner. Originally, the room was simple and restful, with twin beds and dressers, draped in pale blue, and sufficient furniture to make it cozy and spacious in one. Now a strange assortment of objects decorated one half of it, while the other remained as it had been.

Flanking the mirror on one dresser were two bouquets of flowers, arranged with all the perfect artistry of old Japan. Between them, half obscuring the mirror, was a large silver-framed photograph of a gray thoroughbred, loaded with garlands. The dark mark on its back of a saddle just removed, and a jockey holding its head and clutching a silver trophy under one arm, showed that it had just won a big race. In front of the picture was a hammered copper bowl, heaped with ruddy mangoes.

On one side of the dresser three nails had been driven into the wall. From one hung a neatly coiled lasso, the next had a bridle, and the third a small pair of spurs. "Doesn't it look homey?" Pam demanded.

Kulani struggled to keep from laughing. "It's sweet of you to lend Emily your old gear. I know how precious it is to you," she said.

"And here's my little chair." Pam seated herself in a low scarlet rocker. "And I borrowed this red lacquer table from the nest in the living room. It's almost the same color. The little tea-set's just for fun, but it looks cozy. And look, I hung this bull's tail-curl on the lamp-pull, so she'll see it the first thing when she comes in." Her fingers caressed a harsh brown swirl of hair tied to the chain of the shaded light suspended above the dresser.

Kulani fought to control her laughter, then her eyes grew soft and misty. "Is that the first curl old Kane gave you?" she asked.

Pam nodded. "I'm just lending it to Emily," she explained hurriedly. "I wouldn't give it away for anything. I just want Emily to know—"

"Honey, Emily won't have the wildest notion what it is, or what it means to you—"

Pam's face fell. "Well, anyway I do—"

"That's what counts, Pam. To give or lend something precious is being really unselfish. You know that in ancient Hawaii, hospitality was not the choice of an individual, but a sacred obligation of mankind. No matter how humble a person who stopped at a house might be, the owner was expected to give him the finest mat to sleep on and the fattest pig to eat. If anyone was discourteous or niggardly, he was taken out and publicly disgraced, and if he were rash enough to repeat his offense, he might even be taken out and killed by order of the Chief!"

"Mother!" Pam exclaimed in horrified tones.

"It does sound rather dreadful. But the result is that through generations of two-handed giving the Hawaiians have become the most hospitable and generous people on earth. Come, let's sit down on this couch for a few minutes before we dress for dinner and soak in all the splendor."

Pam sighed happily. Her mother always seemed to know exactly what other people wanted to do! They sank into the cushioned seat and gazed across at the half of the room which had been decorated. Pam leaned her head against the flowered cretonne, while she played idly with her mother's capable hand. Through open windows, with tinkling glass wind-bells singing in them, came familiar evening sounds: horses being turned out to pasture, men calling to each other or singing snatches of stirring *hulas*, and behind everything the whisper of the distant sea, murmuring its eternal secrets to the islands.

Usually Pam was out helping the men to wind up the day's work, but tonight she wanted to be still and think of a little girl who was coming across the sea to stay with her for a year.

"The room looks lovely," Kulani remarked after a silence. "It makes me happy to know that my little daughter is a true Islander at heart. I hope you and Emily—"

"Have you any pictures of her, Mother?" Pam broke in. "I'm bursting all of a sudden to know what she's like."

"Dode sent a snap of her a year or so ago. I thought I'd showed it to you—"

"Probably you did, but—"

"I know, with so many ranch things always filling your mind, it didn't register. I think the snap's in one of my dresser drawers."

They went out of the room and Pam carefully closed the door after her, as if she were protecting something precious. When the picture was finally located among some old letters, Pam studied it in silence. She saw a plain little face with wistful eyes which seemed to be searching for something. Emily's mouth was a straight, prim line but her nose and chin were elfish. Two funny, stiff braids, tied with tiny ribbons, hung on her shoulders.

"She doesn't look as if she'd be much fun," Pam announced flatly.

"Probably she's starved for fun," Kulani said. "Dode isn't exactly what you'd call a merry person." Her lashes quivered mischievously.

"What are you thinking about that makes you want to laugh?" Pam asked.

"When your father came from Boston to marry me, Dode came with him. I'll never forget the funny squeak of horror she gave when I met them at the steamer and put a *lei* around your father's neck. When I started to give her one—"

"I bet she ducked!" Pam began to chuckle.

"She did, but your father grabbed her arm and said, 'Wear it, Dode, it makes you feel as if you owned the whole world!' "

"I wish I remembered Father," Pam said.

"I wish you did, too, dear, but you were only three when he died." Kulani broke off to gaze back down through the winding corridors of memory. "I had four happy years with him, so I can never feel poor, Pam, and besides, he left me you!"

"We have more fun than most girls and their mothers, don't we, Kulani From Heaven?" Pam asked.

"Decidedly so! You're my right hand on the ranch, as well. When you're eighteen I'll sit back and you can run Kilohana for me."

"I almost could now, Mother, except the books."

"I'm convinced you'd fill my boots ably in a pinch. Well, it's time we cleaned up."

Pam loved the hour before dinner. Her room and her mother's adjoined and while they bathed and got into silk kimonos, or dressed—depending on whether they were alone or had company—they kept up a running fire of conversation, popping into each other's rooms, laughing and joking. It made Pam proud because Kulani talked to her and treated her as if she were a grown-up. They discussed ranch work, thrashed out problems together, or gloated when things went well. . . .

While she got out of her riding togs, Pam listened to the rush of hot water going into her mother's tub and sniffed the fragrance of bath crystals. Tatsu came in, pulled on the lights and turned down the big four-poster bed while Pam showered. When she came back the Japanese woman held out a blue silk kimono, embroidered with golden dragons. Pam slid into the beautiful garment and Tatsu arranged the wide brocaded *obi* about Pam's taut little waist, then brushed and arranged her bronze hair.

"*Arrigato*, Tatsu," Pam said when the last shining curl was in place.

"No need say thank-you." The woman laughed. "I, too, much like fix you nice."

Pam gave her nurse a quick hug then started for her mother's room. Living away off from everything and everyone on a great ranch which was a complete world of its own made her feel rich and contented. She liked to think of the navy-blue sweep of the sky overhead, studded with fabulous stars; of the dim shape of Hualalai rearing into the night; of horses and cattle grazing in the pastures. In little houses scattered here and there on the flanks of the big green hill, tired men were being fed by their women and playing with their children. Beyond the closed door of her mother's bedroom, Japanese house-boys were scurrying around, putting finishing touches on the dinner table before Ah Sam rang the gong.

Suddenly an odd little feeling of panic streamed through her. Things wouldn't be quite the same after Emily and Aunt Dode came to live with them. The beautiful aloneness she and her mother shared, which kept them so close, would be gone. This would be the very last night for a year that she would have her mother, the old house, and the ranch she so loved, all to herself. It might be fun having Emily, but she was not at all sure she wanted her for such a long time, especially if she proved to be a city-sissy, with no taste for the things she loved —animals, the out-of-doors, and laughing brown and yellow people.

As she entered her mother's room, Kulani turned around and smiled. Pam always thought of a tree standing in strong sunlight on a high hill when she looked at her mother. Her eyes were courageous, her expression serene, as if she knew things other people only guessed at, things which kept her steady and strong, no matter what happened.

"Ready, dear?" Kulani asked.

"Yes, Mother," Pam answered.

"You're quiet," her mother remarked as they went down the long hall toward the dining room. "What are you thinking about so seriously?"

"I'm thinking about having an American girl to take care of —for a whole year," Pam replied, rather gloomily.

"You're American, too."

"I know, but—"

"I understand, Pam," Kulani laughed softly. "But an Hawaiian-born American and a Boston-born American are poles apart!"

CHAPTER II

BIRTHDAY IN PARADISE

EMILY GLANCED AT THE TWIN BED BESIDE HERS. AUNT DODE was still sleeping. A lock of iron gray hair lay across one sharp cheek. The rest of her face was buried in the pillow, as if she were reluctant to wake up and meet the new day walking gladly past the open windows. But Emily was eager and curious to see her surroundings, for she and Aunt Dode had arrived after dark and the instant dinner was over, Aunt Dode had put her to bed.

What she could see of the morning promised beautiful, unknown things. Sliding out of bed, she tiptoed across the room, peered out, and caught her breath in an awed way. Hawaii was not a bit like what she'd imagined it would be when she and Aunt Dode left Boston. She had expected only long yellow beaches with green palm trees leaning over blue water, like the pictures on travel folders.

But outside, a steep mountain that looked violent and wild went looming into the sky. On its rough sides there were dark stains, as if some careless giant had upset a mighty inkpot over it. Emily had seen it from a distance the afternoon before, from the ship which brought Aunt Dode and her to the island, and had asked the Captain about the black marks. He had told her they were lava flows. For an instant the thought of being so close to a mountain that sometimes spouted fire made her feel weak and wobbly, then she forgot to be afraid because there were so many new, thrilling things to look at and listen to.

Now out there, below green sweeping lawns, crowded with strange, beautiful flowers and sweet-smelling shrubs, a solitary rider was chasing horses across the pasture toward some corrals. Men wearing wide straw hats with flowers around their crowns perched on the corral rails and loafed near great saddles slung along the fence, while they laughed and chatted in great booming voices that rolled out new, rich-sounding words. Strong yellow sunlight was tangled in the branches of exciting looking trees and small brown birds with orange legs and bills were screeching and showing off to each other on the grass. The huge island spreading away on all sides didn't seem to be just earth and rocks. It felt alive, like a person, and gave her surroundings a strange feeling, as though everything was moving invisibly forward, down a long road whose end she could not see. . . .

Emily glanced around, hoping Aunt Dode would wake up. She wanted to dress and go out. Pamela would be eleven today. What fun to spend her first day in Hawaii on someone's birthday! It made everything seem richer and more important. She knew by the smell of the morning it was still very early and she wanted to be the first to wish Pamela "Many Happy Returns."

She started for the dresser, then halted in surprise when she saw the strange objects on the wall. One she knew was spurs, the second must be a bridle, but what the coiled rawhide rope was for she couldn't make out. Then she saw a stiff swirl of hair hanging from the lamp-pull and touched it. It was harsh to her fingers and had a wild, strong smell. She jumped back and shivered.

She inspected it from a little distance and concluded it must be part of some animal, but why anyone should want to hang such a thing in a pretty guest-room, she couldn't make out. Her nose wrinkled up with distaste, then she went to her clothes, which she'd laid out neatly on a chair the night before.

When she was dressed she opened the door and slipped out quietly. The bigness of the living room, with its potted palms and great hanging baskets of ferns, astonished her. She had been so sleepy and tired the night before that she had not noticed anything. Glass doors and windows opening outward made the house seem like a part of the garden. Two Japanese boys in clean white shirts and starched breeches were moving about the big room, dusting richly carved furniture, embroidered screens, and tall Chinese vases. Their glossy black hair, yellowish skin and slant eyes made Emily feel vaguely ill at ease, but when they smiled at her and said, "*Aloha* Missie-san," in kind, friendly voices, warmth ran through her. She wanted to ask them where Pamela's room was, but thought they mightn't understand English.

A Japanese woman was going down the wide, matted hall giving on to the living room. Her straw sandals made nice slapping noises against the floor and she carried a large paper parcel under one arm. Probably she was Pam's nurse and was taking a birthday present to her, Emily thought excitedly, hurrying to keep her in sight. She wished she had a gift for her cousin, but she and Aunt Dode were poor. When Aunt Kulani wrote inviting them to spend a year in Hawaii, she had sent a check to buy clothes and provide money for the long trip but there was very little left over.

Emily had no memories of her own mother, but the moment she met Pam's, some inner part of her had gone to her with a rush. When the car that had fetched Aunt Dode and her from the steamer had finally stopped before a big house, a woman had come running to meet them. "I'm your Aunt Kulani," she had said, taking Emily into her arms and kissing her. "I'm happy you're here, dear!"

Emily had felt choky. Aunt Dode was kind in a stiff way, but not demonstrative. Aunt Kulani smelled of sunshine and some faint, fragrant powder that made her seem dear and close.

Emily had been eager to meet Pam, but dinner was half over before her cousin appeared. Aunt Kulani did not seem in the least concerned about her absence, and when she came in asked her about some calf that had been missing, then introduced her to her relatives.

During dinner Pam had hardly spoken to Emily, but had watched her in an odd way, as though she could not quite add her up. It had made Emily feel vaguely uncomfortable, for she was eager to have her cousin like her. Emily saw that Pam was different from the girls she had known in Boston, more vital, and her eyes, though they sparkled with life, had a far-away expression, like a person who is always thinking about beautiful, interesting things.

The Japanese woman vanished through one of the many doors opening on to the hall, and closed it behind her. Emily hurried up, then halted. If she popped in and called out "Happy Birthday!" Pam would know that she was eager to be friends. She took hold of the door-knob, then faltered. Maybe birthday customs in Hawaii differed from those in America. But the sunshine was so bright, the trees looked so happy in the garden that her courage returned and she entered.

Her breath caught with astonishment when she saw the size of the four-poster bed standing up like a sort of island in the big airy room. There was a small hump of bedclothes in the middle, a splash of bronze hair on the pillow, so she knew it was Pam's room.

The Japanese woman was just laying her gift beside Pam's hand, flung across the covers. Hearing Emily, she turned, smiled, and laid a finger across her lips.

Emily nodded and signed that she would be quiet. Her fascinated eyes went to her cousin. Beside her, she felt small and dry and her hair seemed straighter than it ever had been before. "But if only she'll like me, if only we can be friends," she thought. "I won't mind not being pretty, like she is."

She knew she was plain because Aunt Dode was always saying, "Girls who aren't pretty must be clever. I expect nothing lower than nineties on your report card."

A shuffling sound came from outside and Emily looked out the windows. A herd of red cattle was pouring past. Men singing rollicking songs galloped beside the animals, cracking whips and calling orders to each other. She recognized Pam's mother going past on a big dark horse. She looked strong, happy, and busy.

Pam stirred, then her dark blue eyes opened.

"*Aloha*, Pammi-san, Happy Birthday!" the Japanese woman said. "I bring one present for you." And she indicated the wrapped parcel on the pillow.

Pam sat up, ripped off the string, and a loose garment spilled over the white bedcovers. Highly colored beautiful flowers were printed on the heavy silk material. Pam squealed with delight, jumped out of bed and danced her nurse around the room until she was breathless. "Tatsu, you make the loveliest kimonos in the world!" she cried. Sliding into the lovely garment, she surveyed herself in the long mirror.

"Happy Birthday, Pam," Emily said shyly.

Pam flung around like a startled colt. "Thank you, Emily," she said, rather stiffly, then added, "How did you find my room?"

"I followed—her." Emily indicated the Japanese woman. Pam nodded, but didn't seem to have anything more to say. However, after a minute or two she remarked over her shoulder, "Sit down, I'll be dressed in a few minutes."

Emily perched on the edge of the big bed. She had an impression that her cousin felt as ill at ease as she did. She remembered that Aunt Kulani had said at dinner—before Pam came in—that one of the chief reasons she was so eager to have Emily visit her was that Pam had never had an American playfellow for more than a day or two. A little glow went through Emily as she hoped that, maybe, she would be Pam's first real pal.

Going into the tiled bathroom, Pam closed the door and turned on the shower. Tatsu laid out riding breeches, boots, a gay colored silk shirt that had guitars, garlands of flowers and the word ALOHA printed on it. Emily was sure that she had never seen anything quite as beautiful.

While Pam dressed, she tried to think of things to talk about but Pam and Tatsu were so busy joking and chatting that she didn't have a chance to break in. When Pam was dressed, Tatsu took a note out of the long sleeve of her kimono and handed it to her. "Mother give," she said simply.

Pam read the note and the color rose in her cheeks.

"Happy Birthday, Little Daughter:
I've started for Kiholo with the steers. Join me later. And be gracious to little Emily. She's a stranger in a strange land. Remember the old Hawaiian saying, 'If a man be not hos-

pitable to the stranger who halts at his door, his shame shall be broadcast over the land.'

Mother."

Putting the note in the dresser, Pam turned and her voice and manner were less aloof. "Come to the kitchen with us, Emily," she said. "I always eat early. Ah Sam will fix some breakfast for you and Aunt Dode later on. Did you like the spurs and bridle and lasso by your dresser?"

"Oh, yes! But I wasn't sure what the third thing was."

"The picture in front of the mirror is our race horse, Trade-Wind. He won the Hawaiian Free For All last Fourth of July."

"I've never seen a race horse, except in newspaper pictures."

"I'll show you ours tomorrow. We have some of the fastest thoroughbreds in Hawaii."

Emily's eyes shone. She started to ask about the stiff curl when they entered a lofty room where a wrinkled old Chinaman, who looked like a mummy, hovered over a stove the size of a grand piano. It was jammed with huge cauldrons of food and monster pots of coffee. When Pam appeared the old man's dry face cracked into a grin. "Happy Blirthday," he said, and reaching to a shelf above the sink, took down three packages.

Pam pounced on them and tore off the covers. "Ginger!" she cried, holding up a green stone jar, latticed with bamboo. Then she opened a gaily colored cardboard box. "Chinese coconut candy!" Picking up something that looked like a strip of starched tape, she popped it into her mouth and pushed the box toward Tatsu and Emily. Then she carefully examined a bundle that looked as though it might hold a large lead pencil. The old cook watched her expectantly. When the paper was off she gave a cry of glee. "A toothbrush like yours! Oh, Ah Sam!"

"That's a funny-looking toothbrush," Emily said, considering the article in Pam's hand. One end had bristles, certainly, but the opposite end was round, smooth, and narrow, and in the middle the handle widened into a flat blade.

"This is a Chinese toothbrush," Pam announced. "This end is for scrubbing your teeth, the opposite end is an ear-scratcher, and the middle part is for scraping your tongue." She illustrated the uses of the triply useful tool and the kitchen echoed with Tatsu's and Ah Sam's laughter.

While Ah Sam began setting out Pam's breakfast, she started the rounds of straw-lined boxes filling the wide space behind the stove. She swooped on motherless ducklings and chickens, petted a mass of squirming kittens, then pounced on a puppy with a bandaged foot and hugged it to her cheek.

"Do you like puppies, Emily?" she asked, bringing it out.

"Aunt Dode doesn't like me to touch dogs because they have fleas, but we had a kitty once. It was soft, but it scratched me one day, so Aunt Dode gave it away."

Pam looked at her cousin. "Our dogs don't have fleas," she announced. "We keep them clean. You can hold Soap-Suds while I eat—if you want to."

Emily took the little dog rather timidly.

"He won't bite you," Pam said in a rather superior way. "A horse trod on his foot a few days ago."

Seating herself, she began eating while she watched the open door, as if she were waiting for someone to come through it. Emily held the puppy and the old cook snatched covers off bubbling saucepans filled with smoking yellow sweet potatoes, white flaky rice and monstrous stews. Presently the old man glanced in her direction.

"Velly nice you come here, Lil Em'ly," he said. "But you too thin. I make you plenty good-kind for eat. After by and by," his eyes squinched up with smile-wrinkles, "you fat—like this!" And he made imaginary circles in the air which sent Pam and Tatsu into gales of laughter, and even Emily smiled. When Ah Sam trotted into the pantry she turned to Pam.

"At first I was a bit scared of him because he's a Chinaman and looks like a magician, but he's just a kind, friendly old man."

Pam stared at her. "Are American girls afraid of China-men?" she asked, indignantly.

Emily started to explain that she'd never seen a Chinaman close by before, when a step sounded and Pam flung around. An old man with a noble brown face was standing in the door-way, holding up a garland of white, fragrant flowers. Pam rushed to him and he playfully lassoed her neck with the wreath. "O-o—gardenias!" Pam murmured, smelling them rapturously, then her eyes lighted. "What have you got for my birthday, Kane?"

"After you finish *kaukau*," he gestured at her food, "I show you."

Eagerly and proudly, as though the old Hawaiian were a

precious and distinguished person, Pam said, "Emily, this is Kane—my *paniolo*."

"*Paniolo?*" Emily echoed blankly.

"*Paniolo* is Hawaiian for cowboy," Pam explained. "Kane carried me on a pillow in front of his saddle before I could walk. He taught me to ride and swim. He made my first saddle, taught me to rope, play an ukulele and dance hulas. Kane, this is my cousin Emily from Boston."

"*Aloha*, Em'ly," the old man said. "Swell you come to Hawaii. I too glad." And his benevolent eyes rested on Emily as though he'd known and loved her for a long time.

"Hello," Emily said, but the word sounded flat after the way Kane had said, "*Aloha!*"

A bell began tolling and suddenly the kitchen was overflowing with big, brawny brown men who had jingling spurs on their heels, knives in their leggings and wreaths of fresh flowers on their big, battered straw hats. The ceiling echoed with rolling Hawaiian words and booming Hawaiian laughter. They loaded Pam with *leis* and gave her birthday wishes. Emily looked on, feeling small and far-away. Then a paunchy old fellow with roguish eyes saw her. "You Em'ly?" he demanded.

She nodded.

"Here." Removing his hat, he tipped the wreath off it and handed it to her. "*Aloha, Keiki,*" he said. "Me—" he slapped his swelling chest. "Me—Na-lua-hine!"

Emily stood with the flowers in her hands. "What is he saying, Pam?"

Pam said, "My love to you, child. My name is Na-lua-hine."

Emily smiled at the jovial old fellow.

"Why-for you no wear?" he asked, after a few moments, indicating the garland she was holding. "Make like this." Placing the blossoms about her neck, he stepped back to see the effect. "You pritty," he announced in a big hearty voice. "I like swell your hair. Yellow like jasmine flowers." And he gestured at Emily's straight, tight braids.

Emily flushed. She felt magically wrapped in approval, fun and laughter. "Oh, thank you—Na-lua-hine." Her lips went around the strange syllables shyly, feeling their way.

"I got one fine accordion. S'pose you like after by and by I play for you. Come, now us go eat."

Pam and her old *paniolo*, Kane, and the other men were going out into the garden, carrying plates, cups and steaming cauldrons of food. Na-lua-hine motioned Emily to follow him.

"Sit here," he ordered, patting the grass at his side. "I take care on you."

Emily looked around the seated circle. "Are you my—*paniolo*?" she asked, feeling shy and yet a bit important.

"Bet-you-my-life!" the old fellow announced enthusiastically.

The other men shouted approval, then busied themselves with food. Emily watched them pouring rich brown sugar into their thick white cups filled with coffee, piling sweet potatoes and hunks of fat beef and pork onto their plates. Na-lua-hine fixed a plate up and handed it to Emily but she was so interested in what was going on around her that she forgot to eat. Men were drinking coffee with rushing noises, dogs lay on the

grass, waiting hopefully for bones. The sun sprang up suddenly, edging the lava-stained mountain and huge island with
quick gold and a flock of wee butterflies, like flying forget-me-
nots, drifted by.

Emily felt a bit strange, but knew that she was happier than
she had ever been in her life. A flame tree, like a scarlet um-
brella, leaned lovingly over the beds of flowers growing beneath it and saddled horses, tied to a long hitching rail under a
grove of orange trees, stamped, eager to be off.

One of the men tossed a stiff black curl into Pam's lap. "A
curl off a wild bull's tail!" she cried exultantly. "Oh, Moku,
how swell of you to give it to me for my birthday!"

Emily stared at it, fascinated and repelled. It was the dupli-
cate, except for color, to the thing she had noticed hanging
above her dresser. But why, she wondered, should wild bulls'
tail-curls be so important?

Pam's eyes ran excitedly around the seated men. Getting to
her feet, she stuck the curl through her belt in the rear. The
seated men burst into a wild song that sent goose pimples rushing over Emily. Pam raised her arms on each side of her head,
like horns, and began dancing.

Emily watched spellbound. In a dim way she saw that while
Pam danced she was telling a story. After Emily became some-
what accustomed to the strange music, punctuated by shouts
and cries, she began to grasp the imagery of Pam's steps and
movements. Now she was a horse leaping up a steep mountain,
now she was a wild bull lowering death-dealing horns to

charge, now she was a man leaning over his pommel, swinging a rope.

Pam looked like the spirit of Hawaii—always young, strong, gay and beautiful. Her curls gleamed in the sunshine, her cheeks were like flaming roses, and the movements of her arms and body spun magic into the morning. Perhaps, Emily thought, if she stayed a year in Hawaii Na-lua-hine, her *paniolo*, would teach her to dance as Kane had taught Pam. The mere idea of being able to move so beautifully sent prickles of delight all over her and she clasped her hands tightly together.

"Pamela—*what on earth!*"

Emily froze. The flood of absorbing new experiences had wiped Aunt Dode from her mind. Now she was standing on the steps, a scandalized, incredulous expression on her thin, tight face. Emily shrank back and tried to hide behind Na-lua-hine. Pam rolled her eyes wickedly, tossed her curls, then raised her arms above her head, bent over and rushed across the lawn like a charging bull. Aunt Dode recoiled and retreated up the steps, and the Hawaiians rolled on the grass, helpless with mirth. After a moment she recovered herself, pushed up a lock of hair which had fallen down her lean stalk of a neck and opened her lips to speak.

"I'm a wild bull, look out!" Pam cried, warningly, pawing up imaginary dust.

"You're a little savage!" Aunt Dode declared hotly. "How your mother ever allows you to run so wild— "

"I'm not running wild," Pam retorted, her eyes flashing.

"We're just having fun. It's my birthday!"

"Fiddlesticks! Birthday or no birthday—" Aunt Dode gave a faint, disgusted snort, then saw Emily. "Emily, *come indoors at once!*" she cried shrilly.

Emily got to her feet and started toward the house. Her legs were shaky because she knew she was going to be scolded. As she went up the steps Aunt Dode reached out and with a quick jerk broke the *lei* Na-lua-hine had hung around her neck. Emily made no protest. Her hand went up involuntarily, then dropped limply. But the bright morning which had brimmed over with fun seemed to fall to pieces with the flowers drifting to the steps.

A very subdued Emily sat down to breakfast. The things which she had seen and done that morning seemed unreal and far-away. She wondered if she had really worn a garland around her neck and if an old *paniolo* had said her braids were as pretty as yellow jasmine blossoms. Swallowing to ease the ache in her throat, she dug her spoon into the rich golden crescent of some strange fruit which the Japanese serving boy called *papaia*. She watched him disappear through a swinging door that led into the kitchen, to reappear presently with eggs and crisp curls of bacon. He poured coffee for Aunt Dode out of a graceful silver pot and put a glass of foaming milk at Emily's right hand.

Aunt Dode sat with her elbows held tightly to her sides and Emily knew from her quick, precise chews that she disapproved of the luxury around her. It awed Emily, but it was fun having things handed to you, and to be seated at a table of dark, polished wood, set with woven place-mats and finished by a bowl heaped with flowers. In Boston she and Aunt Dode ate in a small, dark kitchen—except when they had company. Breakfast was always a hurried meal because Emily had to go to school and Aunt Dode to work.

A car pulled up to the house. Emily wondered who was calling so early; the clock showed only half past seven. Steps with some strange hesitancy in their sound were coming through the big wandering house. An old man was approaching with heavy unsteadiness, touching the wall occasionally with an outstretched hand. His progress suggested a mammoth ship bucking into head seas, but there was no suggestion of weakness in his movements, rather of great force chained by darkness. He touched a rocker, slid his hand along the edge of a polished table, as if he knew exactly where they were, then halted.

"I'm Pam's grandfather. Kaiko, the Tidal Wave, the Hawaiians call me. Is that you, Dode? I'm delighted you and Emily are here at last," he said enthusiastically. "Hope you had a nice trip. Emily—"

"Yes," she said in a small voice.

"I'm happy you're here. Kulani told me how tough things have been for you both. But you can sew your troubles up in a bag and throw them overboard, now you're here. Hawaii is fine medicine—for all ills."

His big hand found the back of one of the chairs and, pulling it out, he sat down. Tatsu and the serving boy fluttered about the blind man in a glad way. Emily sat as still as a mouse while he and Aunt Dode talked. She learned from listening to their conversation that Kaiko was Kulani's father. He owned a sugar plantation in some place called Kohala but he had a manager to run it and spent most of his time with Pam and her mother.

"I went to Puuiki for a few days but came back because to-day's Pam's birthday," he went on. "Cousin Sally's expecting you for lunch and the night, Dode. She rounded up the clan to meet you and entertain you until Kulani's in the clear. My fine girl works like a man," he said, his dark, sightless eyes shining proudly. "And she's got 'em all skinned when it comes to efficiency. I'll ride herd on Emily—" he placed his kind, heavy hand on her shoulder.

Emily felt picked up. She knew Pam's grandfather was an American, though he was called by a Hawaiian name, but he had a rich, friendly feeling about him, like Na-lua-hine had, as if he had the ability to push drab things aside and spill fun and adventure into ordinary things. Without in the least seeming to hurry Aunt Dode off, he made it appear important that she hasten to see the relatives gathered to greet her.

"If you want to stay on for a week or ten days, feel free to do so, Dode," Kaiko said. "You've worked like a mule. I appoint myself Emily's guardian until you get back."

His fingers closed on Emily's shoulder and it made her want to stand straight and proud, like a soldier who had received a decoration for valor in battle. He didn't seem like a blind person. He was eager and happy, overflowing with life, and under his spell Aunt Dode packed her bag hurriedly and shortly the long Packard which had brought Grandfather Kaiko to the ranch was taking her away.

"This is too fine a day to waste indoors, Emily," Kaiko announced. "Let's go to the corrals and find Pam."

Emily's heart, which had been heavy since her *lei* had been jerked off, felt light again. "Oh, let's!" she said eagerly.

They went into the dazzling sunshine, with voices and laughter pulling them toward the corrals Emily had seen from her window. Pam was doing a sort of war dance about a beautifully carved saddle that old Kane was holding up in one hand. Tied to a post nearby was a golden horse with a *lei* of flowers about its neck.

"Grandfather, look at the new saddle Kane made for me and at the race horse Mother gave me!" Pam called. Dancing over, she flung her arms about the old man.

"Happy birthday, Little Dynamite!" Kaiko laughed, bending to kiss her. "There's a new bridle for you in the house. A horsehair one with tassels on it."

"Oh, *Grandfather*—" and she went rushing off to see it.

"Saddle a horse for me, Moku, and one for Emily," Grandfather ordered.

"I—can't ride," Emily faltered and her heart felt like a winged bird dropping to the ground.

"No matter," Na-lua-hine said in his big, merry way. "I tie one nice soft pillow behind my saddle for you. You hold on me tight and no be scare. I your *paniolo!*" He thumped his chest, gave a whoop, and bustled forward.

Emily watched him in an amazed way. He was a clown, old, funny-looking and heavy, but he threw joy and beauty about him in a wholesale way. Pulling his saddle off a fine young horse, he put it on a fat old mare, folded up a blanket and made a pad which he tied securely behind the cantle of his saddle. When he was settled on the horse's back, he told one of the other men to lift Emily up behind him. She clutched his fat waist tightly and shut her eyes.

When Grandfather and the rest of the cavalcade were mounted they started down the road. Pam came galloping after them, still bubbling over with excitement about her latest birthday presents.

After Emily became a little accustomed to the movement of the horse, the slow ride over old lava flows was enthralling. The seas of black, twisted rock, which had once flowed in molten scarlet to the sea, appeared empty of life, but every so often a band of wild goats went scampering away, their little hoofs rattling like castanets against the rocks: or roving herds of jackasses tore the bright day to shreds with their harsh braying. When Grandfather told Emily that in Hawaii donkeys were called "Kona Nightingales" because of their "sweet singing," she laughed so hard she almost lost her balance.

After three hours of riding they reached a coconut grove, standing out greenly against the blackened land. Through the leaning trunks Emily could see dazzling white beaches. Waves with crests of emerald and azure were crisping toward the sand, or tearing their blue into foamy white lace against rough, out-jutting rocks.

At the far end of the beach there was a corral filled with glossy, restless cattle. Kulani was sitting with her leg around the pommel of her saddle, supervising operations, and when she saw the approaching riders she waved. A big white boat was anchored about fifty feet off-shore and a quarter of a mile away a steamer was smoking slowly. Pam and the *paniolos* galloped toward the corrals while Na-lua-hine slid Emily to the sand, helped Grandfather off and tied the horses in the shade of some lacy green *kiawe* trees. Emily held Grandfather's hand tightly.

"There's a flat-topped rock around here, Emily, where we can sit and watch the fun," Grandfather said.

"Here it is," Emily said, guiding him toward it.

When they were settled on it, Emily pushed up close to Grandfather. The bellowing of the cattle, the shouting of the men and the great splashings when they plunged into the sea were confusing and exciting. The men worked in pairs. One roped a steer and rushed across the sand at full speed. His partner galloped behind and, with great shouts, urged the steer into the water. When the man with the steer on his rope hit the sea, they sank out of sight and, after a breath-taking moment, reappeared. The *paniolo's* assistant watched to see if the steer was swimming for the boat, then rode back to the pen. As the first *paniolo* and his captive drew near the boat, the *paniolo* threw the rope, which was about the steer's horns, to one of the sailors, who lashed the steer's head to the side of the boat. Then the sailor flung him a new rope and he swam back to the shore to get another animal.

While the work went on, Grandfather explained details to Emily. The boat had to anchor in deep water so the struggling cattle couldn't get their feet on the bottom and tear free. Ten or twelve animals, depending on the size of the cattle, constituted a "boat-load." When the boat had its quota of animals lashed on each side, it was pulled out to the ship by a long, circular rope which drew another boat back to land at the same time. When the cattle reached the ship, a sling was put around each one in turn and they were hoisted up into the ship.

Emily hugged her knees to her chest and sat very still, while wind ran its cool fingers through her hair. As the sailors and *paniolos* worked they kept up a shouted conversation, punctuated by quick orders if some steer proved unruly. Finally the last animal was fast and the steamer blew its whistle. Tired men spilled off tired horses and unsaddled them. The animals began rolling luxuriously in the damp sand and the men plunged into the crystal blue water and scrubbed the sweat off their skins.

Pam had changed into a bathing suit and taken the saddle off her horse. Scrambling up his side, she rode into the ocean and began swimming. The horse rose up like a graceful wave, sank, wheeled around, his tail streaming out behind him like a black satin fan. Emily watched in an absorbed way.

"Before long you'll be doing that, too," Pam's mother said, walking over and seating herself on the rock beside Emily and Grandfather.

"Oh, Aunt Kulani!" Emily gasped. "It looks kind of scary."

Na-lua-hine strolled up and announced he'd take her behind him and swim his horse in the sea. Emily gave a horrified scramble backwards and everyone laughed.

"Come on," Pam called. "It's swell!"

Emily was eager to shine in Pam's, and everyone's, eyes, but panic streamed through her. "I don't want to go in. Oh, Aunt Kulani, don't let Pam and Na-lua-hine make me." And she began crying.

Pam glanced at her in a disgusted way and Emily felt forlorn. Kulani put an arm about her and laughed, making Emily's fear funny. "They're only teasing you, dear," she said in her warm way. "After you've learned to ride properly, you'll graduate to swimming your horse in the sea. Actually it's quite easy and if you fall off you can't be hurt because the water catches you."

After a little, Kulani rose to her feet and signalled to her daughter to come out of the sea. "While the men fix food we'll swim in Lua-hine-wai," she announced.

Pam galloped up the beach, slid off her horse and Kane took it and led it away. Pam rushed over to her cousin. "There's a pool in the lava beds, Emily," she said excitedly, "where only girls can swim. It's taboo to men. Wait till you see it!" She bounced eagerly up and down, then started up a dim trail worn into the bluff of black rock.

Pam's mother gave an order to the men in Hawaiian, then took Emily's hand. "Come, little *malihini*, you'll have your eyes opened a few more times today. Probably you feel sort of stranded and left outside, but that will pass." And her brown eyes laughed.

"Oh, Aunt Kulani, how did you know?"

"I was sent to Boston to school when I was fourteen. I'd never been away from Hawaii and if you don't think *I* felt like a fish out of water!"

"What's a *malihini*, Aunt Kulani, that word you called me a moment ago?"

"It means an outsider, Emily. After you've been in Hawaii a while you'll be a *kama-aina*—one who belongs to the land."

They crested the bluff and Emily caught her breath. Wedged into wastes of black lava was a pool like a sapphire-blue mirror, reflecting the sky. When she reached the edge of it she could hardly believe her eyes. Every submerged rock and tiny grain of black sand was outlined with rainbow colors.

"Oh, Aunt Kulani!" she cried. "Isn't it beautiful! What makes the rainbows?"

"Some chemical, or trick of light. Nobody knows actually," Kulani answered.

Pam yipped with glee, dived in and circled around like a small golden fish, while her mother pulled some bathing suits out of a cranny in a rock-ledge and found one small enough for Emily.

"I can't swim, Aunt Kulani," she confessed, feeling hollow and sad.

"You'll learn to before long, Emily. In the meantime, dunk here. This end of the pool is shallow."

Stepping behind some rocks, she wriggled into a bathing suit while Emily took off her clothes and hung them on a bush. Cool air coming off the sea passed over her bare skin. Pam's mother dove into the pool and streaked off, her arms flashing on each side of her head as she hurried to overtake Pam. Emily looked after them wistfully, determining that she was going to learn to ride, swim, dance and do all the other things her cousin did. With her *paniolo's* help, it mightn't take very long.

She touched the strangely beautiful water with one toe, then sank into it, sighing luxuriously. Instead of being cold, it felt like cool chiffon velvet sliding softly up her limbs. She moved, and saw that her body was outlined with rainbows! Little bubbles of happiness seemed to be bursting inside her and she turned her face up to the sky, like a flower giving thanks to rain falling upon it. Presently Pam and her mother came swimming back and sat in the shallow water beside her.

"Like it?" Pam asked.

"It's wonderful," Emily said, like a person under a spell.

"In old times," Pam explained, "Hawaiians believed that any girl who swam in Lua-hine-wai often enough would become as beautiful as a rainbow."

"Will I get to be beautiful like you, Pam, if I come in often enough?" Emily asked very earnestly.

Pam flushed. "Do you think I'm beautiful?" she asked in astonishment.

Emily nodded, her eyes serious.

"Thank you, Emily," Pam murmured, then went on quickly. "But you better get your clothes on or that white skin of yours will be burned badly."

As soon as they were dressed they retraced their steps down the bluff and wandered along the beach toward the coconut grove. The afternoon had a breathless loveliness that made Emily feel as though she were standing on tiptoe inside. Inland, the three big mountains lifted their simple summits into the sky and the deep Pacific, swelling against lava-ledges and hissing up the beaches, whispered of far-off, enchanting things.

When they reached the grove Emily gave a little cry. On the clean white sand coconut leaves were spread, making a green, glossy table. Red hibiscus blossoms, gathered from bushes crowding against a weather-worn house, were scattered here and there. Men were squatting about a fire, moving in an unhurried, contented way, cooking the food they had gathered. Strange edibles sent up tantalizing smells. The day was beginning to drift away. Clouds waited above the beautiful loneliness of the sea, like great white birds with their heads hidden under folded wings. Na-lua-hine was playing his accordion and the music made everything seem boundless.

He signed with his head for Emily to come and sit beside him. She watched him pulling music out of the expanding and contracting box he held against him, while his big fingers flitted expertly over the tiny keyboard. Grandfather lolled against a sandy hummock, a sort of lazy happiness wrapped around him. Emily felt as if she were in the heart of a beautiful dream from which she never wanted to waken. . . . Then someone shouted "*Kaukau!*" and everyone started toward the table.

Emily had been so happy she hadn't realized that she was hungry, but when she sat down on the sand with everyone else she could hardly wait to sample the strange foods placed on the green, flower-decked table. Na-lua-hine established himself beside her and showed her how to eat a sticky substance he called *poi*. At first she didn't like the taste of it but he selected the right sort of food to eat with it and suddenly she found it delicious. She couldn't twist it onto her finger properly and when a dab flew off and stuck to Na-lua-hine's brown cheek everyone shouted with glee, as if she had done something clever.

While Emily, Pam and Kulani had been swimming, the men had caught fish, gathered *opihis*, a sort of limpet, off the rocks and stewed some young hens that they had brought down from the ranch, in the milk of coconuts. For dessert, they had Pam's ginger and coconut candy and finished up with long drafts of sweet water from green coconuts gathered from the grove.

When the last scrap of food had been eaten, everybody lolled around and talked for a while, then Pam went streaking off to the old house and returned with an ukulele.

"Let's play *Nancy-Letta-Go-Your-Blouse*," she cried.

Everyone sat up eagerly and Emily waited. Seating herself crosslegged on the sand, Pam began playing as expertly as a Hawaiian, with lilting chords and lively little runs, and then she began singing.

> "Nancy, Letta-go your blouse,
> *Hemo-la! Hemo-la!*
> Letta-go your blouse!
> If you want a jolly good time,
> Down at the beach at Waikiki,
> Nancy, Letta-go your blouse!"

She started the verse a second time, only instead of singing Nancy, she called Kane's name. His old face lighted up and his eyes ran around the group of singing men. He gave some sort of sign and Na-lua-hine seized his accordion and the men began a wild, shouting hula. Kane got up and began dancing. As he moved, his age fell from him and he looked young and lightened. When he stopped, everyone shouted and clapped, then waited for Pam to sing out someone else's name. One by one she went around the group and Emily watched, spellbound. Grandfather stood up and recited an old *mele* in Hawaiian; Kulani sang; a young rogue of a Hawaiian called Nuhi walked on his hands. The evening seemed to get bigger and more wonderful, then crashed to a stop. Emily realized that her name was being sung!

She felt as if she were falling down a deep, dark well. She wasn't like Island people, who jumped into things and forgot themselves.

> "Emily! Emily! Letta-go your blouse!
> *Hemo-la! Hemo-la!*
> Letta-go your blouse—"

Everyone was shouting, urging her on. What could she do? She didn't even know a poem. Tears swam in her eyes.

"Hey, you no cry!" Na-lua-hine protested and his big arm swept her between his knees. Snatching up his accordion, he fitted her little hands under the straps and slid his big ones over them. Then he began playing. Music jumped and danced into the evening. All at once the tune sounded familiar and dear. What was the song they were playing, Emily wondered. Then she knew. It was *Nancy, Letta-go Your Blouse!* She found herself singing the words, too, and everyone was clapping and applauding.

Pam and her mother sprang up and began dancing together. Firelight threw flickering bronze light on leaning coconut trunks. The air smelled of smoke, flowers and the clean salty breath of the sea. Emily wished it would go on and on forever.

When Na-lua-hine stopped, she dug her head happily against his arm. "Oh, that was more fun than anything I've ever done in my life!" she cried in a high, excited voice.

"You swell kid," Na-lua-hine told her. Snatching up a red blossom from the table, he stuck it behind her ear. "There, now you Hawaiian girl!"

"I'll never forget today, never," Emily said in an awed way when they all started for the horses.

Pam smiled. "I love birthdays," she agreed. "I have a new bridle, a new saddle and a new race horse."

"And I wore my first *lei* today, went into the Pool of Rainbows—what's its Hawaiian name?—"

"Lua-hine-wai," Pam told her.

"Lua-hine-wai," Emily repeated. "And I've half played an accordion and have my own *paniolo!* I feel as if it were my birthday, too!"

"When you can stick on a horse properly, I'll let you have a ride on Kolohi, the thoroughbred Mother gave me today," Pam announced.

"Oh, Pam!" Emily cried, as if she could not believe the world held such bliss.

"But you'll have to ride well, he's dynamite," Pam warned her.

"And when you ride to *my* satisfaction," Kulani said, putting her arm about Emily's neck, "I'll buy you a pair of riding breeches and boots."

"And I'll give you some spurs," Grandfather added.

"And I go up mountain and rope one wild bull and make you one fine lasso when the hide dry," Na-lua-hine chuckled.

Emily felt as if her body was not big enough to hold such an avalanche of bliss.

CHAPTER III

LEARNING THE ROPES

WHEN EMILY WOKE UP SHE KNEW FROM THE SHADOWS GATH-
ered under the trees that it was getting on toward noon. It gave
her a curious feeling of freedom to think that Aunt Dode was
not present to order everything, as she had for as far back as
Emily could remember. There was no one to say, "Emily, tie
your hair ribbons again, they're not straight. And hurry, or
you'll be late for school. . . . I'll have to work late tonight.
. . . When you get back peel the potatoes but don't put on
the lights until it gets dark or you'll waste electricity. . . ."

Emily dug her cheek deeper into the fat, smooth pillow. She felt a little heavy and stiff, then she proudly remembered that she had ridden almost sixteen miles behind Na-lua-hine the previous day. It all seemed like a dream, and she could hardly believe that Pam had said when she could stick on a horse properly she would lend her the golden thoroughbred, Kolohi. Aunt Kulani was going to buy her breeches and boots. Grandfather was giving her spurs. Na-lua-hine was planning to braid her a lasso. How important it all made her feel!

Turning over on her back, she stared at the ceiling, trying to picture herself in riding togs, with spurs ringing at her heels and a fiery horse underneath her. How long, she wondered, did it take a person to learn to be a good rider?

The door opened softly and Tatsu entered. "*Aloha*, Emily-san. I wait long time for you to wake up. Everybody gone, but I take care of you."

"Where has everyone gone?" Emily asked, sitting up.

"*Paniolos* go *hana-hana*—work. Kulani-san go up mountain look the cattle. Grandfather gone with Nuhi to Kohala for see Auntie. Pam, Kane, and Moku go trap wild pigs."

"Does Pam work, too?" Emily asked, astonished and intrigued.

"Sure," Tatsu answered. "Good fun work on a ranch. You like get up now or you like sleep some more?"

"I'll get up."

Emily felt strange and slightly lost with no white people to talk to, but Tatsu's friendliness, her eager questions about how she liked Hawaii, and about life in Boston kept Emily so busy talking that she didn't have time to feel lonely. When she was dressed, Tatsu took her to the kitchen.

"Velly lazy today, Lil Em'ly," Ah Sam greeted her. "Now you be good-girl and eat every-kind I fix for you."

"It's too much!" Emily gasped, looking at a golden half of *papaia*, a tall glass of milk, a bowl of cereal, two soft boiled eggs, a stack of toast and a jar of wild honey, like dark amber, gathered from old *koa* logs in the forest.

"You tly," Ah Sam urged. "Then after by and by no more bones." And he gestured at Emily's thin arms.

To her surprise, she found she could eat it all and it tasted, almost, like more.

"What kind you like make today?" Tatsu asked when she had finished. "You like stop inside house with me and fix flowers, or you like go look her horses and cows?"

Emily hesitated. She was eager to explore the gardens and buildings she had glimpsed the day before, but was rather fearful of her strange surroundings. She heard cattle lowing and occasionally the whinny of a horse, like a clear bugle call.

"I don't know which to do, Tatsu."

"Long time Na-lua-hine wait for you," the woman told her. "He go eat lunch now, but after he finish sure he come back again."

"Oh, Tatsu!" Emily exclaimed. "I slept while my *paniolo* sat for hours waiting for me to get up!"

"He no care. Go outside and maybe you find him."

Emily went to the kitchen door. A fat old cream-colored dog was sitting in the fragrant shade of some orange trees. He had a wide, engaging smile and his pink tongue lolled over his white teeth. Emily set off across the lawn and he followed slowly, wagging a friendly tail. She bent to pat him and he sat down and lifted his paw to shake hands. Japanese yardboys raking up leaves called out, "*Aloha*, Missie-san," then went on working. Trees shook their leaves happily in the light wind and warm sunlight wrapped the earth. Sitting down on the ground, Emily rubbed the old dog's ears and with a sigh of contentment he flopped across her lap.

It was all so different to anything she had ever known, Emily thought, gazing around her. She saw a portly figure swinging down the road from the Office and leaped to her feet. "Na-lua-hine!" she called.

He waved and she ran toward him, the old dog following at her heels. When she was close, she felt shy for a moment but he looked so happy to see her that she forgot that he was a Hawaiian and she an American. They just seemed two people together. A *lei* of white, waxy, fragrant flowers dangled from his hand. "I make you one *lei* of gardenias," he said, giving it to her. "And I wait long time for you to get up." Emily placed the garland about her neck. She had never smelt anything so beautiful.

"What kind you like make today, Em'ly?" her *paniolo* asked when she stopped fondling her *lei*.

"I'd like to learn to ride."

"*Maikai*—good!" he said heartily.

With her small hand tucked trustingly into his big brown one, they headed for the corrals. A fat old buckskin horse with a black mane and tail and a dark stripe down its backbone was dozing in a corner of the dusty pen.

"Pam speak Forty Dollars okay for you," Na-lua-hine told her, opening the gate. Emily hesitated, then followed him in. Taking a rope off the rail, Na-lua-hine caught the horse and beckoned to Emily to come over. The fat dog flopped down in the scant shade and sighed. Emily approached and petted the horse's big shoulder cautiously.

"Forty Dollars little slow, but s'pose you fall off he no kick, and he wait for you to get on again," Na-lua-hine said as he dusted off the animal's back with the palm of his hand. Taking a bridle off the post where it was hanging, he slid his thumb into the horse's mouth so that it opened a little, then thrust the bit in, pulled the headstall over the ears and fastened the throat latch. Emily watched each maneuver avidly.

"After by and by I teach you every-kind," the old fellow promised with bright eyes. Reaching to the fence, he took down a blanket and fitted it to the horse's broad back with deft pats, then he looked down at his small charge. "S'pose you like to ride good, like Pam, better you learn without saddle."

"I'll fall off," Emily protested.

"No. Today, tomorrow, maybe next day, I hold you and us only go slow, inside here." He gestured at the corral.

Emily fought down her timidity and nodded. Sliding his hands under her arms, Na-lua-hine tossed her onto the horse's back. She grasped the coarse black mane and tensed her legs against the swell of his ribs. "Go slow," she cautioned.

"No go any place till you say," Na-lua-hine announced, leaning his elbow nonchalantly on the sleepy old horse's withers. Emily's muscles began relaxing. The *paniolo* pointed out red, black, white and fawn-colored dots on the steep green sides of the big hill and told her they were horses and cattle grazing. He explained that the flutings in the hill were the result of winter rains washing earth away, and the satiny marks winding like paths over the sea were made by Hawaiian gods walking invisibly on the water.

"When can we go around the corral?" Emily asked finally.

"Oh!" Na-lua-hine straightened up as if he'd forgotten a riding lesson was in the offing. "You like to go now?"

Emily nodded. Na-lua-hine placed his hand on her leg to steady her and nudged the sleepy horse, who moved forward. After two or three minutes Emily forgot to be afraid. Na-lua-hine was so close that it was fun feeling the horse walking under her. As they went slowly around the dusty corral, Na-lua-hine explained that learning to ride without a saddle netted the best results in the long run. Legs fitted naturally into the curve of a horse's ribs and when a person learned to stick on without a saddle, his grip was right and balance natural. Emily listened attentively.

"How long before I can trot and gallop—like Pam?" she wanted to know.

"Take little time," Na-lua-hine admitted.

Emily thought of the promised gifts. "Can I go a little faster?" she asked.

"Not today."

Na-lua-hine led her around and around the corral at a snail's pace, until she felt quite relaxed and at home on Forty Dollars' back. When the lesson was over he lifted her down. They spent half an hour bridling and saddling the old horse, over and over again, until Emily became quite expert. She found out that when she slid her thumb into Forty Dollars' mouth in the exact spot Na-lua-hine showed her, there were no teeth that could hurt her. Also, by making a horse open its mouth slightly, a person could slide in the bit without bumping the animal's teeth. Emily nodded. When she struggled to get the leather over the horse's ears he lowered his head to help her and when Na-lua-hine told her that Pam had learned to ride on Forty Dollars she was delighted.

By the time she could get the bridle on easily and pat the blanket correctly into place, the bright afternoon was sliding to its finish. Men were riding in from all directions, calling out to each other, and a pleasant stir crept into the atmosphere.

Na-lua-hine waved at two specks on the steep green hill. "There's Pam and Kane," he told her. Emily watched them cutting out black and white cows from among the other animals. Gradually they collected a herd of about fifty beasts and headed them for a big barn above the other buildings.

"Now us go look the cows milk," Na-lua-hine said, unfastening the rope around Forty Dollars' neck and opening the gate into the pasture.

Emily walked eagerly up the road beside him, the old dog following at her heels. Men were dismounting in front of the Office and when they saw Emily they called out and waved. Kulani was inside, giving orders for the next day's work. To

Emily's surprise, none of the Hawaiians addressed her as Mrs. Garland. They simply called her Kulani, as though she were one of them, but Emily saw that they loved and revered her.

"Had a happy day, dear?" she asked as Emily and Na-lua-hine entered.

"Oh, Aunt Kulani, yes!"

"I'll be through here in a minute, then you can come with me to the barns."

Paniolos were helping themselves to the canned goods on the shelves. As each man got what he needed, Kulani entered it in a big ledger. Emily sat down on a grain sack and the old dog leaned against her and laid his head on her knee.

"Poi, too, much like you," one of the men commented as he hoisted a flour sack onto his shoulder and started for the door. When the last *paniolo* had been served, Kulani pushed a lock of hair off her warm face and came from behind the counter.

"Now for the final job of the day," she said, smiling.

They walked through a fascinating conglomeration of barns, sheds and houses toward an immense building opening at both ends onto corrals. One corral was filled with innocent-faced calves. In the other, big shiny black and white cows waited to be milked. Some stood switching at flies but the majority were lying down, contentedly chewing their cuds. Emily stayed close to Na-lua-hine as they passed among the big warm bodies but she knew from the way Kulani and her *paniolo* moved that the cows were as gentle as the old dog trotting at her heels.

When they were in the dairy Kulani began calling the cows by name and one by one they heaved up and walked slowly into the barn, taking their right places before a long manger filled with grain. As each cow put her head between two stanchions Na-lua-hine or Kulani clicked a latch into place, fastening the beasts into position.

Pam and Kane came out of the feed-room, carrying big tin tubs filled with powdered milk and grain, which they poured into a long manger on the opposite side from where the cows were feeding. When they opened the gate into the calf corral the little fellows rushed in, kicking up their heels and flourishing their tails. Pam's arms were white with powdered milk, her bronze curls gray and dusty but she looked happy and busy. Emily watched Na-lua-hine and Kane wiping the cows off with water and disinfectant, then Pam started down the line, spraying them for flies.

"You want to do this, Emily?" she asked suddenly.

"I'll—try," Emily said doubtfully, but she was glad her capable young cousin had noticed her.

Pam handed her the spray-gun and after a little she got the hang of working it but her arms soon became tired and Na-lua-hine finished the job. By then half a dozen milking machines had been strapped around the first six cows and connected with electric switches. As each cow was finished, the machine was transferred to another, then Pam, Kane, Kulani and Na-lua-hine stripped the first ones by hand, getting down the last rich milk. Rays of sunlight, like dusty searchlights, slanted in the windows; the air smelt sweet and rich and the barn was filled with the sound of contented munching and the muffled click of milking machines.

Emily felt completely contented. She cuddled old Poi's ear. When the rows of big cans were filled, Kulani took a tin cup off a nail and began pouring foaming milk into a flat dish. Poi watched hopefully. Two rangy cats slid out of the feed-room and began lapping daintily. When they had about half emptied the dish Pam said, "Okay, Poi," and the old dog joined them. The cats flattened their ears but did not try to claw him or run away.

Paniolos came tramping in, spurs clanking at their heels, and by twos carried the big milk-containers away. The calves were turned out, the cows loosed, but no one hurried and after the dairy had been sluiced out Kulani sat down on a box and laughed and joked with the men.

"Did you have a riding lesson today?" Pam asked when they finally started down the hill.

"Yes," Emily answered.

"She do fine," Na-lua-hine asserted. "No use saddle."

Pam's eyes lighted. "Good for you, Emily."

"I only went at a slow walk and Na-lua-hine held my leg," Emily confessed.

"That doesn't matter," Kulani broke in. "In a month you'll be able to take short rides with us on your own horse."

Emily glowed.

At the Office Kane put down the milk pail he was carrying and Pam ran indoors and reappeared with a scrawny kitten which she set down on the steps and fed a small saucer of milk.

"How thin it is," Emily commented.

"It'll be fat as butter in a week," Pam assured her, and told the kitten's history.

"What's its name?" Emily asked.

"It hasn't one yet. I think I'll call it Boston because Pili brought it to me the day Mother heard you were coming."

"You give your animals the funniest names," Emily laughed. "Your old horse is Forty Dollars, your dog's named Poi and now kitty is—Boston."

Kane and Na-lua-hine said goodnight and started for their houses. Pam shooed the little cat into the Office and closed the door, then Kulani started down the hill, the girls following behind. Emily was quite tired but didn't want to go indoors yet.

"I'd like to see the race horses. Where are they?"

"You're taking to Hawaiian ranch life like a duck to water," Kulani smiled at her. "We'll drop in at the stable for a few minutes. I want to see our jockey, Opiopio, about something anyway."

Walking off to the right through a grove of orange trees, she went along a path following the swell of the hill and entered a stable fragrant with the smell of hay, grain and clean horses. The structure was lofty and half-filled with dusk. Thoroughbreds reached out their lean heads over the doors of their loose-boxes and, smelling a stranger, whistled warningly. Emily drew back.

"They won't hurt you," Pam told her.

A squat, lean old Hawaiian got off a grain sack where he was sitting and Kulani talked to him for a few minutes while Pam took Emily down the line of horses, pointing out this one and that which had distinguished itself on the track.

"Mother, couldn't we have Malalo out, so Emily can see him?" Pam asked eagerly.

"Of course, dear. Go outside, Emily, where it's lighter, and Opiopio will lead him out for you."

Emily waited in the scented island dusk, listening to voices and sounds in the stable. Presently there was an eager tattoo of hoofs on the wooden flooring between the loose-boxes, then the sound of a man running and then, like a blinding flash of a striking wave, a great gray horse leaped through the door. The old jockey was leading him and Pam danced about the high-spirited animal, calling Emily's attention to his fine points.

Malolo circled about on the tips of his hoofs, whinnying and shaking his head. His tail shimmered in the twilight, a ribbon of light ran from his withers to the base of his ears. He danced, rocked, blew out his rosy nostrils and shook with excitement. Opiopio jerked soothingly on the leading rein to quiet him and Pam embraced the silver head with such vehemence that the horse drew back, startled. A quick hurt showed in her eyes, then it vanished as the thoroughbred reached toward her again, thrusting at her affectionately with his muzzle.

"Isn't he beautiful? Isn't he grand?" she demanded, turning to her cousin.

Emily couldn't speak. The horse was so gorgeous that it hurt. When she could manage her voice, she said, "I didn't know race horses were like that!"

"Wait till you see Malolo on the track the next Fourth of

July! He's going to win the Hawaiian Free For All cup."

"Don't count your chickens until they've hatched, Pam," Kulani advised.

"He's got to win, Mother. Silver-Wings got it last year, Trade-Wind the year before, and when Malolo comes in a winner we'll have won it for three years in succession. An Island record!"

Kulani's eyes twinkled. "All right, Opiopio, put him up," Kulani directed and they started slowly for the house.

When they reached the back veranda Kulani sat down in a rocker and stuck out one foot. "Pull my boots off, sweetheart, I'm tired," she said.

Pam drew them off, placed them in a corner and fetched a pair of Japanese sandals. Tatsu appeared with a tray of tall glasses filled with chilled pineapple juice and sprigged with fresh mint.

"I think maybe you little tired today, Kulani-san, you ride way up mounting. Cool drink taste nice." She set the tray down on a table handy to Kulani.

"Thank you, Tatsu," she said, reaching for the nearest glass. "This will hit the right spot."

The Japanese woman reminded Emily of a quiet moth but it was evident from her expression that she was more than just a servant. She was part of the family. Her service went beyond wages, it was one of love. She asked a few interested questions about the condition of the feed and cattle up Hualalai, then vanished indoors to go about other duties.

"Pull my boots off, Emily," Pam said, her eyes mischievous.

Emily leaped up gladly, but after some tussling discovered that getting riding boots off wasn't as simple as it looked. "Take my toe in one hand, my heel in the other—like this." Pam showed her the hold. Emily tugged again and first one boot, then the other slid off.

"Aren't they beautiful!" she exclaimed, holding them up.

"Longing for your own ones, aren't you?" Kulani suggested.

"Oh, Aunt Kulani, yes!"

"Work hard at your riding and before you know it you'll have a pair, and a big hat, spurs, and a lasso. Then you'll be a real *paniolo*—like the rest of us."

It seemed odd, Emily thought, that only two days ago she had never even heard the word *paniolo*, didn't even dream that such people as Na-lua-hine, Kane, and the other jolly men existed. Now to be called *paniolo* was the goal of her new life, a life so colorful and joyous that it seemed like a glittering dream out of some strange fairy tale.

CHAPTER IV

A CLOSE CALL

EMILY DISCOVERED THAT THINKING ABOUT BECOMING A *paniolo* and actually learning to be one were different matters. Every morning after breakfast, when the rest of the ranch rode off to work, Na-lua-hine gave Emily a riding lesson. After a bit she could go around the corral at a slow walk without the old man holding on to her leg. But when he put Forty Dollars into a trot she was all over his back and would have fallen off dozens of times if Na-lua-hine had not been there to catch her.

"I don't think I'll ever learn to trot without a saddle," she panted, a few days later.

Na-lua-hine scratched his head. "Try one more time," he

61

urged. She started off again but bobbled all over her mount. Her muscles ached, her cheeks burned and finally she called a halt.

"I tink nuff for today," Na-lua-hine told her.

Her face fell. "Could you take me for a ride around the pasture behind you?"

"Sure," the old man said. "And after lunch us try ride in here with no saddle again."

When Emily was perched behind her *paniolo* on a pad, with his thick waist to cling to, she could relax. Sunshine and peace brooded over the island and spread splendor on the sea, sleeping carelessly under the blue arch of the sky. Doves cooed and occasionally a flock of wild geese streaked down from the summit of Hualalai, uttering wild cries as they landed in the pastures and garden. If only she could learn to sit Forty Dollars without a saddle before Aunt Dode returned from her visiting around, she thought wistfully. How proud she would be!

Every night when Pam rode home with Kane to help with the milking she asked, "Well, have you learned to trot yet?" and Emily had to admit that she hadn't.

"Gosh, you're slow!" Pam exclaimed on the sixth night.

"Forty Dollars' skin slips and wobbles so," Emily explained. "Maybe if I had a saddle to hold on to I could do it."

"You'll never be a decent rider unless you learn bareback," Pam insisted, as she dumped meal into the calves' feed-trough.

Emily's small jaw set. She'd do it, yet, she thought doggedly. Poi, who had become her shadow, nudged her leg with his nose as if to encourage her.

Next morning when she and Na-lua-hine got to the corral she stopped at the gate. "Let me ride behind you *bareback*, Na-lua-hine," she said.

"Sure, us can do."

Vaulting on to Forty Dollars, he hoisted her up and they rode in to the pasture. When he put the horse into a trot Emily gripped him fiercely for a while, then, suddenly, got her balance. "I have it!" she squealed joyously. "Get off and let me go alone."

She stuck like a burr for about a hundred yards then her leg muscles went haywire. All at once Forty Dollars wasn't under her any more. She found herself in the grass and was so stunned that she wanted to cry but before the tears had time to come Na-lua-hine was there, dusting her off and Poi was licking her cheek.

"Swell!" the old man cried, tossing his hat into the air. "You do fine. Only eleven more times to fall off, then you *paniolo!*"

"Do you mean I have to fall off twelve times before I'm a good rider?" Emily asked, aghast.

"Sure!" Na-lua-hine said enthusiastically.

Emily felt a trifle daunted, then got up. "Okay," she said. "Put me on again."

During the next two days she got four more falls behind her but she learned to trot, then to canter slowly. Instead of going with her on foot, Na-lua-hine rode his own horse. Emily was sore and stiff when she came in at night but a wild sort of happiness filled her when she loped beside her *paniolo* across the green pastures and old Poi ran at their heels. On the tenth day, she got back to the corrals without a spill and the old dog came up when she dismounted, sat down in the dust and thumped his tail as though he were applauding her.

Every evening when Emily went to the barn to watch the milking, Pam handed her the fly spray in a matter-of-fact way, as if it were her particular job, and Emily felt as if she'd mounted one rung of the ladder she had to climb before she had won her own place on the ranch.

A day or so later there was a rush of work and Na-lua-hine was called off to go out with the other men. A week before Emily would have felt lost and forsaken, but now she was confident that she could catch Forty Dollars and ride alone. How proud everyone would be of her when they came home and she told them about it, she thought as she headed for the pasture where the work horses ran.

Forty Dollars saw her coming and nickered softly. Her heart rushed to him gratefully. She spoke to him, tied the rope about his neck and led him back to the corral. She got the bridle on without trouble, climbed the fence and slid on to his wide back. Poi watched with pleased pantings.

When Emily was settled she realized that she had forgotten the blanket and surcingle, but after a turn or two around the corral, decided she could do without them. Then a thought fizzed through her head like a rocket going off unexpectedly. Everyone had gone around the hill to the holding paddock to collect steers to ship to Honolulu. If she took the trail they had followed, she would meet them coming back. How surprised and pleased they would be to see her!

"Come, Poi," she called.

Riding slowly along in the sunshine with the splendor of the island above and below her, she didn't feel like Emily Price at all. Emily Price had lived in a small, depressing house on a narrow street in Boston. This Emily was riding a cream-colored horse bareback, and had a cream-colored dog following at her heels. This Emily had flowers around her neck and every atom of her sang with happiness and freedom. This Emily was bare-legged and her skin was turning a golden-color from being out-of-doors!

She hummed *Nancy-Letta-Go-Your-Blouse* as Forty Dollars jogged along the path that dipped through the pasture, then swung around the base of the plum-pudding hill. A loop of the road, connecting with the round-the-island highway, almost met the trail she was following. It seemed impossible that it was only twelve days since she and Aunt Dode had driven along it for the first time in the dark.

A car was smoking up the road, leaving a trail of dust hanging in the air behind it. A rush of excitement swept through her. Maybe it was Grandfather and Aunt Dode coming back! She pulled Forty Dollars to a halt and when she was certain that it was the Packard, galloped forward, waving her arm. The Hawaiian at the wheel brought the car to a stop. Grandfather was in the front seat with him. In her glee Emily forgot that Kaiko was blind.

"Look at me, Grandfather!" she cried joyously.

"You ride swell, Emily!" the driver yelled.

Emily felt dizzy with delight and waited for Aunt Dode to

express her approval, but she was piling out of the car, her face bleak with indignation.

"Emily!" she screamed. "Where are your shoes and stockings? What are you doing, riding around alone without a saddle? You'll fall off and get killed. You look like an Indian! I might have known you'd run wild if I left—" Her voice rose into a wail.

"I'm not running wild, I'm learning to be a *paniolo!*" Emily called out indignantly.

"Whatever a *paniolo* is, I won't have you forget you're a lady! Get into the car at once. I'll have no more of this."

"Haul in your slack, Dode," Grandfather advised. "It's good for Emily to ride alone and be out-of-doors, to go barefoot. Kulani sent for you both so the child can be as healthy as she should be."

"Emily's my charge," Aunt Dode retorted hotly. "Her upbringing's my responsibility. Whoever *heard* of a well-brought up girl gallivanting around alone bareback—"

"American girls raised on Hawaiian ranches do," Grandfather assured her soothingly.

"A telegram came from the meat market in Honolulu this morning for an extra shipment of steers," Emily explained, "and Aunt Kulani needed an extra man, or Na-lua-hine would be with me."

"Who is—well, that fantastic name, and what has he to do with you?" Aunt Dode snapped.

"Na-lua-hine's my *paniolo,*" Emily said proudly.

"What on earth may a—*paniolo* be?" Aunt Dode flung the

word from her.

Grandfather explained but it only seemed to make Aunt Dode madder.

"I never heard of anything so preposterous. You're coming home in the car with me, Emily. And you'll spend the afternoon in your room. Just because you're in Hawaii, you needn't—" She was so angry she couldn't finish the sentence.

"Oh, Aunt Dode," Emily wailed. "Please don't make me go home. I was going out to meet everyone and surprise them. This is the very first time I've ever ridden alone and—"

"You'll fall off and break your neck. Or get lost. That horrible horse is much too big for a girl of your size. You should have a small pony!"

"Forty Dollars isn't a horrible horse! He's beautiful and gentle. He comes when I call him and lets me catch him in the pasture." Tears began streaming down Emily's cheeks, then some inner part of her went wild. Aunt Dode, with her tight, angry face, didn't belong in the picture here. The threat of being shut away from the fun and laughter which always filled the out-of-doors was too much for Emily. Wheeling her horse, she dug her heels into his ribs and tore away, Poi running gladly at Forty Dollars' heels.

She knew she was being bad and disobedient but some force, stronger than she was, that crouched in the giant island, pulled her away. Tears blurred the green grass rushing to meet her but the wind sang a song of freedom in her ears. She wondered if she imagined that she heard the laughter of Grandfather and the Hawaiian driver ringing out together but was afraid that if she looked back she might fall off and Aunt Dode would pounce on her and drag her into the car.

When she heard it drive on, she pulled Forty Dollars down to a walk. She was appalled at what she had done. "Well," she thought, "I'll take my punishment when I get home." She saw the small speck of a rider leaving the barns, following a trail higher on the hill. Some *paniolo* who had been busy with other work was taking a short-cut to join Pam and Kulani, who had gone ahead with the rest of the men to round up the shipping steers.

The day, which had been shaken to pieces, settled back into its wide serenity. Emily debated whether to cut across the pasture and fall in with the rider, then decided that if she kept on the trail she was following he would overtake her later. She liked the adventure of being alone. It made her feel the way she imagined Pam felt when she was sent off on special errands up the mountain.

The trail dipped through a hollow and went up a sharp rise. She grabbed Forty Dollars' mane until they regained level ground, then jogged on happily. Ahead was an opening of green grass, surrounded by shrubbery, and lying in the middle of the clearing was a small, very-new red calf. With a cry of delight, Emily slid off her horse and ran to it. The little creature looked up at her with mild, trusting eyes. Forty Dollars began cropping the grass and Poi took the opportunity to rest. The sweet, milky smell of the calf's soft body, as she happily petted it, the sound of her horse grazing, and the old dog panting contentedly made Emily forget everything else until she heard Poi give a low warning growl. Looking up, she saw a cow trotting swiftly down the hill. She was not black-and-white like the dairy cattle, but red like the calf, with a white face. Her movements were swift and light. Emily was still too green to know that range cows are quick to attack anything that goes near their newborn calves. The cow thought she had concealed her baby safely and was angry when she saw a horse, a dog and a human near her precious new darling.

Emily straightened up and said "Come! Come!" trying to make her voice sound like Kulani's when she called the milk-cows into the barn. The cow shook her head angrily. Poi growled and sprang to his feet. His hackles stood up and his eyes narrowed.

Suddenly Emily knew she was in danger. She tried to scream, but her voice died in her throat. She tried to move but her legs were limp and wobbly as wet macaroni. A terrible thought flashed through her mind. God was punishing her for defying Aunt Dode—who had been good to her after her own, strict fashion.

The cow lowered her head and went into a run. Old Poi rushed forward. The cow swerved and charged him and her horn just grazed his shoulder. Poi sprang for her nose and missed it. The cow charged again and he leaped and hung on for a moment, but he was old and his jaws were not as strong as they had been.

He ran in circles, trying to keep the cow's attention, barking frantically, trying in his dog-fashion to tell Emily to get on to her horse. In some strange way Emily understood and rushed for Forty Dollars who had thrown up his head and was watching uneasily. Then she realized there was no fence nearby to climb onto, so she could not mount. Grabbing the horse's mane, she attempted to scramble up his shoulder but it was big and slippery and her arms were not strong enough to hoist her body up. The cow was uttering dull, enraged bellows, trying to toss Poi who was making ineffectual efforts to hang on to her nose. Emily saw from his movements that he was getting tired and winded.

"Poi!" she screamed. "Come here, Poi!" but the gallant old dog would not be called off.

The cow heard her, wheeled and started for Emily and Forty Dollars. Poi dashed around and sunk his teeth into her hind leg. The terrified calf blatted, stuck its tail into the air and shot into the underbrush. Emily hoped that the cow would go after it but she was still intent upon destroying her enemies. She charged around, spinning Poi off her leg, and lunged at him. One horn caught his ribs a glancing blow and tossed him into the air. He hit the ground with a grunt, rolled over twice, regained his feet and rushed in again, but his movements were getting slow and heavy.

Suddenly there was a sound of racing hoofs. More angry cows coming, probably, attracted by the uproar, Emily thought dully, sinking weakly into the grass. Poi would be tossed and trampled, Forty Dollars might be hurt, she would be killed. She hid her face.

Then she heard a shout, saw a man flash by on horseback swinging a lasso. The rope whined, then the noose snapped shut around the cow's horns. With a jerk the *paniolo* flung his horse on its haunches. The rope whanged taut, the cow went head over heels and lay still, the wind knocked out of it. The Hawaiian was off his horse in an instant, rushed forward, tied the cow's feet with the slack of his rawhide, then dashed to Emily.

"You *pilikea*—hurt?" he asked anxiously, picking her up.

She was crying so hard she couldn't answer, but she did manage to gasp, "Poi—?"

"Poi, okay," the man assured her, wiping her face with his dusty bandana.

When Emily could talk she told him what had happened and he explained, gently, that range cows and dairy stock were different. She must never get off her horse or go near red calves when they were new, or the jealous mothers would attack her. When sobs stopped jerking her body, Emily went over to the old dog who lay panting and exhausted in the grass, but he thumped his tail weakly when she hugged him.

"Now you get on top horse," the *paniolo* ordered, "and I let go the cow." He tossed her onto Forty Dollars. "You and Poi go little way up the trail, so the cow no chase you any more. After I let her go I come quick."

Emily's heart was beating so hard that it felt like a bird opening and closing its wings inside her. "I want to carry Poi in front of me," she said, catching her breath.

"Okay, the old man little *pula*—tired," the man agreed, handing the dog up to her.

Emily was still shaking so hard she could hardly hang on to

Poi, but she managed to with a superhuman effort. He smiled a wide, wet smile while his tongue dripped water on Forty Dollars' shoulder. The horse plodded sturdily up the trail and Emily watched apprehensively over her shoulder.

The *paniolo* walked swiftly to the cow, did something to the rope knotted about her feet, sprinted back to his horse, vaulted on, then gave the lasso a quick jerk. The knot slipped open, the cow leaped and charged. The man shouted, brandished his arm, snatched in his rawhide and dashed away, and after some minutes of circling the cow disappeared into the underbrush, following the direction her calf had taken.

When the *paniolo* overtook Emily he reached over and swung Poi to the back of his saddle, where he crouched tensely until he was rested, then jumped off. Emily was weak and shaken and when they sighted a herd of red, glossy cattle coming around the curve of the hill, she froze. Sight of them made her so dizzy that she had to grab Forty Dollars' mane to keep from falling off. The young *paniolo* seemed to know what was happening inside her and spurred close. "No be scare, Em'ly. When fella on top horse, this-kind cattle never make trouble. Us go little up the ridge. After the cattle go by—"

"I'm not only scared of the red cattle," Emily said in a small, shaken voice, "I'm scared to go home. I ran away from Aunt Dode—" she choked and related the incident.

The handsome young Hawaiian exploded into magnificent laughter.

"This-kind no *pilikea*. You tell Kulani. She fix up so you no get into trouble. Anytime anything trouble all fellas go quick and tell Kulani and she make all right."

Emily felt cheered. She had had the same impression, that no matter what might happen, her aunt had the ability to right matters, however tangled they might be. When the herd of fat beeves had passed, the *paniolo* rode forward and told Kulani what had happened.

"Oh, Emily!" she exclaimed. "Thank God you were not hurt. Or old Poi! I never dreamed you'd leave the corral or I'd have warned you to be careful of range cows with new calves. You've had so much to learn and remember these past twelve days that I didn't want to fill your mind too full of details for fear you'd get mixed up—"

"Then you aren't angry with me?" Emily asked.

"Angry? Of course not, dear. You spunky little thing, coming out bareback all alone to meet us!"

"Aunt Dode—" shakily, Emily told what she'd done.

Pam's mother rode along looking thoughtful and Emily's heart began sinking.

"I'll talk to Dode, Emily," Kulani said, finally. "You shouldn't have disobeyed her, of course, but to my way of thinking your bad brush with the cow is punishment enough for one day."

CHAPTER V

BOY DAY

When Pam and Emily were asleep and Aunt Dode had gone to bed to read, Kulani and Grandfather Kaiko sat up talking. Beyond being father and daughter, they were pals. When matters of importance came up, they discussed them and usually brought them to a triumphant conclusion together.

"We've got to figure out some way," Kulani said, "to keep Dode occupied so Emily will be left free to lead a normal island life. Dode's fine, she's worked hard to care for Emily, but—"

"But hasn't the foggiest notion of how to handle a child?"

Grandfather suggested.

"Exactly. As long as Dode's here she'll have fits if Emily rides bareback or goes off by herself. Emily has been kept so close she hasn't had a chance to develop self-reliance or initiative but, given the chance, she will—quickly."

"That's evident from what happened this morning. You could have knocked me over with a feather when we met the little thing out alone on Forty Dollars. She was like a conquering hero with her foot on top of the world—until Dode began telling her off. When she lit out at full speed—" his big frame shook with laughter.

"If we could only get Dode a position on another island where she could earn a good salary—" breaking off, Kulani thought deeply, then her dark eyes lighted up. "I have it," she announced. "Cousin Laura Bell wants to go to New York for a long visit. Leaving a trained nurse in charge of Ruth and Bud is a bit too steep for her purse. She's been hunting around for someone and—"

"In this instance Dode'll fill the bill to a T!" Grandfather broke in exultantly. "The children need discipline and Dode will only be with them for a few months. Tell you what, Kulani, let's you and I each chip in twenty-five dollars a month. That'll boost the salary to a hundred and fifty and make it really worth Dode's while. She'll have no living expenses and can lay away a neat stake to fall back on when she and Emily return to Boston."

"Fixed!" Kulani cried gleefully. "Dode isn't in a position to refuse a chance of this kind. She'll balk about leaving Emily here, but I'll get around that."

"You always manage to get around obstacles, or crash your way through them," Grandfather remarked proudly. "If I were in a real jam, I'd rather have you fighting beside me than anyone I've ever known."

Kulani flushed with pleasure. "Thank you, Father," she said. "How about having a midnight snack while we thrash out details. There's cold chicken in the Frigidaire."

"Bully," Grandfather said, getting out of his chair.

Sliding her arm through his, Kulani started for the kitchen. While she prowled through the spotless shelves, Grandfather sat on the edge of a table, like a big, happy boy. By the time they had made sandwiches and eaten them, everything was fool-proof and before twenty-four more hours, by using Inter-Island radio, matters had been arranged with Cousin Laura.

Two days later a bewildered, pleased, yet slightly annoyed Aunt Dode was shipped to Honolulu. The best she had ever been able to earn giving private French lessons to backward pupils in Boston had been about eighty dollars a month. There would be no living expenses in her new work, so everything she earned could be saved. As well, she was to be mistress in a household run by two capable Japanese servants and had only a boy of five and a girl of six to care for, so her work would be easy.

Emily was fond of her aunt but her new life kept her so interested and occupied that she did not have time to miss her. She was up at five every morning with the rest of the ranch. When Na-lua-hine was needed for some unexpected bit of extra work, she went to the stables to watch the thoroughbreds groomed and taken out for their early canters, but every day, no matter what, she rode for at least four or five hours. As the days spilled by she became more and more at home on horseback and when she was finally allowed to use Pam's old saddle, she felt as if she had graduated into a higher class. The first time she sat in it she felt at sea, then suddenly, as she cantered slowly across the pastures, she discovered that she seemed to be glued to the old horse's back.

"Now am I a *paniolo?*" she asked excitedly.

Na-lua-hine shook his gray head kindly. There was lots to learn still before she earned the coveted title, he told her. Being a good rider did not mean *being a good horseman.* A *paniolo* didn't only stick on a horse, he knew how to care for it when it was well or ill, how to out-think stock, how to act in emergencies, how to make lassos and saddles. . . .

Emily's face fell. "Okay, I'll learn," she said, after a moment.

"Good girl!"

The next day he came for her looking mysterious and important and carrying a rough brown hide in his hand. "Is that for my lasso?" Emily asked hopefully.

Could a man use a rope unless he had a saddle to tie it to, the old fellow asked, with a twinkle. A tingle of eagerness pierced Emily. That was Na-lua-hine's way of telling her he was going to make her a saddle of her very own. She haunted him during the following days, watching him shape wood for the tree, then begin working on the leather. It seemed impossible that anyone would go to such trouble for her! She helped him to prepare the hide, scraping off the hair with a bit of broken bottle, working grease into it, stretching and re-stretching it until it was pliable.

She hung over him while he cut the various pieces that went into the making of a saddle, watched him carving beautiful designs of mangoes, bananas and coconuts on the sweat-guards paralleling the stirrup leathers, on the tapaderos that would cover the stirrups, and on the place where she would sit. Vine and fern leaves were engraved on the cantle and twisted around the pommel. . . .

When the masterpiece was finished, Emily gazed at it in awed silence.

Next Na-lua-hine cut long *latigos* and worked them until they hung limp, dark and lustrous, ready to fasten the black and white horsehair girth he had braided, about the horse's body. Finally everything was assembled.

"*Pau*—finished!" Na-lua-hine shouted triumphantly, holding the saddle up for Emily's inspection.

She could hardly believe such a precious thing belonged to her! Tears filled her eyes, then she rushed at the kind, portly old man and hugged him. "It's beautiful, it's gorgeous!" she cried, choking with happiness.

"I think maybe you like!" he chuckled.

"Like it? I love it!"

The first time Emily rode it she felt like a person in a glittering dream and went around in a daze for hours. When she came in everyone on the ranch crowded about her, praising

Na-lua-hine's work.

"Em'ly help me," her *paniolo* said proudly, patting her foot which stuck out to show the sweeping tapaderos which protected her feet from brush and thorns.

As she grew more expert in ranch ways, Emily felt as if a mighty, invisible tide was carrying her forward, a tide that carried everyone working and living at Kilohana in the same direction. She tried to learn everything she could—watched horses being shod, held buckets of water and creolin when cuts were dressed on horses' legs, remembered to close gates between pastures so stock would not get mixed up, imitated the way men put away their riding gear. . .

The only flaw in her happiness was that she sensed that Pam was unimpressed by her progress. She was friendly and polite but more interested in the mighty work of the ranch than in becoming friends with her cousin from Boston. Emily, on the other hand, thought Pam was the most wonderful human being she had ever known. Watching her rope calves, exercise fiery race horses, handle stock, dress wounds, left Emily limp with admiration. Everyone who knew Pam loved her.

Emily was wise enough to see that it was not only Pam's fire, beauty, and capability that made people worship her. It was her entire forgetfulness of self, her true love for human beings and animals, and her interest in everything going on about her. Emily determined that beyond winning the coveted title of *paniolo* she would learn to be like her cousin. No matter how busy Pam might be, if anyone needed her or if anything went wrong, she was instantly into the breach. When the baby of one of the *paniolos* had convulsions and Kulani was away, Pam phoned the doctor, then rushed to Moku's house and gave the necessary treatment until help arrived. Another day, one of the yardmen almost cut off his hand and she fixed a tourniquet without getting upset at the sight of the blood. She was cool in tight places, leaped into action when it was necessary, and when the emergency was over, sank back into routine work without wasted motion. . . . And still she managed to be a gay, simple little girl, laughing and dancing on her busy way.

One afternoon when Emily was busy rubbing vaseline into Poi's feet, which had been cut on some lava, Pam came leaping onto the Office porch.

"Emily, Tatsu asked Mother if you and I could go to Hilo with her for Boy Day. Her brother is a dentist and has four little sons. Grandfather's going with us."

"What's Boy Day?" Emily asked.

"It's sort of Japanese Christmas honoring the sons in a family."

"Will we be gone long?"

"Two or three days."

Emily's face became thoughtful.

"Aren't you glad to go?" Pam asked, frowning slightly.

"Yes, but it's so important to me to learn to be a *paniolo*— like you—that I sort of hate to take the time for other things."

"If you don't go Tatsu's feelings will be hurt. She asked Mother specially because of you. You still have months to learn to ride in, and Boy Day is such fun!"

Pam always managed to splash her enthusiasm into the

atmosphere and all at once Emily felt as if a wave had lifted her upward. Possibly being away from the absorbing things of the ranch would be a good chance to get closer to Pam.

"I think it'll be fine," she agreed. "When do we go?"

"Tomorrow," Pam answered, bouncing around. Then she bent down and examined Poi's feet. "You're treating them just right, Emily," she announced and went on into the Office. Emily gazed at the garden, feeling that everything looked more beautiful because of her cousin's praise.

Next morning, after breakfast, Nuhi drove the Packard up to the house. When the suitcases were stored in the rear, Kulani kissed the girls and Grandfather good-bye, patted Tatsu's shoulder, and stepped back.

"Have a good time!" she called as the car rolled away.

Emily was silent as they drove along. Her eyes wandered to the great hill, the grazing cattle, the dark cherimoya trees and drooping peppers. "I hate leaving the ranch—even for a day," she remarked.

Pam's eyes lighted. "Good for you! But it'll be waiting here for us when we come back."

"You have it for always, Pam. I only have it for a year."

"I hadn't thought of that," Pam said, then her hand closed over Emily's. "A year's a long time. Don't think of far-away, unhappy things. Let's just have fun."

That was easy for Emily after this first real sign of her cousin's liking and sympathy. After driving for two hours through the ragged, tortured beauty of old lava flows they came to a big gate across the Government road. Pam leaped out and unfastened it and Nuhi drove through. The lava beds ended suddenly and the car rolled through grassy pastures that shivered under the wind. Grandfather roused himself from his relaxed position and sniffed the clean, cold air.

"You know Emily, this great upland grass country was the cradle of cattle raising in Hawaii. We're driving through the historic Parker Ranch."

"Tell me about it," Emily begged.

Grandfather always seemed to get bigger and finer looking when he told of interesting Island things. His dark eyes glowed and he leaned forward like a horse scenting a wind filled with the fragrance of lush pastures. "Few mainlanders realize, Emily, that cattle raising in Hawaii antedates that of the great American West by many decades. The Revolutionary War had only been over a few years and there were still only thirteen states in the Union, in 1792, when Lord George Vancouver, the British explorer, first arrived in Hawaii. His relations with the Hawaiians were warm and intelligent and after spending several months in the Islands he sailed for California, promising to return the following year with some cattle."

Emily listened avidly.

"Previous to Vancouver's arrival, some earlier explorer had told the Hawaiians he would bring them some cows. During the long trip around Cape Horn all the cattle died, but a dozen goats survived and when they were landed the natives thought they were the promised cows. To this day if you ask a Hawaiian to bring you a cow, he'll present you with a goat. The Hawaiian name for goat is spelled K-a-o."

Emily laughed delightedly.

"True to his promise, Lord Vancouver returned to Hawaii in 1793, bringing a couple of dozen Longhorn cows and a bull. He landed the stock at Kawaihae." Grandfather gestured at a blue sweep of bay below them.

"I always get a thrill," Pam burst in, "when I look down there and think of those first cattle making their way up the long, rough slopes to these grasslands. How rich they must have smelled to the poor animals after weeks on shipboard, how free they must have felt."

Grandfather nodded. "The cattle were a gift to Kamehameha, the First. The King put a taboo on them for twenty years, so they could increase. When the time came to round them up, the Hawaiians didn't know how, so *vaqueros* were imported from Mexico to instruct them in ranching and handling stock. The Hawaiian word *paniolo*—cowboy—is derived from the word *Español*, a Spaniard."

Emily's eyes shone.

"The beef cattle industry was well established in Hawaii long before sugar-cane was grown commercially and the Territory at present produces seventy-eight per cent of its own meat supply. Since those first cattle came, the finest breeds of stock have been imported and the Parker Ranch boasts the world's biggest registered herd of Hereford cattle."

"But Kilohana has fine cattle, too," Emily protested.

"Yes," Grandfather agreed proudly. "Kilohana supplies Honolulu with prime Hereford beef and, as well, its herd of Golden Guernseys and Holsteins tops the dairy herd in

Hawaii." As they drove through the splendid windy plateau between Mauna Kea and the Kohala mountains, Grandfather told the girls of the colorful days of the Parker Ranch during his youth. Old Sam Parker, great-grandfather of the present owner, had been a big figure in Hawaii. His hospitality was epic and his mountain home, Mana, was a gathering place for leading Islanders and prominent people from all over the world.

The *paniolos* riding its 600,000 acres were part of the place, as their forefathers had been there for four generations. The mighty swoop of land between the towering mountains had produced cowboys the equal of any in the world. In 1908 Ikua Purdy, born and raised on the Parker Ranch, had gone to Cheyenne to compete in the great rodeo against the cream of American cowboys and had carried off first prize for roping. Angus MacPhee, the man he defeated, who had been the World's Champion Roper for five years in succession, came to Hawaii the following year to win back his title but Ikua defeated him again.

By the time Grandfather had finished talking about the Parker Ranch and its *paniolos*, the car began flashing through cane fields that waved long, jade-green banners in the wind. The cattle country was behind them, the sugar plantations had begun. Around four o'clock the car pulled into Hilo, second largest town in the Islands, where Tatsu's dentist-brother lived. Houses smothered in trees and shrubbery lined the streets, wet and steaming from an afternoon shower. The buildings were a jumble of old-fashioned and modern architecture, suggesting a lovely but rather untidy woman decked out in odds and ends of old and new finery.

Nuhi kept shouting to friends he recognized, who called back greetings in return. The streets grew narrower and more winding as he drove toward the Oriental section of town. Rackety buildings with overhanging balconies reared above the pavements; the lower stories were little shops, the second floors dwelling places. Half-clad babies swarmed on the steps, peddlers trotted past, with wicker baskets hanging from poles across their shoulders, loaded with vegetables and merchandise. Over most of the houses great paper fish, tied to tall bamboo poles, were ducking and floating against the sky.

Emily cried out with pleasure at the beauty they made. "What are they for?" she asked, pointing at the graceful scarlet, purple and yellow shapes twisting and rolling in the wind.

"They're to celebrate Boy Day, May fifth," Pam told her, "and are flown in honor of the sons in a family."

Tatsu was lighted up with anticipation as she directed Nuhi through the helter-skelter streets. He drew up finally before a neat house, set back in a garden that was laid out with elaborate little pools, dwarf trees and bridges made of china, spanning wee streams. Tatsu's brother came hurrying out to meet his guests. After he had greeted his sister, he bowed and inhaled several times and said his household was indeed honored to shelter such distinguished people for Boy Day. His wife was waiting at the door and they all removed their shoes before entering and put on straw sandals which Mrs. Nishi handed out.

The instant the door closed the house became all Japanese. The simplicity of the interior, with its sliding rice-paper walls and matted floors, was restful and cool. A lacquered table, about six inches high, occupied the center of the floor and around it cushions were placed to sit on. Nishi had borrowed a chair for Grandfather, but he insisted he was not too stiff and old yet to sit on the floor for tea!

Pam and her grandfather expressed their admiration for the beauty of the room, according to Japanese etiquette, while Mrs. Nishi began working with tea paraphernalia arranged neatly on a mat beside her: tea bowls, a caddy, whisk, bamboo spoon and other items. When a bowl was handed to Pam she held it in both hands, turned it around three times, and took a swallow. Emily watched and imitated her and everyone beamed.

"You are indeed conversant with Japanese customs," Nishi informed her in his perfect English.

"I watched Pam," Emily confessed honestly and everyone laughed.

When the tea ceremony was over, Grandfather suggested to the girls that they all go for a prowl along the water front, so Tatsu could have an uninterrupted visit with her family. Nuhi leaped up joyously, took Grandfather's arm and headed for the main street of the river-town.

"Swell fun come to Hilo!" he remarked jauntily as he swung along.

He was a sociable soul and seemed to know almost everyone. He stopped at Chinese stores to chat with the proprietors, hailed a big Portuguese, flung a remark at some Filipino dandies, paused to chat with good-natured Hawaiian women sitting on the pavement making *leis* and gossiping. He bought *lichi* nuts and soda pop for Grandfather and the girls, and waited while they loitered in narrow, fascinating little stores, examining curios and beautiful Oriental objects.

The sun had set and the blue sampans riding on the river were doubled in the glassy water. Japanese fishermen squatted in the sterns of their boats, eating broiled fish, rice and spicy vegetables with chopsticks and sipping pale, fragrant tea from small bowls. A sort of dreamy laziness lay upon the town and the distant forests and cane fields crawling up the long slopes of Mauna Loa that reared its faintly snow-crusted summit toward the clouds.

"It will be dark soon, we'd better start back," Grandfather said finally.

"How can you tell?" Emily asked in awed tones.

"A person needn't be blind simply because he can't see," Grandfather answered jauntily. "I know the evening smells from the feel of the air, and—besides, my tummy tells me so!"

On the way back he stopped at a Japanese store and bought four ten-foot paper fish to present to Nishi's sons next morning. Nuhi said he'd take them to his cousin's house, where he was spending the night, to keep them a complete surprise.

Supper was a simple affair at the Nishi home and everyone retired early, to be fresh for Boy Day. Tatsu took the girls to a bedroom and said goodnight. It seemed cozy to Emily to undress with Pam, as if they were sisters and had known each other always. She wondered if her cousin felt the same way but was too shy to ask. They got on to the raised, matted platform across one end of the room which served as a bed. They rolled out padded quilts, which were used for both mattresses and coverings, and went to sleep while the river murmured to the blue boats resting upon it and the Pacific crooned its ancient song to the reefs and beaches.

Next morning they were awakened by a tremendous racket. "*Banzai! Banzai!* It's Boy Day!" was being shouted from all the Japanese houses. Boys were yelling and rushing around, greeting each other and rejoicing in the holiday dedicated mainly to them.

During the forenoon Pam and Emily helped Tatsu to decorate the house with a variety of iris specially grown for the occasion. Tatsu told them that the name of the flower, "Shobu," meant Victory. Relatives and friends kept pouring in to offer congratulations to Nishi and his wife for having four sturdy sons to care for them in their old age. Fun and merriment charged the atmosphere. At an appropriate moment Grandfather signed to Nuhi and he went out and returned with the parcel containing the four paper fish. Nishi's sons, seated like motionless brown images on cushions beside their father, looked interested and eager. Nishi undid the string and inhaled with pleasure when he saw a red, a yellow, a pink, and a purple fish.

"You are indeed gracious, Mr. Grandfather," he said on a hissing breath, as Japanese do when they are pleased. Then he bowed.

Nishi's wife and relatives examined the fish with polite delight and wonder, as if they had never seen such marvels in their lives. After a little the boys' grandfather went off with them, to run up the new fish on bamboo poles for all the neighborhood to see.

The little house had, almost, the feeling of Christmas in it. This was the Japanese time of year to be merry, to spread good cheer, to pay respects and call down blessings on everybody, but mostly on the boys. Incense burned slowly before a small shrine at one end of the room and while Nishi and his men friends sipped *saké* and visited, the womenfolk of his household slipped away to the kitchen where food was being prepared for the feast.

Finally one of the paper walls slid back, and bowing and smiling women urged everyone to come and partake. With elaborate ceremonies, people were seated about the low, laden table. Special foods, served only on Boy Day, had been prepared, as well as more usual delicacies. *Chimaki*, made of beans and red rice wrapped in lily leaves, was handed around. *Hasikiwa mochi*, a rice-cake wrapped with oak leaves, symbolizing strength, was slowly eaten. The food was served on plates only used for the occasion and when nobody could hold any more, toasts were drunk by the adults in hot *saké*.

Once the feasting was over, the formalities, dear to the Japanese heart, were ended—at least as far as the boys were concerned. They raced off to play with their comrades and the uproar coming from the twisted streets told what a happy time they were having. Nishi explained that on Boy Day sons were free to call on playmates without asking leave and to shout and play to their heart's content.

"Would it interest you to see the boys' toys?" he asked hopefully, in his perfect English.

Pam's face lighted. "Oh, Nishi, that would be fun!" she cried and he beamed.

Emily watched her cousin as she examined the tiny images of famous warriors and heroes of old Japan, and saw that Pam's greatest charm was her genuine interest in matters that interested others. She didn't seem like a girl and Nishi a Japanese man. They were just two people, with minds friendly and close.

When the last toy had been examined and replaced before the carved screen, Nishi escorted his guests back to the living room for tea before they started home. The little house had a fulfilled feeling in it. While they sipped tea from fragile little bowls and nibbled at crisp rice cakes, Nishi took advantage of his last opportunity to explain a few more details about Boy Day.

"You see," he said, bowing deeply to Grandfather, "Japanese make Boy Day an occasion in which to inculcate youth with lessons of character, utilizing toys with legends, house-decorations with morals, and even serving food with meaning, like *Hasikiwa mochi*, which symbolizes strength. Even the carp—" he gestured out the open windows to where great fish rolled and dipped against the sky, "have a specific meaning."

Grandfather looked attentive and interested.

"You see, in Japan rivers are swift and strong with many rapids and waterfalls. Of all the fish inhabiting our streams only carp ever reach headwaters. They are powerful enough to breast the strong current, fight up raging rapids, and leap waterfalls blocking their path. Therefore, carp are flown on Boy Day so youngsters may see and remember to be strong and courageous as they swim up the river of life."

"A good example for all of us, not only boys," Grandfather agreed heartily.

CHAPTER VI

A TERRIFYING RIDE

"Wasn't Boy Day fun, Emily?" Pam asked as they drove
away after tea.

"Yes," Emily said rapturously, taking a last glance at the
blue sampans along the water front and the great colored fish
floating in the breeze. "I can't really believe I've slept in a Japanese house with paper walls." She giggled. "If Aunt Dode knew
she'd have a fit!"

"Dode'll get over race-prejudice after she's been in Hawaii

for a while," Grandfather announced. "Hawaii is the world's greatest adventure in friendship. For over a hundred years people of all nationalities have been living and working peacefully together. Each race that came in brought its own religion, ways of eating, thinking, and living and after a while borrowed something from other races in return."

Emily listened intently.

"In the Orient Japanese and Chinese are shooting each other but in Hawaii it's a common sight to see a Japanese boy carrying a Chinese girl's book to school. In Europe different nations watch each other suspiciously. Here Germans, English and Americans are friends. The Hawaiians are largely responsible for this condition. Their spirit of *Aloha*—love—for their fellow men has paved the way to better understanding between everyone and mellowed and broken down people's conviction that their particular blood is superior to all others. Each race, each individual has something to give and something to learn from the other fellow. When people say "*Aloha!*—My love to you!" —every day of their lives to everyone they meet, and are greeted with the same word, the spirit of it gets into the atmosphere, making life more like the beautiful thing God intended it to be at the start."

Emily weighed Grandfather's solemn words. They were true. Seven weeks ago, while she was still in Boston, if anyone had told her she would miss a funny-looking old brown man like Na-lua-hine, or a skinny old Chinese cook like Ah Sam, she would have thought they were crazy. Now she could hardly wait to get back to them. They were precious friends she loved and wanted to be with. She listened to Tatsu and Nuhi joking together in the front seat. This magic word, *Aloha*, drew everyone closer together in some mysterious, powerful way. It made the afternoon holy, the sea and mountains more beautiful and strangers loitering along the streets friends.

Pam bent over and whispered in Grandfather's ear. "How careless of me!" he exclaimed. "Of course Emily must see the Naha stone."

He spoke to Nuhi in Hawaiian and he turned off the main street. They drove for a few minutes and finally pulled up. Against a background of huge green land-taro leaves and hibiscus bushes covered with blossoms like storms of gaudy butterflies, lay a long slab of black lava, roughly resembling a coffin. Something awesome and impressive lingered about it that sent goose flesh prickling over Emily.

"That's the famous Naha stone," Grandfather explained as they went to look at it. "According to legend, any warrior who could lift the end of this ponderous block of lava was destined for royalty. Kamehameha performed the feat, so the story goes, and won the other chiefs to his support."

"But a man couldn't possibly lift that rock even an inch," Emily protested.

"Sure," Nuhi insisted. "Long time before the Hawaiian *Aliis* —chiefs—lift up the Naha stone. My great-great-great-grandfather see Kamehameha pick up with his own eyes."

"You try, Nuhi, you're strong as a bull," Pam suggested.

"I no can make. I no *Alii*," Nuhi said with a gorgeous explosion of mirth. He wrestled with the great block until his face was purple, then stopped.

"Why were chiefs stronger than common people?" Emily asked, turning to Grandfather.

"They were given special food and exercises to develop their muscles and increase their stature," Grandfather explained, "and, at first, early explorers took them for another race of people. Most of the men and women were over six feet and graceful in proportion."

They lingered about the great stone in its luxuriant setting, then Grandfather began sniffing. "It's getting on toward sunset," he announced. "We've a long way to go and must get started. Wait, I've an idea. I'll phone Kulani and tell her we're staying at Puuiki tonight."

"What's Puuiki?" Emily asked.

"That's the name of my sugar plantation. This is a good chance for you to get acquainted with sugar cane. The grinding season is on and the mill's going full blast. We can spend the morning looking around and get back to Kilohana in time for dinner."

"Who takes care of the plantation when you're at the ranch with us?" Emily asked.

"I have a manager."

It was dark by the time Grandfather finished telephoning from the hotel. The car purred through the night, which smelled rich and damp, as if its arms spilled over with earthy offerings. Finally Nuhi turned off the highway and drove down a long road toward winking lights at the dark edge of the sea.

Next morning before daylight the house began jerking back and forth. Windows rattled, furniture jumped about.

"An earthquake," Pam remarked, sitting up and switching on the light. "Probably Mauna Loa's going to erupt."

"Oh, Pam!" Emily's voice collapsed with terror. "How terrible! I can't imagine a mountain spouting fire."

"You've got to get over being afraid of things if you're ever going to be a *paniolo!*" Pam said, a trifle shortly.

Emily swallowed. Pam, who had seemed so close during the past two days, was far-away again. "I'll try not to be a 'fraid-cat, Pam. I want to be like you."

"Like me? Why?"

"You're so wonderful."

"Don't be silly," Pam retorted, looking uncomfortable. "We might as well get up and dress. It's almost four and Grandfather'll be ready to take us through the mill before long."

Just as they left the room another shock passed through the earth. Emily's knees felt weak with terror but she managed to keep walking along as if it didn't bother her. Grandfather had had his coffee and was on the veranda waiting for them. As they stepped through the door, Emily gave a stifled cry. On the dark slopes of the mountains behind the plantations long fires were burning with a red, awful light.

"The volcano has erupted," she gasped, grabbing at Grandfather.

He laughed and put his arm about her. "Those fires aren't the volcano. You'll see them on any plantation in Hawaii during the grinding season. Sit down on the steps and I'll tell you about them."

Emily sank down weakly and, feeling the shaking of her slight body, Grandfather placed his big, comforting arm about her.

"Years ago there was a disastrous cane-fire on the island of Maui. It burned thousands of acres of sugar cane, which was just ripe and ready to turn into sugar. The manager of the plantation determined to grind all of it he could, anyway. He discovered that cane which was run through rollers within forty-eight hours from the time fire was put to it was uninjured. As a result, the old, laborious, costly method of stripping the long leaves off the stalks by hand was abandoned. Instead, quick fires are run through fields ready to be cut. They are lighted about three in the morning, before the wind rises, so that the flames can be kept in control. Then the stalks are rushed to the mill in the correct quantity to be ground within the appointed time of forty-eight hours."

Emily's fright had faded into the background by the time they started for the big mill with its brilliantly lighted windows and solemnly smoking stacks. Step by step they went through the process of sugar-making from the start.

Silly little engines puffed importantly and gave squeaky whistles as they pushed flat cars piled with cane to mighty rollers that crushed it to juice. After the juice rushed out like water it poured along a sort of flume into giant boilers that cooked it until it was thick and dark. The molasses went into centrifugal whirlers until it dried, then it came out rich brown sugar that poured into bags which machines stitched up. The bags moved along a big leather belt which spilled them neatly onto freight cars. These cars were then pushed down to the landing and shipped to California, to be refined into white sugar.

Emily moved warily among huge spinning wheels, plunging pistons, and revolving leather bands. Her heart beat until it choked her when they walked across narrow bridges and looked down into the huge, busy mass of machinery and men moving methodically about their special tasks. She tried to remember what Pam had said about being scared of things and tried to forget her awe in the wonder of what she was seeing.

By the time they had gone through the mill, which ran day and night during the grinding season—lasting from early summer until late fall—daylight was coming. Gangs of blue-clad laborers of a dozen nationalities were starting for the fields with hoes over their shoulders and wicked-looking cane-knives dangling from their belts. As they passed each other they kept calling out *"Aloha,"* then went on jabbering in their own tongues. Big Hawaiian *lunas* on fat horses rode ahead to oversee the gangs of workmen assigned to them. The Manager, who was watching everything, stopped to confer with Grandfather about different phases of the work, but the activity and bustle never stopped. Pam talked to people she knew, asked questions and explained confusing details to Emily.

Finally Grandfather mounted an old white horse and the girls climbed onto young animals which were saddled and waiting for them.

"We're going into the fields, Emily, so you can see how cane is grown and cultivated," Grandfather said as they jogged along. "Sugar is the basis of Hawaiian prosperity and nowhere in the world is it so scientifically raised and studied. There are laboratories in Honolulu and experimental stations where new varieties of cane are grown and tested and antidotes for pests and blights are studied."

Grandfather's horse stumbled and he jerked it up expertly.

"Plantation laborers in Hawaii are well housed, provided with water, wood, and electricity free of charge. The children are given free milk and the plantation maintains a doctor and hospital which can be used without cost to anyone below a certain salary.

"Each plantation, each field has a specific irrigation system. In this section of Hawaii, the windward side, the slope of the country is so steep that the cane is planted on a slant, while the mills are built at sea-level. Because of the heavy rainfall, deep gorges have been gashed into the mountains. Long detours and costly trestles and bridges make it impractical and expensive to build the usual narrow-gauge railroads to carry cane to the mills. Instead, wooden flumes filled with swiftly rushing water float the stalks to the yards. Bundles of the right size to move freely inside the flumes are thrown in at spaced intervals and taken four or five miles."

Pulling up his horse, Grandfather listened to the hiss of water flowing by in one of the flumes he was describing. "When I was a boy my brothers and I thought it fine sport to ride cane-bundles from the fields to the mill," he said.

"Oh, Grandfather!" Pam cried. "Could we try? But maybe

you'd be scared to, Emily," she added, not unkindly.

"I want to—if you do," Emily said in a tight, small voice. "It looks kind of—" she broke off hastily and added "fun."

"It is," Grandfather agreed. "While not actually dangerous, it needs a cool head. Once you're on a bundle and get going, *you have to stay there.* If you try to get off and out of the flume you may be hurt, because of the speed at which the water's travelling."

"Shall we try?" Pam asked rather breathlessly.

"Yes!" Emily said violently. "I don't want to miss any fun —while I'm here!"

"That's the ticket," Grandfather said. "Make hay while the sun shines and you'll have a fine lot of memories to take back to Boston."

Emily's face went all white and bleak for an instant. "Please don't talk about Boston, Grandfather. I don't even want to think about it any more."

Pam flashed an amazed look at her cousin. "I didn't know you loved Hawaii like that."

"I love it so much I can't even talk about it," Emily said, catching her breath.

Grandfather called to the *luna* overseeing the gang and told him to order one of the men to take the girls' horses back to the stables. Pam jumped down and Emily dismounted slowly.

"This-kind hard for make," a knotty Japanese told Pam, whose cheeks were burning with excitement.

"Yes," she agreed, her eyes following the fall of the flume before it curved along a steep bluff and crossed a trestle spanning a deep, narrow gorge. "But I'd like to try and make it one time."

"Okay. I make Number One strong bundle for you," the man said, lashing a generous armful of stalks together.

"I feel kind of empty inside," Pam confessed, turning to Emily. "But if Grandfather and his brothers did it, I can. Maybe you'd better not try."

Emily swallowed. "I want to," she insisted.

"You're swell!" Pam cried. "I'll go first. Hang on with all your might and if you get frightened shut your eyes and hold on tighter."

While the Japanese made up the extra-special bundles the girls stood close together, looking on. Emily felt curiously pleased because she and Pam were sharing the same experience for the first time.

"Well, here I go," Pam said when the Japanese put her bundle into the water and held it strongly against the side of the flume.

"Draw your legs up high, as if you were riding in a horse race," Grandfather directed, "or you'll scratch them against the sides of the flume."

"I'll remember," Pam called out. Grasping the bundle fiercely, she mounted warily, as she would mount a snorty horse, arranged her legs in jockey-position and yelled, "Let go!"

She caught her breath as she felt the water seize the bundle of cane-stalks, tossing them up, then shooting them forward down the steep slope. For a few moments she had to close her eyes until she adjusted herself to this new way of travelling. Then she glanced back to see if Emily were really going to follow. She had just been turned loose. "Emily is a sport—way down inside," Pam thought.

Then she had to concentrate on what she was doing. The bundle bobbed, leaped, gave dismaying little half-rolls under her, like a bucking horse. Water swooshed up when the bundle ducked and fell away when it reared up. The flume turned sharply and she was forced to lean out as though she were taking a thoroughbred around the curve of a track. Panic pierced her briefly. Emily had never ridden a horse at full speed, she might not know how to balance and be shot off like a slingstone. Instinct told her Emily was doing this only because she had told her that morning she must get over being scared of things.

The flume dropped down a slope and the water gathered speed. The bundle zipped along at a furious rate, then slowed a little as the flume levelled to follow the curve of a bluff. Because Grandfather was blind he probably didn't realize what a risky flume this one was to ride, Pam thought, as she closed her eyes so as not to see the drop on her right hand, and her worry for Emily increased. She managed a backward glance. Emily's eyes were shut, her face pale and she was hanging on for dear life.

Pam hastily closed her eyes again as the flume crossed a high trestle, spanning a deep, narrow gulch. When the changed sound of the water told her she was safely across, she risked another backward glance. Emily was just starting over the trestle. "Don't open your eyes!" Pam screamed and Emily gave a grim, silent little nod as she whirled on.

When her cousin was over without a mishap, relief surged through Pam. The rest of the ride wouldn't be so risky. She could see the brown flume, filled with tossing silver water and bobbing bundles of cane, twisting ahead, down the slope of the land toward the smoking stacks of the mill. The water gathered fresh speed as it pitched down a hillside. Faster and faster it rushed. Then, as the fall of the land grew less, it lost impetus and the bundle slowed up until it bobbed serenely along the narrow, shining ribbon of water gurgling inside wooden walls.

Men hooking out dripping cane looked stunned when they saw a small girl riding in. A lean Chinaman snatched her off and, shaky and thankful, she found her feet on the ground. Emily came floating in, deathly pale, eyes shut tight. When she was lifted off, she sank weakly to the grass.

"Never again," she gasped. "But I did it!"

"I can't get my breath yet," Pam said. "It'll take Grandfather an hour to get in. I bet we made it in less than twenty minutes. My, but you're swell, Emily. Maybe because I'm so accustomed to Island things I can't quite understand how you feel, or how they seem to you. Mother has told me about the subway trains that rush underground. I'd hate that. It would scare me."

"It wouldn't, after once or twice," Emily insisted.

Pam looked at her cousin. She didn't seem like a timorous sissy any more, she was dear and close. Her plain little face was beautiful with that lighted, eager expression.

"I'm glad you're here, Emily. I wasn't at first. I was afraid you wouldn't like riding and the ranch people and I'd have to stay with you and miss a lot of fun. But you like everything and love Hawaii. Maybe there'll be times, still, when I'll get a little impatient when you're slow and make mistakes, like the other morning when you left the gate open and the calves got into the horse-pasture."

"Oh," Emily said in a thin voice, afraid that she had forfeited her cousin's nearly-won friendship.

"It doesn't matter. I sorted them out. You've showed me you're game by riding the flume."

"I felt as if I had no insides," Emily admitted and their laughter chimed together and floated toward the rumbling mill. Emily lifted her face to the fresh wind. She was happy all the way through. Friendship shone in Pam's eyes and the comradeship of sharing a thrilling adventure.

CHAPTER VII

EMILY WINS HER SPURS

Almost anyone who has lived near the ocean has hunted for shells on the beach, but few people have searched for them in tree-tops. However, that's exactly where you look for them in Hawaii—on the under-sides of new leaves. Before Grandfather lost his eyesight, he had assembled a magnificent collection of shells which ranked with those made by Lorrin Thurston and Montague Cooke. Being the kind of man he was, mere darkness did not daunt him or dampen his enthusiasm and he was always on the lookout to see if some new variety of land shell could be found.

When he and the girls reached home, Emily and Pam hurried up to the barn, for it was milking time. The afternoon had retreated to deep valleys and was hesitating on the hills. Men were collected about the Office and the peace of a day full of accomplishment lay over everything.

"Isn't it wonderful to be home!" Pam exclaimed, as she and Emily made their way among the big, slow-moving cows, waiting in the corral for their turn to go in and be milked.

Emily was so happy that she could only nod.

After joyous greetings all around, the girls went to work and the clicking of machines and the rich sound of milk going into buckets filled the evening with contentment.

Just as they turned out the last cow and were giving the barn cats and Poi their milk Grandfather came bolting through the door. His dark eyes, which saw nothing, were full of light and fire and his movements were excited.

"One of the *paniolos* has brought in part of a land shell unlike anything in my collection," he said, and everyone crowded up to see the fragile fragment he held in his big fingers.

"It's gorgeous," Kulani said. "A sort of pale green, with a coral colored mouth and looks like a rosebud which has just opened."

Grandfather breathed as if he'd been running.

"I'll need the bright eyes of you girls tomorrow to track this down. Kimmo marked the tree where he found it on the grass. It's way up Hualalai. If there's a broken shell of this variety under the tree there are live ones in the branches. No one is going to beat me to this one, if I know it!"

His eagerness got into the atmosphere and the girls promised to go with him to try to find the new beauty. Ah Sam had lunches ready at daylight and in the freshness of the early morning Kane, Grandfather, and the girls set off up the steep slopes of Hualalai.

Emily had never been up the mountain and was eager to see what lay behind the bulge of the hill. When they topped it, they halted to wind the horses. Empty reaches of country went away toward the vast shape of Mauna Loa. To the right, Hualalai flung its cinder cones against the blue sky and in the east Mauna Kea showed its snowy summit.

The silence of the wide morning was broken by the silvery maternal nickerings of mares to their colts, by the distant bellowing of fighting range bulls and the high sweet whistle of plover. Red *iiwis*, black and red *apapanas* and green *amakihis* called to each other from *lehua* trees, where they sucked honey, and occasionally one darted to a new branch, flashing like a jewel against the sky.

As they rode slowly up the winding trail Grandfather told the girls about the native birds of Hawaii. Before white men imported mynah birds to the Islands, the native varieties had been plentiful, but the mynah birds from India had practically destroyed them, tearing their nests to pieces and tossing the young to the ground. Little by little, the native birds had been driven farther and farther back into the mountains and forests.

In olden times each family of noble birth kept a retainer who spent his entire life in the forests, gathering feathers to fashion the magnificent red and yellow feather cloaks and helmets worn by the chiefs on ceremonial occasions. The feather-gatherers smeared a sticky substance on the branches of trees where the birds sucked honey, then waited until the birds were caught. The rarest and most prized feathers of all were yellow ones, which were not as plentiful as the red.

The now extinct O-o bird, which was brownish in color, had only two yellow feathers under each wing. The Mamo bird had more yellow feathers on its body. After the birds had been robbed of the colored parts of their plumage they were turned loose to grow more feathers. It took several generations to collect enough to make the specially prized yellow helmets, cloaks and neck *leis* which could only be worn by the highest-ranking chiefs. When, at last, enough feathers had been collected they were painstakingly stitched to a net made of coconut fiber and when the garment was finished it fell in soft, sumptuous folds to the ground.

"Some day, when you go to Honolulu, Emily," Grandfather concluded, "you'll see some of the helmets and cloaks in the Bishop Museum. In the use of feathers for garments, the Polynesians surpassed all other people and Hawaiian feather cloaks rank with Persian rugs as masterpieces of human skill."

They rode along slowly, pushing farther and farther inland. The country grew steadily wilder. Grazing herds were left behind. The forests became quieter and deeper. *Ohelo* bushes, dangling jewel-like clusters of berries, flanked the thread-like trail. *Palapalai* ferns and prickly *akala* berries filled the moist hollows. *Ohia, olapa* and *kolea* trees sprang triumphantly out of crumbling lava flows which had once overwhelmed this portion of the island. Occasionally flocks of wild turkeys went sailing away on widespread wings, or herds of wild sheep and hogs bobbed off through the brush.

"No one's after you today," Pam called out when a razor-backed sow took off as if she were intending to win a Marathon. "We're hunting for little shells living in the tops of trees."

Finally they reached the altitude where land shells were plentiful. Everyone dismounted in a grassy opening and tethered the horses to trees. Grandfather lolled against a fern-bank and Pam and Emily got ready to climb trees.

"For land-shell hunting, Emily," Grandfather explained, "you need sharp eyes and strong bodies. Sometimes you have to do some pretty stiff climbing and go deep into the forests. But there are no snakes or poisonous plants or insects to be scared of. We're still miles below the region where wild cattle roam—so go to it and get me the shell that I want!"

Kane gave the girls their share of the lunch and they started off into the amber and jade of forest sunlight and shadow. "You'll know which trees have land-shell colonies living on them," Pam explained, "because there will be dead shells lying on the ground underneath. Dead shells are no good for a collection because they've lost their luster."

The sound of horses grazing and the voices of Kane and Grandfather grew fainter and fainter. The forests grew more sweet and secret. Pam went ahead, pausing every so often to examine the grass under certain varieties of trees.

"*Achatinella* shells are spiral," she told Emily, "pointed, and usually rather plump in shape. But sometimes you find long, slender ones, which are more rare. Some are striped red and white, like peppermint candy; others are white flushed with pink; some are coral-colored, some sulphur yellow. But the one Grandfather's after today must be pale green with a coral-colored mouth."

"I've only climbed a few trees in my life," Emily confided, "but even if I'm slow, I'll look hard."

"Isn't it lovely here?" Pam asked, pausing to look up through the green tangle of branches overhead.

"Yes," Emily murmured, like a person under a spell.

Finally Pam gave a little cry and pounced on a dead shell in the grass. "This tree has *achatinella* on it. You climb it and I'll find another one."

Setting down a Mason jar with a screw cap, Pam began searching the grass under another tree.

"What'll I do with the shells when I find them?" Emily asked, as she began scrambling into the branches.

"You have to put them in your mouth. Land shells have a habit of crawling out of pockets and when you're hanging on by your eyebrows to a branch you can't reach into the tight pockets of trousers to drag out a box or glass container."

Emily looked horrified.

"Don't be like that!" Pam said. "Land shells are clean as pins. They live on young leaves and dew."

Emily hoisted herself higher into the tree and began searching on the under-sides of new leaves, as Pam was now doing in a nearby tree. After a little she found a small, striped shell. "I've got one!" she cried.

"What does it look like?" Pam asked from her leafy perch. Emily described it. "That's a common variety. Grandfather has lots of that kind but if you find any of the sulphur yellow or coral-colored ones, keep them. They're rarer."

For a while the forests were very quiet, except for the occasional whistle of some shy native bird winging its way higher up the mountain. After a tree had been carefully gone over, the huntress moved to a new one. At the end of a couple of hours they had collected some fine specimens and put them into the glass jar.

"Let's rest for ten minutes," Pam suggested. "Then we'll find another grove. There's the tree Kimmo marked with his bandana. I've searched it hard and there isn't a trace of another shell on the grass underneath it, or in the branches. That land-shell family must have moved on somewhere else."

Emily studied the jar which was now about a third filled with graceful, delicately colored pointed shells. Their beauty thrilled her. "They're the jewels of the Hawaiian forests," she said, turning her flushed, eager face to her cousin.

"Yes," Pam agreed. "Now if only we can find the new one Grandfather wants, he'll be full of glee. Every land-shell collector likes to beat his rivals and it will be a feather in Grandfather's cap to find an entirely new variety. Come on, let's hunt again."

Clouds began settling down on the dark summit of Hualalai and the forests grew sleepy. Birds stilled their songs. Turkeys, sheep and hogs crept away for their noon rest before going out to feed again. The girls climbed tree after tree, speaking to each other in hushed voices.

"I don't like to go back without the shell that Grandfather wants," Pam announced, sliding down a trunk and landing in a bed of deep fern. "Are you tired, Emily?"

"No," she said stoutly.

"Fine. Let's cross this little gully and try on the other side."

They slid down through banks of damp fern and scrambled up the far side. "That tree's in line with the one where Kimmo found the green *achatinella*. You take it and I'll go over this other one. I wonder where the rascals went when they moved along?"

They sat down to eat the lunch that Ah Sam had prepared, then Pam glanced at the sky and clouds.

"It must be around two o'clock. We'll have to start home about three. It takes two and a half hours to get home from here. Let's keep on hunting for another fifteen minutes."

Emily was so busy hanging onto a limb while she looked under some new leaves that she could only nod. Her arms ached, her eyes were tired but she was determined to keep pace with Pam. Pam went shinnying up a new tree with as much vim as if she had just begun hunting. They both worked busily. Then suddenly Emily gave a choked, excited little cry. "I think I've got the one we want!"

Pam swung easily to the ground. "Come down quickly and let me see it."

Emily descended cautiously and held out the shell she had found.

"It's the right color, anyway," she said.

Pam studied it carefully. From working with Grandfather, she was expert in distinguishing new varieties of shells, not only by color but from the shape. After a few tense minutes she jumped up and down with glee.

"It *is* the new variety, Emily! Grandfather'll bust, and—" she broke off.

"And what?" Emily asked.

"You'll find out later," Pam announced mysteriously.

Putting the precious find in the glass jar, they went rushing back through the trees like mad things.

"Grandfather, Grandfather, Emily found the shell you want!" Pam screamed when they reached the cool opening where the horses were grazing.

The old man bounced up from the grass. With the aid of Emily's and Pam's eyes, he registered details of coloring. The shape and details of formation he recorded with his expert finger tips.

"Well, Emily," he said, his big, booming voice shaking with excitement, "when a new variety of *achatinella* is discovered and classified it's usually named after the finder—"

Emily squeaked with delight.

"But we've got to be absolutely sure first." Reaching into his pocket, he took out a microscope and handed it to Pam. She noted each feature carefully and recited it.

"It's a new species all right," Grandfather said in glad tones. "So I'll call it after you, Emily."

Emily hugged him.

"You'll be distinguished in Hawaii by this discovery," Pam

said. "I'm proud of you, Emily."

"We all are," Grandfather broke in. "I think maybe when you wake up tomorrow morning you'll find a spanking new bridle at the foot of your bed!"

When Emily opened her eyes next morning it was there! Shiny new bit, long limp-leather reins, sassy little tassels on the cheeks and one dangling from the throat latch. Snatching it up, Emily looked it all over, then hugged it to her so tightly that one of the buckles hurt her, but she was too happy to care. She had her own saddle now, and her own bridle. She was two rungs up the ladder. If she tried hard in every way to meet all the qualifications, some grand day she'd wake up to see boots, breeches, and spurs announcing to the world that she was a full-fledged *paniolo!*

Her methodical little mind went slowly over items, checking them off: she must be a good horseman, as well as a good rider; she must know how to care for animals, well or ill; she must be cool in tight places and act swiftly in emergencies.

She had been tired out from climbing trees when she came in the night before and she knew now, from the quality of the sunlight outside, that it must be around ten o'clock. But the after-glow of finding the rare land shell, plus the joy of having her own bridle, made her feel as if the riches of the world were hers. What did it matter if everyone had gone off about their work? People couldn't feel lonely or left out when they were as full-up with happiness as she was. She'd catch Forty Dollars and ride around the pastures to celebrate.

After she had shown Tatsu and Ah Sam her treasure, she hurried through breakfast and headed for the corrals. She looked around for Poi, who usually was waiting for her under the orange trees, but he was nowhere in sight. Maybe he had gone off to try and kill a mongoose in one of the stone walls. He seldom got one because he was old and slow but he always had the fun of thinking he would. She skipped along, swinging the bridle so that sunlight flashed off the beautiful new, unstained bit that looked as shiny as silver. How proud Forty Dollars would feel with it in his mouth!

Na-lua-hine had left him in the corral for her while he made his round of water troughs below the big hill. The air was sweet with the scent of trees, flowers, and fat stock and the slopes of the island poured seaward with leisurely, magnificent abandon. Emily was so happy she felt dizzy. Her bare feet pressed the earth with passionate affection.

What a beautiful world it was, she thought rapturously, how close God seemed at Kilohana. She felt His presence in the trees, earth, and air. "Oh, please, make something happen, God," she prayed, "so I won't have to go back to Boston!" And as she skipped along in the sunshine she felt as if her prayer were already answered.

Opening the corral gate, she closed it carefully behind her. "Look Forty Dollars!" she cried, holding up the new bridle. The old horse nickered softly and took a few steps toward her. She slipped in the bit, slid the headstall over his ears, fastened the throat-latch with its dangling tassel, then stepped back to get the effect. "You look like a race horse!" she told him, scampering to the fence for her saddle.

Her daily *lei* that Na-lua-hine made for her was dangling from the pommel and she put it about her neck. She sang little songs of happiness as she fastened the girths around Forty Dollars, pulling them until they were right, then making nice flat knots with the *latigos*. It was easy now, and fun. She had stepped back and slapped down the stirrup when the bray of a mule startled her. It came from the pasture where the work-horses ran.

Climbing the fence, she looked in the direction from which the sound came. Sure enough, there was a mule. She knew that the pack-mules, used for trips up the mountain to bring back wild game for the ranch larder, had no business there. They were kept in an enclosure higher up the hill and apart from the other animals. Na-lua-hine had explained that mules could not produce young of their own. There had to be a Jack-father and a mare-mother to get the tough, onery animals which were particularly suited to hard, slow work. Many mules had twisted, warped dispositions and loved to worry small creatures. The lives of colts and calves were in danger if they ran in a pasture where mules were.

Emily knew from its pricked-up ears that the beast was watching something in the deep grass. No colts or calves ran with the work-horses. It must be watching a mongoose. However, she determined to drive the mule out and put it back where it belonged.

Jumping off the fence, she mounted Forty Dollars and started for the gate. It seemed years since she had gone out

alone bareback for the first time. Days spilling over with fun
and beauty lay behind her like a full harvest. She no longer
feared the red cattle, for she was becoming wise in the ways of
a Hawaiian ranch. She knew a dozen or more Hawaiian words
and Na-lua-hine had promised to teach her to play his accordion and sing Hawaiian songs.

Suddenly the morning was shattered by a terrible sound, unlike anything she had ever heard in her life! The cry came
again. Rage was in it and a frenzy to destroy. She froze in the
saddle and Forty Dollars threw up his head. Then she saw the
mule at the far end of the pasture rush forward, shaking its
head. Its ears were laid back, its teeth bared. A small cream-
colored object went flying into the air and when it fell back to
the ground the mule brayed again and made another savage
rush at it. Again the small animal was flung upward. A long
yelp of terror reached Emily's ears. It was Poi!

For an instant she could not move, then she drummed her
heels against Forty Dollars' ribs and tore across the pasture.
When she got closer she screamed and screamed. Every time
the old dog hit the grass the mule struck at it with its forefeet,
then seized the dog and threw him into the air again. Poi's
shoulders were torn and bloody but he was fighting gamely.

Emily leaped off her horse and rushed in, trying to scare
the mule off but it came for her with bared teeth and she
dodged behind Forty Dollars while she looked about wildly
for some stick to beat the infuriated animal. Lying in the grass,
was an old slip-rail which had been used in a temporary gate
between the horse and calf pasture. It was about eight feet

long and quite heavy but Emily snatched it up as if it had been a twig and rushed at the mule.

It charged her, roaring with fury. Poi crawled away a few yards and rolled over. The mule went after him again. Screaming at the top of her lungs, Emily dashed to the old dog's rescue and banged the mule's chest with her pole. There was a hollow thud and it sprang aside. Back and forth, around and around they went. Emily's breath ached in her lungs, her arms shook from the weight of the pole. Surely, someone would hear the uproar!

But nobody came. Emily settled down grimly to the struggle to protect the dog and defend herself. "I mustn't get frightened," she thought. "I must keep cool and fight till I can't go any more. Poi fought bravely for me against the wild cow."

Suddenly she heard above the braying and her own screams the sound of racing hoofs, then a noose whizzed past like a striking snake and closed about the mule's throat. Emily dropped the rail and saw Pam taking a swift turn about her pommel. Then she flung her horse on to its haunches and the mule lurched over into the grass. Pam circled about, choking the beast down, and Emily flung herself upon Poi.

When the mule was still, Pam dismounted, dashed in and tied his feet, then she flew to her cousin. Tears were streaming down her cheeks.

"Oh, Emily, you might have been killed," she cried, clutching her.

Poi groaned and Pam released them both. Emily was incoherent, sobbing and shaking as she bent over the mangled dog. Pam examined him hurriedly.

"One leg is broken. His skin cuts will heal. I don't think he has internal injuries, but if you hadn't come the mule would have torn him to shreds," she said in unsteady tones. Gathering the old dog gently into her arms, she stood up but when Emily tried to rise her legs were useless.

"I can't move, Pam," she said, trying to control the sobs jerking her body.

"I'll wait till you can. I'm shaking, too," Pam swallowed. "I'm sorry I ever thought you were a city-sissy. I love you. You're brave. You were in terrible danger, Emily, more than you'll ever know—"

The mule began thrashing to break its bonds and Pam directed a baleful glare at him. "I hate mules," she cried. "But you have to have them on a ranch. Let's leave him here for a while, for punishment. There's where he got over the stone wall. I'll send the yardboys to fix it up at once, so he can't get out of his pasture again."

When Emily was able to stand up they mounted their horses and carried Poi home. Emily got creolin out of the Office and put some in a bucket of hot water, then washed and dressed Poi's wounds. Pam made a splint for his broken leg and placed him in a straw-filled box behind the kitchen stove.

When he was comfortable and had been fed some warm milk, Pam walked up to her cousin in her straight-forward, boyish way and placed her hands on Emily's shoulders. "I'm going to ask Kulani From Heaven to give you a horse of your very own, Emily, a lively one! Come to my room. Your breeches and boots and spurs are all here. I'll help you to dress up in them and when everyone comes back from work, they'll see that the ranch has a new *paniolo!*"

CHAPTER VIII

THE LONG SHADOW

DURING THE FOLLOWING WEEKS EMILY SEEMED LIKE A WAN-
derer who has returned home, rather than a visitor at Kilohana.
She learned to swing her small lasso, helped to groom the thoroughbreds, assisted Na-lua-hine and Kimmo in trapping wild
hogs to be salted down and added to the larder. When steers
were shipped from Kiholo she swam her horse in the sea and

after work applied herself to learn to play the accordion under Na-lua-hine's instruction. They kept the matter a secret, for he wanted to spring it on everyone as a surprise when she was expert. He taught her the chant which had been composed in honor of the ranch and to do a simple hula.

In an unexpressed way, Emily realized that there were no reservations once Islanders took you into their hearts. She was one of them now, part of the splendid acres which welded the various nationalities working on them into a unit. They were all members of the human family pushing toward a common goal. She ate rice and sipped tea with Tatsu; munched sour bread and black sausage with the two Portuguese who repaired the stone walls dividing the pastures; laughed and sang with the Hawaiians, and in the evening after dinner listened to Island-born Americans discussing matters of importance about Hawaii.

Complete happiness had made Emily's plain little face lovely. With spurs ringing at her heels, a lasso at her pommel and a big straw hat circled with flowers, she was as much of Hawaii as anyone about her and the knowledge that Pam loved her like a sister made her feel invincible.

When letters came from Aunt Dode a chill brushed her but she thrust it away and prayed to God for a miracle to keep her at Kilohana forever—and she had a child's faith that it would be so.

One hot noon, Emily and Pam rested their horses on the hill before descending its steep side to fetch the mail. Ranch sounds drifted up through the thin, clear air: the singing of a horseshoe being hammered, a dog's bark, the lowing of cattle making their way across the pastures far below. The three great mountains slept in the sun and the majestic breathing of the blue Pacific came faintly to their ears.

"Emily," Pam said suddenly, "would you like to live here for good?"

The look in Emily's eyes was answer enough.

"I'm glad. It seems as if you'd been here with us always. I'm going to ask Mother to make Aunt Dode let us adopt you."

Blood rushed into Emily's face. "Oh, Pam—" she began, but could get no farther.

"Aunt Dode will probably raise a howl," Pam said in a matter-of-fact way. "But Kulani From Heaven can do anything. I'll talk to her about it the first chance I get and before your year with us is up— Oh, goodness! I see the dust of Pili's truck. We must hurry or we'll be late for the mail!"

Leaping on to their horses, they shot down the hill, raced across the pastures to the big gate shutting off the lava flows. Emily opened the gate from her horse, like a professional, while Pam shifted her saddle, which had slipped forward, back into place. Then they tore on down the road, dust flying from their horses' heels.

Pili was waiting at the roadside. "I lick you this time!" he gloated. "I wait more from five minutes!"

"I've waited hours for you," Pam retorted as he handed her the letters and papers.

"Is there anything from Aunt Dode?"

Pam glanced through the envelopes before she slid them into

the leather bag. "No," she announced, and Emily felt as
though she were safely adopted already. She was fond of her
aunt but no single human could mean to her, now, what Kilohana and its people did.

When they entered the Office, Grandfather and Kulani were
there, she seated at her desk, Grandfather on a grain bag. Pam
tossed her mother the mail and examined Poi's leg, which had
recently been taken out of its splint.

A sound so slight and so quickly smothered that it was like a
ghostly whisper in the dark came from Kulani. Both girls
looked up and Grandfather asked sharply, "What is it, Kulani?"

She did not answer for almost a minute. Her dark eyes had
a strange hurt in their depths, as though someone she loved
and trusted had struck her unexpectedly. Pam rushed over.

"Please Pam— I must be still for a moment."

"Is someone you love dead?" Pam asked anxiously. "Oh,
Mother, your face looks all drawn and funny—"

"I'm all right, dear. I've had a jar—" she glanced at the type-
written sheet of paper in her hand, as if the words written on
it were in a foreign language. Pushing back her chair, she
walked mechanically to the door and looked at the gardens and
buildings, her face calm but white as chalk.

"Mother, what *is* the matter?" Pam cried, rushing to her.
"You've got to tell me. I'm your partner—"

"Of course I will, Pam. It was absurd of me to go off the
deep end as I did." Going back to her swivel chair, she sat
down, facing the big dusty room filled with homey ranch
things. Grandfather leaned forward, Pam clung to her moth-

er's hand and Emily sat absolutely still, hugging Poi.

"Father knows, though possibly you don't, Pam, that our family has held Kilohana on a ninety-nine year lease. We're the third generation of Storms who've lived here. Many Island estates are held on similar terms and when the time-limit expires the lease is automatically extended for another ninety-nine years. This letter—" her strong, tapering fingers spurned the paper on her desk, "is from Napier Kingsley, who holds title to our land. Our lease expires in eighteen months—and instead of re-leasing Kilohana to us, he wants to take it over."

The words hung in the air like a puff of smoke from a gun which had been discharged accidentally. Grandfather made an odd sound, Pam flung back her head.

"*Mother*—" she cried, and the word was like pain made visible. "He—he can't have it! If we had to go away from here, I'd die!" And she burst into terrible tears.

Kulani seized her and shook her with fierce gentleness. "Get hold of yourself, Pam. The matter can be adjusted, someway." The steadiness of her voice was more upsetting than tears. "I'll write to him, explain how we feel about the place. Kingsley's grandfather was here in the early days. He bought the property but returned to the East in his old age and none of his family has been to Hawaii since then. This Kingsley hasn't the slightest notion how Islanders feel about ranches like Kilohana. His health is poor and the doctors have advised a mild climate."

Pam gestured wildly, then seeing her mother's steady eyes, stopped in her tracks like a horse jerked down by an expert hand. "Write to him quickly, Mother," she said in a stifled voice.

Grandfather rose to his feet in his slow, big way. "This matter's going to take a deal of figuring out, Kulani. If Kingsley's obdurate, I'll sell the plantation and we'll offer to buy Kilohana outright. Kingsley's a New Yorker. Money will talk to him as nothing else can. There are lots of other places equally good for his health."

"Oh, Grandfather!" Pam rushed to him thankfully and he put his hands on her rigid shoulders.

"Don't get in a lather! Puuiki is worth a lot of money, but I grew up here, so Kilohana's more valuable to me. The plantation was just an investment. On any market it should bring a cool million. I think Kingsley will be quite willing to talk our language—if it comes to a real showdown." He gave a deep chuckle.

"I think, Father, it will be best to send the girls to Kona for a few days, while we figure things out in detail and frame a letter to Kingsley."

Pam looked rebellious but before she could speak Kulani reached out and took her hand. "Lamb," she said in her rich, vibrant voice, "you can help me best on an occasion of this sort by leaving me free to concentrate on the business at hand. Grandfather and I will have to see Mr. Banks, our family lawyer, and arrange with him to put Puuiki up for sale, if it's necessary. I don't want you, or Emily, to say anything about this to anyone. There's no use distressing and upsetting the ranch people over something which can probably be adjusted.

You know how Hawaiians and Japanese carry on when old family places break up. Ours won't be broken up, if I have any say in the matter, and I'll have plenty to say!"

"Are you sure it'll be okay, Kulani From Heaven?" Pam asked unsteadily.

"Don't I usually accomplish the things I set out to do?" Kulani teased.

"Dern tootin' you do," Grandfather said. "You zipped Dode out of the picture in nothing flat and she's as happy as a cricket in Honolulu."

The day which had been full of darkness and terror suddenly resettled its bright plumage and went on its way as if it had absolute confidence that the valiant woman had ability to keep the wide acres of Kilohana intact for the people who loved it and looked to it for support.

"Find Kane and Na-lua-hine. I'll phone Aunt Mag and tell her you'll be over to visit for a few days. And Pam, promise me you won't worry, or even think about all this. It will come out all right. With your two old *paniolos* to ride herd on you, you girls won't be too much trouble."

"What'll we take over to Aunt Mag?" Pam asked, trying to be as steady as her mother. "Moku killed a wild pig yesterday, it's fat as butter—"

"Take a side of it over and you might as well put in two wild turkeys and the ducks we were going to have for dinner tonight. Grandfather and I will be heading for Hilo to see Mr. Banks as soon as the milking's over."

"Is there anything else I can tend to for you before we go?"

Pam asked, fighting to keep her voice normal.

Kulani counted off a dozen errands, then added, "Emily can attend to some of them for you." Her eyes caught up the small figure on the steps, making her one of the family. "And Pam—" grasping her daughter's hand, she gazed deep in her eyes.

"I know. Chin up! I'll keep it up, Mother, because you always do. You're—" She could not continue.

"So are you!" Kulani said, mischievously, and they went into a clinch.

If Kane and Na-lua-hine had not been along, the drive to Kona might have been a rather dismal affair. But Kane's calm pleasure and Na-lua-hine's noisy glee at the thought of going to Kona picked up the girls' spirits. Na-lua-hine, dressed up in his best store suit, stuffed his accordion into a corner of the ranch Ford and settled himself behind the wheel. Putting his big bare feet on the pedals, he said,

"Let's go! I got plenty friends in Kona. Kona jolly-fun!"

They had made a rather late start and darkness came down before they were through the miles and miles of old lava flows that had poured down Hualalai until 1801. Pam was quiet in the back with Kane, but Na-lua-hine kept tossing jokes into the air and by the time they entered the lush forests swathing the southern end of the island, she was more like herself.

Na-lua-hine kept up a running fire of conversation for Emily. Kona, he told her, was the most lush and luxuriant district in all the eight islands, as well as the most beautiful. It had been beloved by the chiefs of old. It was known as the Land of the Setting Sun and the Land of Hanging Rain. In Kona people were kinder and laughed more loudly than in any other place in Hawaii. Flowers were bigger and more fragrant, fruit juicier and more plentiful than anywhere else in the Pacific. If you were very still at night, you could hear land shells singing in the forests and gods rustling through the coffee. . . .

He finally turned the car into a lavish garden and drew up before a big, brightly lighted house. Aunt Mag, Kulani's older sister, came out to meet them, and Emily fell in love with her instantly. She was big and strong but her laughter sounded like the chime of silver bells. Her home was an exquisite old place, and Emily learned that it had been built by Pam's great-great grandfather, who had been one of the first missionaries in Kona.

The original part of the house had been New England in architecture but with added wings and porches it had gradually become all-Hawaiian in spirit. The plaster walls were made of bleached white coral, pounded to fine powder and mixed with white *kukui* ashes and had a beautiful, satin-smooth finish. The *koa* beams and graceful balustrade leading upstairs had been dragged from the mountains with lassos, then shaped and polished by hand.

After the girls had been established in a room with a mammoth four-poster, they went down to dinner. Later, Aunt Mag showed them the treasures of the old house. A worn Bible, a spinning wheel, and a spinnet, which had come by sailing-vessel around the Horn. A *Mamo lei*. . . . Emily caught her breath when she saw the fine yellow feathers which had been gathered two by two. They were soft as chiffon velvet in her hands and the thought that the feathers were hundreds of years old and had been worn countless times by great chiefs made her shiver with pleasure. Their luster was undimmed and they had the sheen of pale sunlight coming out of a sky freshly washed by rain.

Then Aunt Mag showed them polished *koa* spears, twelve feet long.

"In ancient times *Ooihe*—spear-throwing—was part of every warrior's training," she said. "Each spear had a name and was supposed to possess its own *mana*—spirit—which endowed it with supernatural qualities. It was this power that guided the shaft in its flight. Spear-drills were a fine art and every movement had to be in perfect coordination. Some warrior-chiefs were so expert that they could turn away a dozen spears hurled at them, with the one spear in their hand.

"And this," Aunt Mag went on, taking up a wooden shaft about the size of a broomstick, but widening into a blade at one end, "is an *O-o*—a spade. It was used to cultivate taro and sweet potatoes. The Hawaiians have a proverb, which goes as follows," she turned to Pam. "You say it."

Pam, who had been rather silent, brightened up.

> *"O ka ihi i ka make*
> *O ka O-o i ke ola!"*

"That means," Aunt Mag explained:

> "The spear is symbolic of death,
> The spade of life!"

Next morning when Emily awakened she was tingling with eagerness to see the land of Kona. Pam was still sleeping, her face buried in her arm. A warm, happy feeling stole through Emily. Sleeping with Pam made her feel as if they were really sisters and being in such a big bed with a frilly canopy around the top made it seem as if they were both princesses in some fabulous story.

Sliding out of bed, she hurried to big windows opening onto a tiny railed balcony. The morning was sweet with the fragrance of ripe mangoes and guavas and smelt vaguely of drying coffee beans, gardenias, sugar-cane and the strong odor of forests growing out of wild, wet earth. Beyond a dome-shaped mass of magenta bougainvilleas, long moulten slopes poured down to a spectacular coast-line. Here the island was all green forests and a sort of secret splendor wrapped everything. The whisper of the sea against the shore seeped into the room like faint, eerie breathing. A sound made her turn. Pam was sitting up in bed, stretching.

"Isn't Kona beautiful?"

"It gives me a queer, excited feeling, as if something wonderful was going to happen in a minute," Emily confessed.

"Yes, even when nothing happens, it's still exciting. Maybe because of all the stirring things that took place here long ago." Getting out of bed, Pam stretched. "I had bad dreams last night—"

"Don't worry, Pam, Kulani From Heaven can do anything. She won't let Kilohana be taken from us."

Pam's face suddenly looked like her mother's. "Nor will I!"

she announced.

A merry hail came from the garden. "Hey, you kids, what-for you sleep all day? Little more seven o'clock. Come down quick and us go Honaunau and have jolly-fun."

"Na-lua-hine!" Emily exclaimed, her eyes lighting. "But what's Honaunau?"

"The City of Refuge. Kane'll tell us all about it when we get there."

Breakfast over, the four of them rode down through glossy coffee plantations toward the sea. White flowers like a dust of snow grew along the branches of every tree and between the blossoms ruby-colored, shiny berries showed. Gangs of Japanese and Filipino laborers were gathering them into bags to take to the mill. Pam insisted that they stop their horses for a few minutes so Emily could see the red pulp being washed off and the beans made ready to dry on great tin roofs. Two kinds of coffee grew in Kona, Pam told her cousin, Guatemala and Arabica, but because of the richness of the volcanic loam, both types had a richer flavor when grown in Hawaii than in the lands where they originated.

It was nearing noon before they reached the shore. Here the forests thinned out and coconut groves leaned over white beaches set in low headlands of lava which had poured over Kona centuries ago. As they rode slowly along the shore, they kept running into tiny Hawaiian villages. Women called out "Aloha" from narrow verandas where they sat braiding mats. Men offered spicy items of gossip as they mended fish-nets under the purple shade of mango trees. Na-lua-hine exchanged rib-nudging jokes with gray-beards who had been boyhood friends. Bevies of girls in clinging wet *mumus*—a sort of loose slip—offered them shell-fish they had gathered off the rocks, and skittering flocks of naked children, splashing and laughing in the blue water and tumbling up the beach, uttered cascades of giggles and ducked their heads when Pam joked with them in Hawaiian.

At last, Kane, who rode in the lead because Na-lua-hine always wanted to linger too long with his friends, halted on a flat lava spit jutting into the sea. About a mile across was a similar spit and between the two lay a wild stretch of tossing water, where waves rushed shoreward, trailing their long white manes in the sun. On the far side of the bay, high black walls of lava-rock stood up against lacy green *kiawes*, brooded over by tall coconut trees.

The walls looked grim and awesome and Emily pressed her horse close to Kane's, eager to hear about them. As Kane's English was too sketchy to give the full flavor of the place, he spoke in Hawaiian and Pam translated.

In ancient times Honaunau, he told them, was the holiest place in Hawaii. The biggest and most impressive of all the temples was within its walls. The highest priests lived there and in the *Hale o Kiawe* were the most powerful idols. Human sacrifices were offered to the gods and secret ceremonies performed to insure the proper outcome of mighty undertakings.

Also, if a person committed a crime, or was accused of committing one, if he could escape from his enemies and reach the City of Refuge no one could molest him. The City could not be approached from the land, only from the sea. If a man or woman swam across the shark-infested water between the points and reached the far shore in safety, he was taken in by the priests and remained for a stated time. Then he could go forth in safety, for having swum the Gauntlet of the Gods without being destroyed, man might not harm him.

Even as mighty a King as Kamehameha, who conquered all the Islands, dared not violate the laws of the City of Refuge. Once in a great rage, for he had a violent temper, he threatened to kill his favorite wife, Queen Kaahumanu. Terrified, she fled to the City and claimed sanctuary, as she had made the swim successfully. Kamehameha came over but dared not enter the enclosure for refugees, who were wards of the gods. He pleaded with Kaahumanu to return to him, looking so handsome in his towering yellow feather helmet and sweeping feather cloak that she almost weakened. However, she told him that her time in the Walled City was not up, making her person inviolate, and she did not trust him. He vowed on the gods of his forefathers that he would not harm her, but she was adamant. His face was shamed before his people, so he sent his warriors away in order to talk to her alone. He wept and implored and because Kaahumanu loved him and did not want to destroy his prestige, she finally came out and after that had almost equal power to his in the land.

Emily listened spellbound and when Kane finally stopped talking they circled the bay and lunched in the coconut grove behind the old walls. The day was so peaceful and lovely it was hard to imagine that long ago people with terror in their hearts had swum among sharks to reach protection, while priests offered up human sacrifices and asked for guidance from their gods, and warriors, bold in battle, with spears in their hands, dared not break the taboo which protected the weak, innocent and unfortunate.

Na-lua-hine, who had brought along his accordion, told Emily to play it and Kane and Pam listened, astonished. When Emily played and sang the Kilohana hula without a mistake they were speechless with admiration.

"You Hawaiian girl now," Kane commented, when she finished.

"Bet-you-my-life!" Na-lua-hine yelled. "I think never you like to go away from Kilohana, Em'ly."

The invisible thread linking them to the throbbing past of Hawaii snapped in mid-air, jerking the girls back to the vital present. Involuntarily, their eyes leaped together. Go away from Kilohana—the words sounded hollow in their ears. Pam's face twitched, then recalling her mother's command, she controlled the words that beat against her lips. The ranch people must not know about the long shadow that had fallen on Kilohana, a shadow that reached thousands of miles, across a whole continent and ocean. Emily's small face looked bleak and empty of warmth and joy, but the secret she and Pam shared wrapped about them both, binding them more tightly together.

The man wandered off to borrow spears from the caretaker of the City of Refuge and Pam turned to Emily. "The instant we get back to the house I'm going to phone Mother. If I just hear her voice I'll feel braver. Whenever I begin thinking about—"

"Me, too," Emily said with a shiver. "Let's make our *pani-olos* hurry with their fishing so we can find out what Mr. Banks said."

When they got in, Aunt Mag told Pam that Kulani wanted her to phone her in Hilo.

"If she and Grandfather are still with the lawyer—" Pam could not finish.

While Pam phoned, Emily sat in a small huddle on the steps, looking at the blue-flush of the Kona sea melting into the sky. Maybe nothing could be done, she thought, a dry sob jerking through her. "When I see Pam's face I'll know." But it didn't take that long. The instant Pam got off the polished floor of the living room she skipped down the long veranda. "Mother says Mr. Banks feels certain everything will be okay. They've drafted a letter but it may be a month before they get a reply. She and Grandfather are going to Puuiki tonight and will remain there tomorrow. Next day we can go home."

"Oh, Pam!" Emily cried, leaping up, and they went into a bear-hug.

They were merry at supper on the wide *lanai* overlooking the sea. The sun set, the fierce light died in the west and muted whispers, like gods walking solemnly over the water and pushing through the tangled undergrowth, filled the coming night with mystery and magic. After supper Na-lua-hine made music on the steps and Emily and Pam sang. Sometimes Kane joined in with his thin old voice and Aunt Mag added her rich contralto when they finished with the Kilohana hula.

Next morning they were off in a shell-pink dawn to ride down to Napopo. All the beauty of the world lay on land and sea, and in the south Mauna Loa stretched its mighty shape across the sky, sleeping above the fires burning in its heart.

"Ke-ala-ke-kua," Pam pointed down at a sapphire blue bay below them, "means the Highway of the Gods. Captain Cooke, who discovered the Islands, was killed there. We're going to see the monument erected to his memory."

Emily had read about the British navigator in a Hawaiian history Pam had sent her one Christmas and knew how the Hawaiians had revered him as a god at his first visit. Then later there had been trouble between the British Tars and the natives, which resulted in Cooke being killed on February 13th, 1779.

Kane borrowed a canoe and they paddled across the fierce blue water. Na-lua-hine pointed at blocked cave mouths in the grim face of the bluff. In the caves the great chiefs of ancient times were buried with their war canoes, spears, feather cloaks and helmets, he told them. Kane nodded. The caves were taboo he explained. Legend had it that an eerie rite was repeated at dawn, sunset, midnight and noon, when the spirits of the Ancient Dead rose up and walked in an awesome procession through the towering caverns. Anyone foolish enough to try and see it died or went mad. . . .

A sort of chill descended like a cloak over the four in the

canoe as they paddled along, then Na-lua-hine gave a grunt. "Why-for us talk only this old kind stuff? Yesterday is finish, tomorrow not come yet, us only have today for sure. Us got plenty food, accordion to make music, better us have happy-fun!"

CHAPTER IX

THE FOURTH OF JULY

PAM GLANCED AT THE STOP-WATCH CRADLED IN HER PALM, then looked at the blanketed thoroughbred being led up and down the ranch race track. Last year it had been the gray stallion, Silver Wings, who had been in training for the Hawaiian Free For All cup. His great heart and mighty stride had captured the coveted trophy which now sat on the grand piano in the living room. This summer it was his son Malolo—The Flying Fish—who was a perfect replica of his father.

Pam's eyes, which had been filled with the keen delight of a born horse-lover watching a fine animal, filmed over suddenly and a far-away expression crept into her face. At heart she was an optimist, but she had her mother's gift for thinking in a straight line. Because of the possibility that this might be the last time a horse would carry the Kilohana colors to victory, the training of Malolo was a solemn, as well as a thrilling, affair. Though Pam said little, there was hardly an instant of any day that she did not think of the dark shadow that lay upon the bright acres of the ranch which had been, and would always be, a vital part of her. Her allegiance to the ranch went beyond devotion to individuals and animals. It embraced rocks, trees, wind, the rustle of dawn coming up over the big hill, the shape of Hualalai and the force throbbing in the soil underneath her. She'd never be the same if Kilohana went out of their hands.

She gazed at the acres she loved like a person under a spell, then gave herself a brisk shake. "I mustn't keep wondering if Mother was able to put on paper how we feel so a man in New York will understand why we just must keep the ranch," she thought. "Malolo's ready to have his last try-out before we go to Maui. Only three days till we sail. I've got to get on my job." Her eyes swept the green pasture and picked up the specks of two approaching horsemen.

"Okay, Opiopio, warm him up," she called out. "Mother and Grandfather are coming."

The dozen figures which were moving about a couple of dozen horses, waiting in a knot a short distance away, were stirred into sudden action. The two Japanese gardeners who had saved up and bought "dace-horses" of dubious ancestry, led them off the track. *Paniolos* took the two top-horses of the work string, to be ridden in the Cowboy Relay race, and tied them to nearby trees. Opiopio, the grizzled jockey who had ridden Keloliana horses for as far back as Pam could remember, took the plaid blanket off Malolo and prepared to mount.

The horse knew what was in the wind. He circled about on the tips of his hard black hoofs. He shook his mane in the sun and whinnied. His tail shimmered, a ribbon of light ran from his withers to the base of his small, shapely ears. He rocked and danced, blew out his coral-lined nostrils. Opiopio jerked gently and soothingly on his bit while Mahiai, his groom, put on the tiny pigskin saddle.

Kulani and Grandfather rode up. The old man looked like an eager boy and Kulani's dark, thoughtful eyes lighted up briefly as they noted the young thoroughbred's beauty. "He looks in tip-top condition, Opiopio," she said, her voice warm and approving. "Get up. Pam, you've got a stop-watch to time him?"

"Yes, Mother," she answered.

"I think we'll run him alone. If he makes the time he should without a horse against him, he'll knock it down several seconds when he's on a track with a big field to spur him on. I've another watch so we can double check."

A great hush came down as Opiopio walked Malolo on to the track. The vital youngster was mad to run but because of his fine schooling managed to control himself. Opiopio tensed in the saddle, got into position and loped slowly around the half-mile track, then began pushing his mount as they neared the starting point.

Pam's heart began hammering in her side. Emotion always surged through her like a great tide when she saw a thoroughbred running, gripping her throat until it ached. Kulani gave the signal to break and both watches clicked down, as Malolo hurled himself forward as if he had been shot from a gun. With expert hands the old jockey steadied him along the curving ribbon of track. Magnificent limbs stretched out, small hoofs flung the turf disdainfully behind until he seemed to stream over the earth like a thought speeding to its destination. He flashed past the half, the three quarter. . . .

"Push him, Opiopio, push him!" Pam yelled, jumping up and down. Her eyes were starry, her cheeks crimson, and her hair danced a mad dance with wind and sun. She knew that because three times in succession a Kilohana thoroughbred had returned to the big island of Hawaii with the Free For All trophy that the Collins, who were the chief thoroughbred owners on Maui, were out to win the cup this year. She and her mother always stayed at the Collins plantation. They had written with honesty, openly stating that they had imported a horse and a jockey from America to take the cup away from Kilohana and bring it back to the island of Maui, which was the cradle of island racing. This fact, added to the possibility that the present Kilohana colors might never be carried again, made Malolo's victory assume terrific importance.

"How he's going!" Kulani gasped, glancing at the watch in her hand. Grandfather strained forward, listening to the blurred roar of Malolo's hoofs swinging against the earth. The gray streak whizzed down the home stretch, flashed over the line.

"What did you get, Pam?" her mother asked in shaken tones.

Pam glanced down, tried to speak, then began laughing on a wild, high note. "Mother—a mile in 1.44—flat! On this track. *Am I crazy?*"

Kulani shook her head and blinked moisture from her eyes. "I got the same time!"

Grandfather whooped with delight; Na-lua-hine began turning absurd handsprings; Japanese yelled, *"Banzai!"*; *paniolos* beat each other on the back. When the tumult of excitement died down, Kulani looked at her small daughter. "If he can do a mile in that time here, he'll mop up everything on a good track with a big field against him."

Dismounting, she hurried forward to consult with Opiopio and help with the blanketing. As a rule, Pam would have gone over but thoughts too deep and moving had her in their grasp. With the astuteness of the blind, who have the gift of snatching invisible things from the air, like a radio, Grandfather knew what was in her heart. Getting off his horse, he walked over to her and placed his hand on her shoulder.

"Child," he said in his deep, vibrant voice, "take a mental broom and clean all those thoughts from your mind. If you keep thinking about a thing all the time, you draw it to you. For thousands of years, men have known this for a fact. I know what Kilohana means to you. It means the same to me and to your mother. It simply isn't on the books that the ranch should go out of our hands—"

"Oh, Grandfather, do you really believe that?"

"Yes," he gazed at her with his blind eyes. "Watch yourself. Guard your thoughts. Keep your mind off the possibility of losing Kilohana. You know the old saying, 'The thing I feared has come upon me.'"

"I don't want to think about it, Grandfather, but it sort of keeps creeping along the edges of my mind, like mildew."

"Get out that mental broom I spoke of a moment ago and brush the mould off your mind, shake it out, hang it up in the sun and—let's get on our way. We've got to clean up on the Free For All cup again, beat the outside horse and jockey that's been imported to upset our cart of apples. There are dozens of things to be seen to before we take off in three days."

Pam nodded cheerfully and butted her head against the old man's arm, like a playful calf.

"That's my girl!" Grandfather said approvingly. "You know, it's an odd thing but I've discovered during the many years I've lived, that if people don't look back at yesterday, or fret about tomorrow, but just concentrate on making today as full and worth while as possible, that life sort of takes care of itself as it goes. *In the present, you're taking care of the past and building the future*—at the same time. Do you understand what I'm driving at, Pam?"

"Yes Grandfather. Na-lua-hine said the same thing in different words when we were in Kona."

"Then there's nothing to be afraid of, Small Fry, except—" he gave a chuckle.

"Except what?" Pam demanded.

"The problem of keeping old Opiopio sober the day of the race. He's been pretty good since he took the pledge, but—"

"I'll lock him up in Malolo's stall for twenty-four hours before the race is due to come off," Pam announced with a peal of gay laughter.

Three days later a magnificent cavalcade left Kilohana. Seven horses in padded trucks rolled down the road: Malolo in solitary grandeur, with his jockey and stable boy to quiet him; the two horses for the Cowboy Relay race came next; then the two thoroughbreds that Pam and Emily were to ride in the Girls' Race; and, last, the two Japanese yardboys with their 'dace-horses' in a smaller truck. Kane, Na-lua-hine, Shibu and Oka, and Kimmo and Nuhi, who were the Relay riders, jammed in the Ford, and last came the big Packard with Grandfather, Kulani, Tatsu, and the two girls.

It was like a royal procession rolling solemnly over the island to Hilo, the only port on the island where the horses could be walked onto the ship instead of having to be tied to boats and swim out to it. During the six hours the steamer was crossing the rough channel between Hawaii and Maui, the *paniolos* stayed in the bow with the horses, watching to see that they did not get frightened and beat about in their stalls. Pam and Emily looked on anxiously until the ship reached the lee of Maui and the water was smooth again.

Next morning before dawn, the steamer blew a hoarse blast, announcing that the port of Kahului was coming up. People dressed and poured on to the lighted decks, to be served coffee and sandwiches before landing. As light welled gradually up over the curve of the earth, Emily saw an awesome mountain filling the sky.

"That's Haleakala—The House of the Sun," Pam told her, as they hung over the rail in front of the bridge and looked down into the bow where men bustled about horses, getting them ready to land.

"It looks higher than Mauna Kea and Mauna Loa," Emily said.

"It isn't," Pam asserted. "Haleakala is only ten thousand feet high, Mauna Kea is almost fourteen, but Haleakala seems bigger because it stands alone."

The ship warped into the lighted wharf, jammed with people down to meet incoming friends. A clear hail came from the crowd, "Pam! Oh, Pam!" A tall boy of about fifteen, with a curious lounging grace of movement, was waving madly.

"There's Ted Collins, Emily. The old gentleman with the red face, standing beside him, is his grandfather." Pam waved. "Ted and I are friendly enemies. Hi—Ted!"

The boy signalled that he saw her.

"Stay where you are," Pam called excitedly. "I'll come down by the gangway." Grabbing Emily's arm, she whispered, "Now we'll have some real fun."

Rushing to her cabin, she picked up the tall cup Silver-Wings had won the previous year. It could only be the property of the winner for a year, then went back to the track to be raced for again. Whoever won it kept it for another twelve months.

Snatching it out of the chamois bag it travelled in, Pam dashed to the railing and held it up for Ted to see.

"How'd you like to be holding this?" she cried.

"I will be in a few days," he shouted back.

"That's what you think!" she taunted.

"That's what I know," Ted insisted in a laughing voice. "When you see our new race horse, Dark Victory, you'll ship your old nag back to the ranch to be a pack horse."

"You won't be talking so loud—*after* the Fourth of July," Pam asserted, tossing her head.

"We'll see!"

After seeing the horses established in their loose-boxes at the Kahului track, the Collins took their guests home. Their plantation was at the mouth of the Wai-kapu Valley and the name, Forbidden Waters, fascinated Emily. Ted told her that the valley cutting back into the breath-takingly lovely West Maui mountains was so narrow that the towering walls almost met overhead. If people ventured up it they had to walk in single file and speak in a whisper, else the echoes of their voices, travelling upward, might dislodge boulders and bring them crashing down into the stream winding its narrow way along the bottom.

The house was entirely unlike Kilohana in appearance but had the same gracious, hospitable atmosphere. There were no grazing animals about it but big stables lay off to the right, and to the left a sugar-mill, set in flowing seas of jade green cane, rumbled away, like a well-fed beast contentedly purring on a warm hearth. And off in the east rose the mass of Haleakala with a white pillar of cloud, like a mammoth god, sitting on its blue forehead.

Every morning during the four days preceding the races the entire household went to the track and in the afternoons there were picnics and swimming. The Collins were a large, noisy family, always playing the piano, joking and singing as if life were an unending party.

Young Ted, turning sixteen, was the idol of his tribe but had managed to remain unspoiled. He rode like a centaur, swam like a fish, played, sang and danced like a Hawaiian. Though he ragged and teased Pam until her eyes flashed, he adored her, but when it came to races and thoroughbreds they were mortal enemies. Pam taunted him about the Free For All cup. It would be hers again, she insisted. "Like fun," Ted retorted.

"Look at Dark Victory," he said one morning at the track when he was being 'breezed.' "He's bigger, deeper in the girth and longer in the shoulders then Malolo."

"But Malolo's cannons are shorter, his pasterns longer and he has more driving power in his quarters," Pam flashed back.

"Well, the proof of the pudding's the eating," Ted insisted. "When the big race is over, you won't crow so hard. The Free For All cup isn't going back to Kilohana *this* Fourth of July! Kilohana horses aren't going to romp off with it again!"

Pam's face changed subtly and a far-away expression crept into her eyes. Ted sensed the change in her at once. "What is it?" he asked quickly.

"Nothing," she retorted, "but the cup *is* going back to our ranch again." And she stamped off, her head held at a fighting angle. Tears blurred the green paddock, with knots of men wandering down the long line of loose-boxes flanking it, inspecting the sleek, gorgeous creatures inside. "I mustn't think about that," she told herself, "or the thing I fear will come upon me."

But when the morning of the Fourth dawned the specter that possibly this might be the last time the Kilohana colors would stream around the Kahului track, tagged on her heels until her nerves were jittering. It made her short with Emily when they got into their racing togs and she snapped at Ted all the way to the races. He was bewildered by her mood, for usually she was a good sport about races. The winning or losing was always among friends.

When they arrived crowds were milling about the bleachers and grandstand. Swarms of laborers from outlying plantations and picturesque *paniolos* from ranches on the slopes of Haleakala were swarming in. Laughing Hawaiian women, like vast calico sacks, grabbed at their hats when the brisk wind threatened to snatch them off. Japanese *Mama-sans* hoisted the babies strapped on their backs to more comfortable positions. Portuguese bragged and showed off. Filipinos in gaudy silk shirts jabbered excitedly. The Royal Hawaiian band, imported from Honolulu for the day, was throwing noisy music into the air, stepping up the excitement charging the atmosphere. Iron-muscled horses were being given brief, last-minute workouts, but the two main contestants for the big race were locked in darkened loose-boxes.

Pam's face was grim as they made their way through the crowd toward the paddock.

"Not feeling quite so cocky today?" Ted asked in friendly,

teasing tones, as he took hold of her elbow.

Pam made no reply. In her white doeskin breeches, white silk shirt and black patent leather boots, with her bronze curls dancing in the wind, she was an arresting little figure. Everyone knew her, everyone called out to her as she passed but she hardly heard them. Her whole being was focussed on Malolo and Opiopio. As she neared the loose-box where the Kilohana thoroughbred waited, she fished in her pocket and drew out a key.

"What's that for?" Ted asked.

"I locked Opiopio in Malolo's loose-box last night so he couldn't get drunk," she answered shortly.

Ted went into gales of laughter and his grandfather slapped his side with delight.

"Gal after my own heart," he shouted. "Takin' no chances that there'll be a last-minute slip-up. That's the spirit, Pam. Fight, fight like blue blazes for the things you want. Then you'll get 'em, one way or another."

Pam flashed a quick look at the jovial old man. "Does it always work, Uncle Bill?" she asked.

"Ninety times out of a hundred, Pam."

"Okay," Pam thought, "I'll fight to win this race; fight to keep Kilohana." Striding forward, she took hold of the lock and slipped in the key. Opiopio came out grinning. "Malolo top-notch, Pam," he announced. "Just all same dynamite. Sure he *Letta-Go-His-Blouse* when he run today."

Stepping into the knee-deep, fragrant hay, Pam looked the noble beast over. He was nervous from the excitement tensing the atmosphere but his eyes were dark, steady and full of fire. Her hands went over his iron muscles with fierce affection. He was in tiptop shape, not over-trained and not too soft.

"You sleep good last night, Opiopio?" she asked.

"Sure, sleep like young fella. Lucky you lock me up las' night. Everyone make plenty foolish round here, have good fun and if I not inside with Malolo sure I forget and take little drink."

"Have some coffee." Pam turned. "Emily, give me the thermos."

Emily handed it over and they waited until the old fellow had drunk three cups, then Pam said, "In you go again, Opiopio, we've got to win today."

"Sure. Us win easy, Pam, you no scare."

Ted made some playful remark and Opiopio retorted. "Okay you laugh on me but Pam smart like anykind to lock me up. If no—" he made an expressive gesture of holding a glass to his lips that sent everyone into gales of laughter.

The key clicked and Pam slid it into her pocket and turned away. After a few last-minute instructions had been given to the men taking part in the various events, the Wai-kapu party made its way back to the Grandstand to watch the Parade which opened the race meet.

The bugle blew, the band struck up the *Stars and Stripes* and everyone stood up. A big Hawaiian rode on to the track on a black horse, carrying the American flag. Behind him came *pa'u* riders, two by two—girls with unbound hair and flowers around their necks representing the different islands. Each girl wore yards and yards of different colored silk wrapped around her and flowing back from her stirrups, and all the proudly stepping horses had flowers braided into their manes. Behind the girls came *paniolos* from the different ranches which were entering riders in the Cowboy Relay race; then came Japanese jockeys on nervous "dace-horses." Once around the brown track they rode while the wind pulled at the flag which seemed to beckon to everyone, irrespective of nationality, to follow it.

The crowd grew tenser as the minutes passed. Sounds seemed unnaturally loud, the music of the band crashed against the mountains and an invisible river of excitement swept the multitude and island on relentlessly.

The first race on the program was the Japanese race, which always afforded the greatest fun, if not the keenest excitement. The Japanese methods of training race horses were unique. Instead of oats, they fed their animals barley, mixed with dozens of eggs, and instead of giving their horses water, they had nothing but weak tea to drink for weeks before the races. Their overwrought animals behaved outrageously and inexpert jockeys were all over their backs. They were called back by the judges half a dozen times to start again and get off evenly. Finally the thrilling cry, *"THEY'RE OFF!,"* burst from the spectators.

And were they! Some of the horses jumped the rail into center field, others balked, others occupied themselves throwing off their jockeys. People shouted with laughter, yelled advice and finally the race was won by a solitary Japanese riding doggedly in the opposite direction from that in which he had started!

Other local races followed, then the Cowboy Relay, with teams representing the different Islands, was run up. Pam waited in her seat, tense as a spring. As if she suspected how wrought up she was inside, Kulani reached out and took her hand.

"Don't get all worn out before the Girls' Race," she cautioned.

"I can't help it, Mother, I want so badly to have Kilohana win everything—this time." Her dark blue eyes met her mother's brown ones.

"I—understand, dear," Kulani said in low tones and their unspoken thought hung between them for an instant. Then Kulani whispered, "Stout fella, Pam."

"All right, Kulani From Heaven," Pam whispered. "I'll try not to forget to be a good sport."

"You couldn't be anything else, but under the circumstances, there's a possibility you may get your values distorted."

Pam nodded. The cowboys came on to the track in pairs, leading their horses and carrying their saddles and bridles. Each team took its appointed position and waited tensely. At the signal from the starter, the riders slapped saddles on to their horses' backs, slid on their bridles and tore away, leaving their team-mates holding the horses which would run the next half mile. Spectators yelled and urged the men on. Horses flattened out, riders bent over their withers. As they began sweeping into the home stretch, men leaned over and unfastened their girths as they raced. After crossing the finish line, they jerked their horses on to their haunches, vaulted off and ran to their next mounts, carrying their gear in their hands. Once, twice, three times around they streamed, hoofs flying, men shouting, grandstand roaring. . . .

Maui came in first and Pam became silent. Ted bent over.

"Well, we got it this time," he gloated, "and we'll win the Free For All, too."

Pam glared at him.

"Hey!" Bill Collins exclaimed. "In Hawaii races are all in the family, so to speak. This year it's our turn, last year was yours. What does it matter?"

"If you knew it might be the last time for your colors, you'd care, too," Pam thought darkly. Her lips trembled as she pushed the thought away, but by the time the Girls' Race was called her little face was grim and white. Emily was so shaky when Na-lua-hine put her in the saddle that he had to make knots in her reins so they wouldn't jiggle out of her fingers.

"Ride race easy," the old fellow said encouragingly. "Just like when you race me at the ranch. No ride too fast at first, then when you half-way round—*Letta-Go-Your-Blouse!*"

"All right," Emily murmured.

There were seven contestants, the race was tight and the pace hard. Pam came in an easy first, Emily a brave third.

"Good for you, Emily, you rode like a veteran," Pam cried as they came off the track.

"Swell, you ride swell Em'ly! I proud on you," Na-lua-hine gloated. "After us go home I write Montgomery Ward and buy you fine new accordion."

"Oh, Na-lau-hine!" she squealed, half-dizzy from the excitement of the race and delight at the praise from Pam and her *paniolo*.

"Tell Mother I'm not coming to the grandstand for lunch, Emily. I'm not hungry and would rather be near the horses."

Emily looked a little anxiously at her cousin. Pam's manner was overwrought and she suspected that Pam was in some lonely world of her own where no one could reach her. If only Malolo would win she'd feel better.

"Make him win, please God," Emily prayed, as Na-lua-hine took her back through the ground to the grandstand. When Emily gave Kulani Pam's message she nodded.

"I understand how she feels and she's better off with the *paniolos* and horses than sitting here getting tenser and tenser as the minutes pass."

"I'll take her some sandwiches," Ted said.

"Don't, Ted," Kulani advised. "For the time being you're a red rag to her bull. I'll get hold of her before Malolo goes out to run."

When the lavish lunch-basket was emptied, Kulani rose. "I'm going to see my man up and my horse out," she announced.

Grandfather and Emily rose to accompany her and the Collins Clan followed suit, leaving their guests to look on from the grandstand. As they entered the paddock, Kulani lengthened her stride. Blooded horses which were to take part in the big event were being led out of their boxes; jockeys were being boosted on to their backs.

"All the jockeys, except the one on Dark Victory, are Hawaiians," Emily remarked in astonishment to Grandfather.

"Yes," he agreed. "Almost always they are. Racing isn't a money-making event here. It's sport among friends. Each family has some one man who rides for them and while they don't quite rank with professionals they're expert enough. Old Opiopio has ridden for us since he was fourteen and now he's almost fifty, but still wiry and tough as a nut."

Malolo was out, running in wide, eager circles, while his groom, Mahiai, hung onto the great-ringed snaffle bit, trying to hold him down. But when Kulani and Grandfather and Emily came closer they saw a crowd about the door of the empty loose-box and high excited voices all talking at once. Kulani pushed through the massed bodies. Pam was in the center of the hay-filled box, her face scarlet, her eyes wet. Kane was arguing with her and a *paniolo* stood nearby with the crimson jacket and cap of Kilohana in his hands.

"What has happened?" Kulani asked.

At the sound of her voice, Kane broke into a torrent of Hawaiian. Opiopio's leg had been broken a few minutes ago, while he was getting Malolo ready to go out. Maddened by excitement, the horse had lashed out at the side of the stall and shattered Opiopio's knee. An ambulance had already taken him to the nearest hospital. Pam was going to ride in his stead but it was madness for a girl of twelve to compete against men.

Pam rushed to Kulani. "I've got to ride him, Mother. All the Maui jockeys are up on other mounts. *Paniolos* are too heavy." She was struggling into her racing colors as she talked.

"Steady Pam, steady," Grandfather said from the door.

Pam didn't even hear. "But it isn't fair, the odds aren't even any more." Pam insisted in an overwrought way. "Dark Victory is being ridden by an American jockey who came with him from Kentucky. Malolo's being ridden by me!" She blinked tears out of her eyes.

"Pam, Pam," Kane protested, trying to calm her. "More better scratch Malolo this time. Next year run him again. Big risk for small girl like you to ride long mile race. If only half mile maybe you can make. But sure you tire out—"

"I'm going to ride him. There may be no next year!" Pam said stormily, then her eyes leaped to Kulani's, remembering she had cautioned her to say nothing of what was in the wind. Kulani suddenly put out her hand. "Let her go, Kane," she said. "She can try her luck. There *isn't* an extra jockey to be had—"

"Oh, Mother!" Pam cried shakily. "Thank you for letting me try."

She charged through the knot of men about the loose-box just as Ted appeared. Word of what had happened had spread like wildfire. He took hold of her arms. "Pam, you're crazy. You can't ride against that big field. Fifteen horses are running. Put someone up. I'll help you to find someone—"

"There isn't anyone," Pam cried.

"Then scratch your horse. He hasn't a fair chance under the present conditions. A strange rider knocks seconds off a race horse's time—"

"I know it," Pam said, her small face tragic.

"Wait," Ted said, excitedly. "I want the Free For All cup as badly as you do, but I'll ride Dark Victory against you. Then odds will be even. Both horses will have strange jockeys."

"Oh, *Ted!*" Pam gasped. "What a *sport* you are! Oh, Ted, you're swell!"

"I'm going to beat you," he warned, gaily.

"We'll see," Pam retorted.

Tearing off his coat, Ted leaped on to Dark Victory's back. Kane, looking like a disapproving mother hen, gave Pam a leg up on to Malolo. With a wild leap into the air, Malolo tried to break for the track, but Pam curved his neck down and brought him to order. A running mob of grooms and paddock hangers-on followed in her wake. From mouth to mouth the news flew, reaching the grandstand and bleachers before the horses were on the track.

Kulani's hand found Grandfather's. "My baby's off on her first solo flight," she said in low, moved tones. "But under the circumstances I had to let her try her wings."

Grandfather blew his nose. Emily's throat ached.

While the horses were lining up for the start, they went back to their seats in the grandstand. Jockeys were sparring for position. Pam's face was crimson and strained. Ted's face was tense and watchful. Pam felt like cutting at the riders jostling her with her pliant whip, to help Malolo from being bumped, but controlled the outlaw impulse. Malolo was wild to be off and got away three times, and had to be brought back. His gray coat was blue with sweat and Pam's eyes were stormy. She was riding for Kilohana,—which might be no more—and riding to win.

Then the great, stirring roar, *"THEY'RE OFF!"* jarred the

atmosphere. Bunched together, Dark Victory well in the lead, the horses swept around the first turn. Pam's start had been poor and for a while she felt like a small cork in a choppy sea. She rose in her stirrups and leaned over Malolo's withers, then felt his valiant spirit coming to meet hers through the reins. Reassurance, confidence returned and a tremendous love surged through her for the magnificent beast she rode. Eagerly, joyously, the horse flung himself forward with a stride as strong and rhythmic as the plunging of a perfect machine. Generations of noble animals bred to this one end went into the making of it. . . .

Once around the half-mile track they swept, the front horses bunched together, much in the positions they had held when they started, but Dark Victory still held the lead and was not, as yet, extending himself.

"*Letta-go-your-blouse*, Pam!" the Kilohana *paniolos* yelled as she tore past the bleachers.

Her face was tense and strained as she flashed by. The pace was terrific. She dared not break through the bunched horses for fear of a foul, which might disqualify Malolo, and as they approached the next turn she swung wide to take the outside. She was light and could afford to risk it. Dirt pelted her face, stinging like bullets; horses struggled into the lead, then dropped back. Positions began changing and Dark Victory stretched out as Malolo began creeping up on him.

Pam saw, with relief, that the last horse was behind and settled down to fight. Assuring herself that the two lengths, demanded by racing rules, gaped between her and the bunched horses, she swung in recklessly and took the rail. The track blurred before her, rushing to meet her like a destroying flood. Wind roared in her ears and Malolo's pounding hoofs flung the earth behind him. Lower leaned the girl, faster sped the horse.

They were one! They were one! They were one!

So the impact of flashing hoofs rung and playing muscles sung as they leaned out to take the turn. A metallic clash roused her from her spell. Side by side with touching stirrups, Dark Victory and Malolo raced. Pam's arms felt as though they were tearing out of their sockets, her head reeled. Faster, faster, faster. . . . Pam rode with her cheek against Malolo's neck. Ted's chin was almost between Dark Victory's ears. Neck and neck, flank to flank, the great horses raced and the ringing hoofs and straining lungs of their gallant ancestors echoed to each stride and gasp as they smoked down the track with the rest of the field far in the rear. A roar struck Pam like an appalling blow. Spectators in grandstand and bleachers rose like a man. Pam swayed in the saddle but drove her teeth into her lip.

"Malolo! Malolo! Pam! Pam!"

She felt clubbed, stunned as the blurred roar of voices shook the atmosphere.

"Dark Victory! Dark Victory. Ted!"

The judges' stand rushed up and flipped behind. They were over the finishing line and she did not know who had won, or if it was a dead heat. Malolo, knowing the race was over, swung around and Pam dropped exhaustedly forward on his reeking shoulders, then straightened herself.

Loving hands pulled her from the saddle—Kane's. Mists billowed and rolled before her eyes, filled with the dim shapes of horses and people. Then the haze began clearing away. Kane was hurrying her along the track, jammed with excited people. Hot thoroughbreds were being led away. Kane was crying in a glad, excited manner. "Good girl, good kid, you ride swell! Never I seeing one race swell like this."

Dark Victory was standing before the judges' stand, Ted beside him. "Come Pam," he cried in a breathless voice. "We've got to be weighed out."

People seemed out of their heads with delight and excitement, as they loaded Pam and Ted, Dark Victory and Malolo, with *leis*. Pam swallowed. It had been a dead heat then. That meant that the race would have to be run off again later in the day and she doubted if she had the strength for it.

Ted jumped off the scales with his saddle on his arm.

"Weights all correct," the clerk of the scales announced. "Now you, Miss Garland."

Pam stepped on. Kane handed her her saddle.

"Correct," the clerk said again. Outside the crowd was yelling "Malolo! Malolo! Pam. Welakahao! Whoopee!"

"Hurry up, they want you! They're cheering you," Ted cried, grabbing her arm and hustling her forward. "I don't give a hoot if you won. It was only by a nose. Wasn't it swell? Wasn't it glorious?"

Swinging her on to his shoulder, Ted waved his cap. Pam felt dizzied with happiness. The cup was going home to Kilohana—once more! She looked down and saw Ted grinning up at her. Tearing off one of her *leis* she put it around his neck and kissed him. The crowd went mad. Victor and vanquished applauding each other. Friends! Hawaiians yelled and cheered, Japanese Banzai-ed, whites hurrahed.

"Oh, Ted," Pam gasped. "Someday, maybe, I'll be able to tell you why I wanted so badly to get the cup this year."

Ted bounced her down, linked his arm through hers and bolted through the seething crowd toward their box in the grandstand. "To heck with who won. We're lucky to have ridden in a race of this kind. Wasn't it *swell?*"

Pam nodded. "And you're swell, too, Ted, to—to do what you did. "Not many people would have. You're my—"

"Favorite enemy?" Ted suggested in his gay way. Pam nodded and they began laughing together.

CHAPTER X

THE HOUSE OF THE SUN

"No visit to Maui is complete without making a trip up Haleakala," Uncle Bill Collins announced a day or so later, when the excitement of the races had abated a little. "I've arranged for horses and a guide to meet us at the end of the automobile road at Olinda, to take us through the summit." His merry eyes began twinkling. "And as long as we're there, we might as well ride through the crater and on around the island. Pam, you've been to the top, and of course Kulani has, but Emily here hasn't—"

"So we'll all pay our respects to the House of the Sun," Kulani agreed, "and see the windward side of Maui to boot. The horses will have to rest for a week and old Opiopio's leg won't be healed enough to move until at least that time, so there's nothing to prevent us from following Uncle Bill's plan!"

"Oh!" Emily breathed. "Sometimes I'm scared I'll wake up and this will all be only a dream!"

The next morning automobiles took them through the great sugar plantations covering the isthmus which joined the eastern and western halves of the island together. Then the cars crawled up through grassy ranch lands where sleek horses and cattle grazed. Pam sat in a blissful haze, re-riding the race in her mind and thinking about the trophy she would carry home. Grandfather kept humming snatches of the Kilohana hula; Ted and jolly Uncle Bill Collins chatted and laughed with Kulani, and Emily leaned back, happily silent.

Halfway up the mountain the automobile road ended. Horses and a guide were waiting in some corrals under tall, somber eucalyptus trees. As they started up the vast, sloping flanks of the dead volcano, Kane told the girls legends about the demi-god, Maui, for whom the island was named.

Maui was a hero. In olden times the Sun went across the sky so quickly that Maui's mother complained that she didn't have time enough, or light enough to braid the fine mats for which she was famous. Maui went up the mountain and argued with the Sun about the matter, but the Sun rolled on his way, ignoring him. That made Maui angry. He went to the lowlands and braided a mighty lasso, crept up the mountain at night and lay in hiding, waiting for the Sun to emerge from the crater, where he lived. As the Sun came up slowly, Maui leaped from his place of concealment, lassoed him and cut off his longest leg, and ever afterwards the Sun moved more slowly, giving men and women more time to go about their work.

As they mounted, the horizon seemed to swim higher and higher into the sky. Far below, the island spread out, a palette of color, and ahead rudely uptilted cones showed red and purple against the blue sky. Drifts of ash and rivers of congealed lava lay on all sides. Slowly the long procession of horses and pack animals toiled up the rough slopes and after a sharp scramble finally landed on the sheer brink of the crater.

Emily could not believe her eyes! She had memorized the dimensions of the vast pit at the summit of the ten thousand foot mountain. She knew it was twenty-seven miles in circumference and in places almost a thousand feet deep, but she had not been prepared for its beauty.

Immense, silent, rimmed with cyclopean walls, splashed with barbaric color, and harboring strange shadows beneath its overhanging cliffs, the vast bowl cradled its seventeen giant cones. The day was breathless, but sudden winds came up out of it with gusty swirls and peculiar roaring noises, just as gases had come out in ages past. Precipitous crags brooded above the distorted landscape, perhaps remembering a time when mad flames had danced demon-dances beneath crimson-dripping crags and shaking lava islands had grated against seas of melting rock. Across the farther rim, in contrast to the color and chaos at her feet, the serene mountains tops of Mauna Loa and Mauna Kea showed above packed masses of Tradewind cloud, drifting at the five thousand foot level. Emily's heart caught, seeing them, and her eyes leaped to Pam's.

"In a week we'll be home," she said, gazing at the snow-crusted summits a hundred miles away.

"I can hardly wait," Pam said.

After they had looked their fill, the party pushed on, following a narrow trail winding just below the rim of the mighty pit. Finally the trail curved sharply toward two big cinder cones standing like sentinels to right and left. Riding into stone corrals, everyone dismounted to rest the horses and eat lunch before beginning the descent into the crater.

Kane and Na-lua-hine took the girls up the side of the cone to the left of the trail and showed them breast-high stone fortifications covering the rough slopes to the summit. Below was a rock quarry which, through successive generations, rival chieftains had battled to possess. In the eerie stillness of the mountain top it was easy to picture the tawny, mighty warriors, squatting there, fashioning weapons of peace and war; adzes to shape canoes, sling shots. . . .

> "O ka ihi i ka make
> O ka O-o i ke ola!"

Na-lua-hine quoted.

"I know what that means!" Emily said. "The spear is symbolic of death, the spade of life!"

"You smart like any-kind now," Kane chuckled. Pointing across the crater, he recited the names of peaks that recalled the carnage of long ago. "That one," he pointed at a high cliff, "is—" he regarded Emily with smiling eyes. "You say, Em'ly, slow, after me—"

Emily took a deep breath. "I'm ready."

"Okay, that place name—Puualiokakoanuiokane!"

Emily's tongue got all tangled up before she was halfway through and everyone laughed. "What does it mean, Kane?" she asked.

"The Soldiers of the Mighty Army of Kane," he said in ringing tones.

A delicious sense of remoteness from the world stole over them all as they began descending the trail winding down the Sliding Sands. The walls rose higher, colors grew more violent, the silence more impressive. Desolation lay on every hand. Solid lakes of cold lava, masses of smelted rock, sphinx-like cinder-cones lifted their heads above the cluttered crater floor. Now and then strange cries came from the crags as herds of wild goats, swarming ant-like on the ridges, began working down after their noon rest, to search for feed on alluvial flats. Dust rising from their sharp little hoofs looked like brown steam rising from volcanic cracks.

Ted pointed at strange glittering plants growing on the slopes of certain cones and took Emily over to see them. "Those are Silver Swords," he told her. "They only grow in the crater of Haleakala and in a remote spot in the Himalayas. Feel how soft they are." Dismounting, he waited for her to come over. "It's illegal to pick them, now that Haleakala's a National Park. See the silver particles on the leaves. They're soft as the down on a moth's wing."

Emily touched one of the slender leaves, like a slim dagger, and caught her breath with surprise.

They pushed on slowly, winding between towering cones and making their way over lava flows. The trail threw a loop and crawled up the vivid cinder slope between a cone of gray ash and one of poisonous-looking scoria. Ted spurred his horse up to Emily's. "In old times, the Hawaiians buried their High Chiefesses in this cone," he gestured at the gray one, "and that one is called Haalii—the Passing Place of Chiefs. Inside there are rock platforms containing what remains of their bones."

Emily gazed at the awesome heap of violently colored, tortured rock. She shivered involuntarily, then said in her small, quiet way, "What a place to be buried in—the House of the Sun!"

Ted nodded.

The trail dipped down between the great cones and Uncle Bill Collins pulled up his horse. "There," he said, pointing out a strange, low breastwork of highly colored, brittle lava, "is the Bottomless Pit."

Emily saw a black, gaping hole some twenty feet across. Everyone dismounted to peer into it. When one of the *paniolos* pitched a big stone into it, everyone waited expectantly, but there was no sound of it hitting bottom. Emily drew back a step and Pam laughed.

"It is scaring, isn't it?" she said.

Evening was beginning to creep into the crater and Uncle

Bill said they must hurry on to camp. Some of the *paniolos* had gone on ahead with the pack animals to get everything ready for the night. It was restful, after all the turmoil and excitement of the races, to ride along slowly, listening to hoofs crunching cinders and to conversation drifting back over peoples' shoulders.

The first chill of night was drifting into the vast, quiet pit. Terrific blue shadows were lengthening across the floor, swinging walls were silhouetted sharply against the sky, washed with apricot color in the west. The trail twisted around the end of a lava flow and suddenly ended at a small grassy plain and golden-green forest. Tents were pitched and a campfire uncurled rosy smoke spirals. Men were busy with pots and pans and the fragrance of coffee drifted by on a faint breeze coming up the Kaupo Gap.

"Grandfather," Emily exclaimed, "why is there a forest here when the rest of the crater is just cinders, ash and lava?"

"This, my dear, is the oldest end of the crater. Volcanic activity started here, then moved on across the floor. Behind the tall cliffs are miles of damp forests. The Trade Wind blows over them, spills over the crags, hits the cold air in the crater and precipitates rain."

Because it was her first experience camping, Emily rushed about trying not to miss anything. She went with Na-lua-hine to water the horses from a small pool a short way up one of the cliffs. The water had to be bailed out with a bucket and spilled down the sloping rock into a small water trough. She helped to get firewood, covered the saddles with slickers to keep off the night dew, and hovered about the fire watching supper cooked.

She was so happy she could hardly bear it. The sound of horses grazing, voices talking, the bubbling of sea birds in the cliffs, the sense of being so high up in the sky, filled her with a strange exhilaration. Fierce color burned above the ragged rim-line in the west and chiffon-blue shadows hung limply under crags. A majestic peace lay like a benediction over everything. Climbing on to a rough lava heap, Emily clasped her hands about her knees and drank it all in.

"What are you thinking about, Emily?" Pam asked, coming up behind her.

"I'm soaking everything in so I'll never forget it."

Pam sat down beside her and gazed at the crater, too.

"I feel about as big as an ant, Emily," she remarked, after a silence.

"Me, too, but isn't it marvelous?"

Pam nodded.

Next morning they started down the Kaupo Gap. The gap was a five-mile break in the mighty granite walls which some awful convulsion had blown into the sea, far below. After two hours of slow riding down over lava flows the trail ended on a wild coast with the sea breaking whitely against it. They rested the horses for a while under some wild orange trails, then set off on a narrow path of shiny cobblestones that ran up and down the sides of terrific gulches and wormed its way along hog's-back ridges that fell away sharply on both sides. Grand-father told Emily that this trail that wound along like a mam-moth serpent, with stones for scales, had been built in ancient times for the Kings' Runners. The pebbles had been polished by bare flying feet carrying messages of peace or war and royal ultimatums.

About noon they halted in a deep canyon, where a river crossed the ancient trail. The *paniolos* tied the horses in a grove of *ohia* trees. Under the dark, glossy leaves luscious fruit, shaped like apples, hung in thick clusters. Emily bit into one and found the meat was more juicy than real apples and had a sherbet-like consistency. Wild bananas hung in yellow bunches from bending trees. *Papaias* flaunted their ripe, golden fruit. Pam, Ted, and Emily clambered through the dense, moist undergrowth, collecting a little of everything to add to the lunch the *paniolos* were spreading out on green fern leaves.

When they had eaten they made their way up the gorge to a pool where a waterfall leaped from the lip of a cliff, sending thunderous clouds of spray into the air. Everyone bathed and had shouting fights with wild ginger blossoms, whacking each other with the thick buds that sprayed water and honey— which, of course, necessitated another swim.

When they finally rode on, Emily felt as if she had been in another world of sunshine, green things and clean water where no one had ever been before. The trail began its mighty winding up and down more gorges yawning their mighty jaws on the sea. Occasionally they passed through tiny villages where Hawaiians ran out to meet them with gifts of *leis* and fruit. On and on and on they pushed through increasingly beautiful country until they picked up a bold headland jutting into the Tradewind driven sea. This was the settlement of Hana, the most northern and easterly point of Maui.

There was a rumbling sugar mill, a sleepy little town with streets starred with yellow *frangipani* flowers that the wind had shaken off the trees. Rackety Chinese stores were here and there, with wrinkled grandfathers sitting on the steps watching the antics of their littlest grandsons crawling around their feet.

Uncle Bill Collins took his party to a small hotel run by a fat, jolly Chinaman. The *paniolos* went off with the horses to the plantation stables, then drifted away to visit friends. After supper, in the scented purple twilight, everyone sat on the veranda listening to the deep-sounding voice of the sea. Starlight gleamed on dark leaves and the mighty headland of Kawiki jutted into the sky. Behind all the beauty of the locality there was a weighted feeling of sadness lying upon everything.

Pam remarked it and Uncle Bill Collins straightened up.

"I'll tell you why, Pam," he said. "Once there was a very great family named Calhoun, who lived here and owned all the land. They were lawless, splendid people. Royal livers, prodigal, open-handed. They spent their money on race horses and good times and by and by there wasn't any left."

Uncle Bill drew on his cigar and the ocean gave a sudden angry crash, as if it were crying, "I remember!"

"The Calhouns mortgaged their land and went deeper and deeper into debt. They loved Hana passionately but couldn't come down to earth and take care of the land they owned. Finally, far-sighted business men figured that the water, conserved by the great forests swathing this northeastern end of Haleakala, could be collected in ditches and taken around to the central plains of Maui to grow cane. They came over and offered to buy the Calhoun land. The Calhouns didn't want to sell, for they loved Hana as only Islanders can love land. But they had reached the point where they hadn't a choice. Old Man Calhoun died before the deal went quite through. His son Dick signed it and in a moment of mad remorse shot his stableful of race horses. The shock killed him. You'll read their story some day, for it's been written into a book."

"Oh, Uncle Bill," Pam gasped, "how could anyone do such a terrible thing as to shoot all his race horses?"

The old man moved slightly and his wicker chair creaked. "You're too young to understand yet, Pam, that when a person loses everything he loves in one swoop—"

Pam caught her breath. "I'm not too young to understand, Uncle Bill," she cried. "Only I wouldn't kill my horses. I'd— I'd fight. I'd make the man who was trying to take my place—" Breaking off, she looked around in a wild way and rushed out into the dark.

"What on earth—" Uncle Bill began.

Kulani rose. "I'll go after her, Bill. She's still keyed up from the races."

Kulani found her lying on the grass, shaking like a horse that's been ridden to the limit. "Pam," she said, kneeling down and bending over her.

"Oh, Mother, Mother," she sobbed.

Kulani gathered her daughter into her strong arms. "I know what's troubling you, Pam, but you mustn't go to pieces. You and I have to keep steady and cool through the next few months and swing Kingsley into our way of thinking. Just suppose the worst happened, we still have to set an example to our people. What would you think, what would they think of me, if I behaved as you're behaving now? You're my partner, Pam, and partners don't fail each other. You're crossing bridges which we may never get to. . . . Tearing off hunks of agony that will probably never come."

Pam choked.

"I need you now, as I've never needed you before, Pam. I have no husband to fight with me, only my daughter. Don't fall down on me, or on Grandfather. He's convinced, as our lawyer is, that Kingsley will be willing to sell if he won't release. Kilohana is just a name to him. I'm sorry now I told you. I thought you could take it in your stride."

"Oh, Mother, I will, I will!" Pam cried.

"Will you give me your hand and word upon it? Not let your mind race around in circles?"

"Yes, Kulani From Heaven! I don't know why I blew up like this. I never have before."

They were sitting on the grass, facing the clean wind blowing across thousands of miles of heaving blue water. Pam lifted her hot face to its cool, steady touch, felt it pour through her hair. She saw her mother's profile against the stars, two white gardenias resting like pale flower-spirits above her ear. The lost peace that had gone from her in the Office when Kingsley's letter came was seeping back into her, in a deeper, stiller way.

"This is the first real crisis in your life, Pam," Kulani said. "If you handle it like a man, you'll come out on top. If you crumple up, when the next crossing comes, you'll crumple easier. I love Kilohana as much as you do, but *because* I love it I'm going to click on all twelve cylinders, every minute. . . . Else I'm of no use to it, else I can't jiggle things around until they come out the way I want."

Pam gripped her mother's hand fiercely.

"Trouble is the real test of a person, Pam. It's no trick to be gracious, generous, kind and strong when things are easy. But when things grow difficult, if you can go on with a smile, believe when apparently there's nothing to believe in, fight when you can't see a step ahead, laugh when crying's easier, have fun when there's nothing to make fun with, then you're a hundred per cent worth while. People will come to you for help when they're in trouble, rush to you to share their joy, count on you to go all the way in emergencies. If a person can be like that, and anyone can be—if they want to *enough*—then you'll be that most splendid of all things—A Happy Warrior!"

Pam gazed into her mother's steady dark eyes. From their depths Kilohana was looking on her, counting on her. She opened her lips to speak but Kulani kissed her forehead.

"You don't need to say it, Pam. I know you will!"

CHAPTER XI

KITCHEN MAGIC

WHEN THEY FINALLY GOT BACK FROM HANA TO WAI-KAPU A few days later, Opiopio's broken leg was sufficiently improved to make it possible to move him back to Hawaii. Horses were gathered up, good-byes said, and the Collins issued invitations to come over again for the next Fourth of July.

Back at Kilohana, with determination worthy of an adult, Pam set out to apply her mother's philosophy to daily life. "We've got to believe everything will work out right, Emily, even if it doesn't seem possible. We've got to have courage, have fun, work, laugh, and pretend there's no Mr. Kingsley and no Aunt Dode who can take you back to Boston when your year is up."

"Six months of it are gone already," Emily remarked in a

small, dry voice, staring in front of her with a stony face.

Tawny sunlight was stalking arrogantly over land and sea, piled clouds held mighty conferences above the strong horizon. Doves cooed in the orange trees growing outside the kitchen door and a parakeet whistled three shining notes and darted for the summit of Hualalai.

"I can't believe I'll have to leave all this," Emily said, gesturing around her. "When I do, a part of me will stay here forever."

"When your time is up Kulani From Heaven will figure out something so Aunt Dode can't take you away from us," Pam asserted staunchly. "And when our lease is up on Kilohana she'll fix it so Mr. Kingsley won't take it. It's sissy of us to stew over things which aren't here yet. You've learned to be a first class *paniolo*. Now if you're a real Island girl you must learn to cook, arrange flowers and housekeep. Tatsu can show you the last two and Ah Sam will teach you cooking. Mother's going to show me how to keep track of food sales in the store and when I'm smarter and older I'll learn bookkeeping."

Emily gripped Pam's hand. "When I'm around you, I always feel brave and strong, but sometimes at night, when I'm lying in the dark, I begin thinking that maybe Kulani From Heaven won't be able to make Aunt Dode agree to let me stay with you."

Pam's jaw stuck out. "We've got to help each other to be strong, Emily. I'll tell Tatsu to move your things into the room next to mine. Then if you get lonely at night, or I get to thinking in circles, as Mother calls it, we can go to each other and remind each other that we mustn't think about things we don't want to happen or we'll pull them to us. Let's not waste time, let's start today to be Happy Warriors. I'll go to Mother and ask her to show me how to keep the Sales Record book and you tell Ah Sam you want a cooking lesson."

"Okay," Emily agreed, bouncing up.

Pam streaked off toward the Office and Emily headed for the kitchen, old Poi at her heels. "I'll give you all the food I spoil, Poi," she promised and the old dog wagged an enthusiastic tail.

Ah Sam was seated at the back door, smoking his funny, short, three-sided Chinese pipe that had a wee brass bowl half-way up the stem. Emily told him what she wanted and he nodded.

"Sure, I like velly much teach you to cook, Em'ly. What-kind you like number one to eat?"

Emily checked off a dozen or so of her pet Island dishes.

"After you little smart I teach you make those kinds. Today, I show you how to make Sampan Soup. It velly easy for small girl to fix."

They went into the kitchen and Ah Sam put on a kettle of water to heat and chatted with Emily until it started boiling. "Now us make Sampan Soup," the old man said, smiling and going to the stove. Emily hovered close, watching the old man's every move. Putting some green tea leaves into a pot, he poured water over them and let them steep.

"I thought we were making soup," Emily remarked.

"Sure. Sampan Soup make from tea. Now us put tea in-side two bowls and add one tablespoonful of Shoyu—what

Amelika-style mans call Soy Sauce." When the dark, salty fluid was stirred into the tea, Ah Sam told Emily to taste it. She was a bit dubious, but took a sip.

"Why, it's delicious!" she exclaimed. "And so easy to fix. You simply couldn't make a mistake."

Ah Sam's eyes squinched into smiling slits. "Now if got velly high-up people for dinner, make like this." Peeling an avocado, he diced it and added a generous quantity to each bowl. "Now tly again."

Emily sampled it. "Why, Ah Sam, it's the most delicious boullion I ever tasted."

"Not so bad," he agreed. "If no can get avocado, take a few pieces of chicken breast and cut with scissors, velly long and thin, and put inside the soup. That China-style."

"I bet that would be good, too," Emily agreed enthusiastically.

"Tomorrow us cook rice. That easy, too. Bime-by you smart like enny kind and cook one dinner for surplise family."

Emily radiated happiness. "Couldn't I see you cook rice today?" she begged. "I can't forget how to make Sampan Soup; it's Green tea, rather weak, Shoyu, and diced avocados or sliced chicken breast, if you want to be stylish."

"Smart girl," Ah Sam praised. "Sure, I show you how to cook rice, Island-style."

Measuring four cups of rice—there were eight for dinner and one cupful of rice fed two persons amply he told her—he washed the rice thoroughly three times in cold water. That removed the powdery surplus starch, which made the grains stick together, Ah Sam explained, and Emily saw that the water was almost clear after the third washing. Draining the rice thoroughly, Ah Sam put in two cups of water to each cup of rice, covered the pot tightly and set it on the back of the stove where it would cook very slowly. In about fifty minutes he lifted the lid off. The rice was dry and each kernel free of its mates. Setting the lid a little crooked, so a crack was left, he allowed the rice to steam off for ten minutes so it would get still drier. Less rice took less time to cook, he explained, one cup about twenty minutes, two or three about forty.

"Well, it's no trick to cook rice, either," Emily commented gleefully.

Each day she went to Ah Sam and learned a new dish. The next was bananas fixed in the popular Island way. Greasing a large, heavy frying pan generously with butter, Ah Sam sliced bananas length-wise until it was almost full. When the fruit was fried a light brown, a matter of only a few minutes, he sprinkled on a generous layer of shredded coconut and topped it with marshmallows. Covering the delicious-smelling concoction, he let it stand for a couple of minutes, until the marshmallows melted, then put generous portions on the plates going into the dinner table, with sizzling steaks and neat heaps of green beans piled beside them.

The following day Emily learned how to cook beans so they were always green, tender and tasty. Instead of breaking them up or slicing them fine, Ah Sam cut them in half from end to end, placing them in neat piles, sufficient for individual servings. Each heap was tied around the middle with a piece of string and dropped into a large saucepan of furiously boiling, salted water, to which he added a wee pinch of soda just before the beans were dropped in. In about twenty-five minutes they were tender. Lifting the bundles out, Ah Sam drained them, plastered them with butter, put them on the serving plates, and cut the strings.

After a week or so he informed Emily she was expert enough to cook Chicken Avocado and told her to write down each step so she wouldn't get mixed up. Slicing a large onion, Ah Sam mixed it with a cupful of diced celery, including a few top leaves. Cutting up two stewing hens, he put them into a saucepan of lightly salted water, and added the onion and celery. The hens must simmer in a covered pot until they were tender, he explained, and the vegetables gave them a richer, sweeter flavor.

While the chickens were cooking he showed Emily how to make the cream sauce. Melting a heaping tablespoonful of butter in a frying pan, he added a tablespoonful of flour and stirred it in, then poured in a whole can of milk. Canned milk, he explained, made richer, smoother sauce than fresh milk. After the sauce thickened, he set it away until the chickens were ready. Draining off the juice, he placed the sections of fowl in the middle of a large platter and poured the re-heated cream sauce over it, like a snowy blanket. Around the edge of the smoking heap he arranged cup-moulds of rice and between each white ball he placed a quarter section of avocado. Then to complete the green-and-white effect, he sprinkled the dish with a little finely chopped parsley.

The right salad to go with Chicken Avocado was watercress, romaine and hearts of artichoke, Ah Sam said. Taking the small, inner leaves of romaine, Ah Sam arranged them so they radiated from the center of the salad plate, like wheel-spokes, then made a little green nest of watercress and inside he placed three small artichoke hearts.

"They look like green eggs in a green nest—laid by a green bird," Emily cried delightedly.

"Mebbe-so-yes," Ah Sam chuckled. "But us no finish yet." Taking cubes of pineapple, he dotted them around the artichoke hearts and sat a fat white marshmallow on top.

"Oo, I bet that's good," Emily gasped.

"Sure velly fine," Ah Sam agreed. "Now little French dressing pour over all and any fella eat-up 'em up quick."

"What dessert goes best with this meal?" Emily asked.

"Banana and coconut fritters," Ah Sam announced. "But this too hard for little girl to make. After by and by when you got fifteen year I show you." He chuckled.

Emily grew suddenly quiet and thoughtful. "But I won't be here," she said in a sunk way.

"I think sure never you go back to Boston, Em'ly," Ah Sam said. "Kulani From Heaven make some kind so you stay with us."

A few days later Ah Sam, Emily, and Tatsu planned a surprise dinner, which was to be made up of the dishes Emily had learned to cook—with the right dessert, which Ah Sam would cook.

While the family was busy about ranch work, Tatsu and

Emily set the table and arranged a floral piece of gardenias in the center. The menu was to be: Sampan Soup with diced avocado in it, for the first course. Then Chicken Avocado and rice, watercress, romaine and artichoke salad, finished with pineapple and marshmallow, and coconut and banana fritters for dessert.

While Emily worked about the kitchen, preparing the dishes she knew, Ah Sam smoked his pipe and watched. "You so smart, Em'ly, mebbe I no cook enny more, but go back to China," he remarked.

"Oh, Ah Sam, no!" she cried. "It would be awful without you. I love you and Tatsu and the *paniolos*."

"I only making foolish. You tink I like go away from Hawaii. Over in Orient Japanese and Chinese fellas fight. In Hawaii they flens. Hawaii number one good place. Everyman got plenty *Aloha* and make jolly with other-kind mans. Swell, s'pose make this way in every country."

"Yes," Emily agreed.

When everything was ready to serve, Emily dashed off and dressed for dinner.

When the meal was finished Grandfather pushed back his chair in a large, satisfied way. "Well, Ah Sam certainly outdid himself tonight," he announced.

Tatsu and Emily began to giggle, then Ah Sam popped his head around the door and announced proudly, "Emily make dinner tonight."

"Except the dessert," Emily said in her honest way.

"Dessert no-count," Ah Sam chuckled and everyone laughed.

All through the evening Emily glowed with pride. She had really done something—and done it well—the whole family agreed heartily about that.

CHAPTER XII

AN IDOL IS FOUND

"Let's fish for *ULUA* and squid before we start home," Kulani suggested one warm noon as they swam in the rainbow-spinning waters of Lua-hine-wai. "We've got off an extra big shipment of steers today and a little fun will do us all good."

"Oh, let's!" the girls cried delightedly.

"It's silly," Emily said, an impish expression flitting over her face, "I don't feel like a plain orphan any more. I feel loved, beautiful and—important. Maybe the water of Lua-hine-wai's working on me, or maybe I'm just plain crazy," she finished with a laugh.

"You always were beautiful, loved and important," Kulani asserted. "But when you came to Hawaii you were shut up in-

side yourself, like a butterfly in a cocoon. Now you're free.
That's the only difference."

Emily gazed at her aunt with worshipping eyes.

"Happiness is the greatest beautifier in the world, Emily
dear, so when you make others happy you're helping to spread
beauty over the world. But come, the tide's just right for good
fishing." And she started down the trail leading back to the
beach where *paniolos* were loafing beside their horses.

When Kulani told them she wanted fish they jumped up and
hurried like eager boys to a ledge in the lava where they kept
spears and nets for just such occasions. In pairs and singly they
drifted up the beach. Everyone began searching rocks and looking into still pools. Na-lua-hine went after *wana*, a species of
sea-urchin he loved. It tasted like salty marrow and butter and
when he found one he opened it and gave it to Emily to suck.
Other men collected *limu*, a flat, reddish brown edible seaweed and put it into small bags. Pam pried *opihis* (a sort of
limpet or shell fish) off the rocks with Kane's legging knife.

Moku, who was expert with a spear, went on ahead to watch
for *ulua* and Kimmo searched quiet pools for squid. Emily had
eaten it, stewed in coconut milk, but had never seen one alive,
so she kept close to him. Presently he froze to attention and
pointed.

"*He'i!*" he announced excitedly.

Out of a crevice a long tentacle showed.

"You like see close, Em'ly?" Kimmo asked.

She drew back, but nodded.

Gently lowering a pole into the water, Kimmo touched the

waving arm. Instantly the squid wrapped its tentacle about it. Kimmo teased it some more and another tentacle took hold of the pole. He manipulated the stick again and after a little all the long arms with their sucking cups were fastened to the staff. Kimmo drew the squid gently through the water to the edge of the pool in order that Emily might see the creature at close range.

Its body resembled a small, dirty gray sack, its mouth was like a small opening in the sack, with a circular lip and parrot-like beak, which was almost hidden at the moment. Fiery round eyes glared up at them. Kimmo jiggled the pole. The squid retained its hold, but began changing from slaty gray to red with black mottlings.

"He's *hu-hu*—mad!" Kimmo chuckled, and made a quick movement of his right arm.

Feeling the menace of the gesture, the squid began to un-writhe, but Kimmo drove the small spear he carried in his right hand into its body. Instantly the clear pool was filled with a cloud of sepia the creature ejected and tentacles rushed up the spear with incredible swiftness and wrapped about Kimmo's wrist. Emily recoiled, but Kimmo laughed. Seizing the hideous writhing mass with his free hand, Kimmo bit the squid between the eyes. It relaxed its hold and Kimmo nonchalantly stripped the slimy tentacles off his wrist.

Squatting down, he stuffed the squid into a small bag tied about his waist. "More good from crab or lobster," he announced, patting the dead squid gleefully. Then going on, he began searching for others.

A faint hail from Moku sent Pam and Emily scampering after him. When they got to him, he pointed over a lava ledge. "*Ulua*," he whispered in a tense voice. He measured the water with narrowed eyes, then nodded in a satisfied manner. Straightening up, he began tying his big spear firmly to his wrist with a stout cord.

At first the girls could see nothing, then, fathoms below, they saw a streak like quicksilver, cruising back and forth and gradually working nearer to the surface. Peering down through the water, which was like blue glass, they saw a strange and beautiful world. *Wana*, sea-urchins, like huge spiny orange cactus-dahlias blossomed on rough black lava ledges. Pastel-colored coral, like graceful shrubs, grew in a golden-blue garden of fine-ribbed sand. Scarlet and yellow fish, fish blue as electric lights, and striped black and white fish about three inches long nibbled at invisible growths on the rocks. Occasionally a whole school of them flashed here and there, like flocks of brightly colored birds. Suddenly the *ulua* struck and the little fish exploded in all directions. Moku poised his spear, braced back and threw. The line to his wrist whanged tight and the water was thrown into terrific confusion as the *ulua* raced around, fighting to get free.

Kimmo rushed up and locked his arm through Moku's and they danced and teetered along the edges of the rocks. For a few breathless instants it seemed as if the monster fish would drag them in, but it began losing strength and came nearer and nearer to the surface. One moment it was electric blue, the next like a silver-white palm leaf flashing and turning from side

to side. Plunging and leaping, it came to the top and after a
fierce, brief tussle Moku and Kimmo landed it.

It was about a yard long and weighed eighty or ninety
pounds. For a few moments it slapped the rocks with its tail,
leaped into the air, rolled over and over. Moku managed to
strike it a deft blow on the back of its head. It stiffened, quivered, arched over, and the light went out of its scales.

The men were panting but their faces were eager and happy
as Hawaiians always are when they're getting food. While they
squatted down to clean the fish, Emily wandered on. She pried
opihis off the rocks with Na-lua-hine's knife, scooped them out
of their shells and munched them. She gathered seaweed and
nibbled it and enjoyed the wind blowing against her face. Behind her, happy voices came faintly to her ears, like voices in a
dream—the beautiful dream that is Hawaii.

Mighty clouds were heaped above the summits of the sleeping volcanoes, little golden beaches wedged themselves in between black lava outcroppings. Small groves of coconuts moved
their glittering fronds in the sun. She strolled on like a happy
sleep-walker for a while, then stubbed her toe against a hard
object. Bending down she saw it was a stone, unlike any in the
region about her. After digging the sand away, she unearthed
an image with a frightening face. It must be an idol, she concluded, and might be valuable. Hoisting it into her arms she
started back toward figures bending over rocks and peering into
pools, all too occupied to notice what she was doing.

"Look what I found," she called triumphantly when she got
within earshot. Setting the shaped stone down on the sand she

wiped the perspiration off her face and waited expectantly.

The Hawaiians crowded up, then recoiled with horrified expressions on their faces.

"No good fool with shark god!" Na-lua-hine cried. "Bring bad luck. Where you find?"

"In the sand," Emily replied.

"More better put back quick in the *heiau*." Na-lua-hine pointed at a crumbling heap of lava slabs, which Emily knew from its prominent position on the shore line had been an old temple.

"It's only a piece of stone," Emily protested.

"No talk like that or bad trouble come to you," Na-lua-hine said reprovingly, making a quick sign to avert evil. "Us go put the *akua* back where he stop before and give some nice fish."

Lifting the image reverently, he spoke to his fellows in Hawaiian and they hastily selected some of each type of shell fish they had collected, a tentacle of squid, a slab of *ulua* and put them in an extra flour bag.

"You bring, Em'ly, and come with me," the old man ordered.

Pam and Kulani, sensing that something unusual was afoot, came hurrying up and the men told them what had happened. Kulani listened without comment until they finished speaking, then said in quiet tones;

"Run along with Na-lua-hine, Emily, and put the old god back where he belongs, then we'll gather up our plunder and go home."

Emily felt a little solemn trudging beside her *paniolo*, who looked silent and worried. She wanted to ask about shark gods but decided it wasn't the right time. As if suspecting how she felt, Na-lua-hine took a big breath and explained that it would not be wise to delay making peace with the old god.

"Why?" Emily asked.

"Because," Na-lua-hine said, "the moon is in *Ku!*"

Emily did not understand the significance of his remark but the words held some malevolent quality. She asked Na-lua-hine to explain and he told her that when the moon was in its dying quarter Hawaiians believed that supernatural forces held ascendency on earth.

Emily shivered involuntarily. Of a sudden the dark lava flows pouring over the land looked sinister instead of thrilling, and the voice of the sea, instead of being a song, seemed menacing. She stood as still as a mouse while Na-lua-hine propped the idol up between hunks of loose lava. When it was firmly in place, the old man laid the offerings before it, murmured a long prayer, and rose.

"There," he said in relieved tones. "Now maybe trouble no come, but I no like when this-kind thing happen."

Emily did not refer to the matter riding home but felt a trifle awed and uneasy because the *paniolos* were not as gay and noisy as usual. When they dispersed and went to their homes she hurried across the Office.

"I didn't know it was bad, Kulani From Heaven," she said.

"It wasn't, dear, and no harm will come from it. I believe in being tolerant of the way other people believe, that's why I let Na-lua-hine take you with him to put the image back. He'll feel better about it and it did you no harm. Don't be uneasy, nothing will happen that wasn't going to anyway. Now you and Pam run along and have your baths and I'll look through the mail."

The girls scampered down through the garden, Poi at their heels. Halfway to the house they met Grandfather heading for the Office. He was walking slowly and looked thoughtful.

"Grandfather, something's happened!" Pam exclaimed. "Has—has Mr. Kingsley—"

"We've had no word from him yet, but a radio came from Aunt Dode today."

Emily froze.

"Cousin Laura's returning from New York sooner than she planned and Aunt Dode was notified that she has been made heir to a legacy from a distant relative, which makes it unnecessary for her to work for her living any longer."

Emily's eyes went to the dark slopes of Hualalai. There was a suggestion of treachery to the leaden forests and dark lava flows. The sea was so still it seemed dead. She was conscious of Pam's fingers gripping her arm and of Grandfather speaking to her, but nothing was real. Her mind had come to a full stop.

"I won't go away. She can't make me go back to Boston," she said, finally, in a dull way, then her voice rose to a wild note. "I'll run away— I'll hide where no one can find me. I won't go away—from Kilohana!"

"Hush, hush," Grandfather said gently, placing his hand on her shoulder. "We'll talk to Dode, Emily, make her understand what it means to you to be here, and for us to have you."

Kulani came swinging down through the twilight and Pam rushed to her and told her the news. "Do something, Kulani From Heaven, so Aunt Dode can't take Emily from us," she said explosively.

"Steady, Pam," Kulani said. "Grandfather and I have discussed the idea of adopting Emily and intended to put the matter up to Dode when Emily's year is up with us. Instead, we'll do it immediately. I'll write her at once so that when she arrives she'll be prepared to discuss the matter, after giving it thought."

"Don't let her take me away!" Emily begged.

"Probably Aunt Dode will be glad to let you stay with us, dear. Bringing up a child is a difficult and bewildering task for her and she can't fail to see how being at Kilohana has agreed with you. It will be all of three weeks, probably a month, before Laura gets back and Dode is free to come here."

Emily did not reply and Kulani gave her a gentle reminding shake.

"Chin up, Emily. Remember the old saying, 'The happy heart goes all the way.' "

"I'll try to remember, Kulani From Heaven."

"I will, too," Pam put in.

But in spite of their best efforts, the girls wandered around in a lost way for a few days, then hope and faith picked them up and they went on their way feeling more normal.

When Aunt Dode arrived she proved obdurate. Hawaii was well enough for a holiday, but Emily was Boston-born and belonged there. Now that she had means, Emily could have the advantages of good schooling, instructive trips, and they could move into a small, attractive cottage. Besides, hadn't she been a mother to Emily? Hadn't she slaved and sacrificed for her? Hadn't Emily any gratitude, or loyalty? How could the things of the past six months, and people she'd only known for a brief while, mean more to her than the aunt who had brought her up?

"It isn't that Emily's ungrateful or disloyal," Kulani and Grandfather argued. "You don't understand, Dode, at all—"

"I certainly do not," she retorted. "And to be frank, I don't approve a bit of the way Island children are brought up. They've too much freedom and run too wild. Why, on a ranch like this they've no companions except Hawaiians and Japanese. How you educate them—"

"Pam has had a governess every year from September until June," Kulani explained. "This past year she's been growing so fast that I let Miss Ames go East, but she'll be back the first of next year."

"Well, bring Pam up the way you want. Emily's going back to Boston with me," Aunt Dode said flatly.

And that was that! No amount of pleading on Pam's part, or arguments on Grandfather's or Kulani's could budge her. Emily went around with a dead face and the ranch was inconsolable. Na-lua-hine tried to talk Aunt Dode into revoking her decision, but without success. The spanking new accordion arrived from Montgomery Ward's and the old man presented it to Emily.

"When you play the Kilohana hula in Boston, think of me,"

he said, with tears in his eyes.

Emily felt as if something inside her was tearing to pieces. "I couldn't play the accordion in Boston," she choked. "I'd die—"

Aunt Dode engaged passage on the liner which had brought them to Hawaii, paid parting visits, returned to the ranch and packed their trunks. There were terrible scenes over Emily's saddle, bridle and lasso. She wanted to take them but Aunt Dode insisted they must remain behind. Suddenly, only two more days remained until they would leave. Emily wandered around like a white-lipped ghost, holding Na-lua-hine's hand.

"It's absurd, fantastic of you to carry on like this," Aunt Dode said angrily when Pam and Emily came in silently to dress for dinner. "Why, you'd think someone was dead!"

Emily looked at her as if she did not see her and started up the hall. Aunt Dode rushed after her and seized her by the shoulder. "This has gone far enough, Emily. I might have known you'd get out of hand if I left you here. Why, in six months you'll have forgotten all about Kilohana—"

Emily tore free and dashed into the twilight-filled garden.

"You're a cruel, wicked woman!" Pam said hotly. "Emily will die if you take her away. Why do you want her to go away from everything she loves and from the people who love her? She belongs to us now. Even if you make her go, she'll still belong to us. You'll only have her body—"

"My dear Pamela, I know far better than you do what's best for Emily," Aunt Dode said icily.

"That's what you think!" Pam raged. "When Emily's of

age she'll come back here. You see!"

Aunt Dode smiled in a superior fashion. "Long before Emily's eighteen she'll have forgotten Hawaii completely. I'll see to that. She's going to be a lady, like her mother was."

"Just because my mother wears breeches and works like a man you needn't think she isn't one," Pam said fiercely.

"Oddly enough, Kulani remains one, in spite of the way she lives," Aunt Dode conceded. "But that is neither here nor there. Emily is my trust and I shall not fail it. That's the end of it." And she swept down the hall toward her room.

Pam hurried off in search of Emily and found her wandering around the garden.

"I'm all burning up and dry inside," Emily said dully. "I can't go away. I *can't!*" she kept repeating, without tears. In little jerks her eyes moved over the wind-ruffled sea, followed trees, went up to the green hill, then rested with pitiful despair on stock grazing across the pastures below the house. "Oh, Pam, I love it so. I love it so!" she said in a low, breathless voice.

Pam fought tears which kept rising in her throat, choking her.

"I'm going to run away and hide where she'll never find me," Emily whispered.

"When?" Pam asked eagerly.

"Tonight!" Emily looked around wildly, then with a stifled cry threw herself on the grass. "I want to stay here," she clutched the turf. "I want to smell Kilohana, feel it, keep it close to me."

Pam grew pale around the nostrils. She knew how Emily felt. "Don't cry," she begged. "I'll help you." Pam whispered instructions to Emily and the old garden seemed to inch closer around them, as if it intended to be party to the plot to keep Emily in Hawaii.

That night, while the household slept, Emily crept from her bed and tiptoed out of the house. She had told Pam she would leave about three, then decided it would be wiser to go earlier, as she could get farther away before her loss was discovered in the morning. Poi got up from under the ferns where he was sleeping and followed her silently. She ordered him in a whisper to go back and he sat down and looked after her in an understanding way. She felt bereft at the thought of going without saying good-bye to Pam, or having her near when she set off. But, to her delight, when she got to the corral, Pam was there. Forty Dollars was saddled and a gunny-sack of food and a gallon jug of water were slung from the pommel. Pam's horse was saddled, too.

"Are you going with me?" Emily whispered.

"Only down to the sea. I'll head you in the right direction, then come home. After Aunt Dode leaves, I'll come and get you."

They led their horses quietly out of the corral into the deep grass of the pasture, so hoofbeats on the road would not rouse the family. When they were halfway across the pasture, Pam glanced back. "We're safe now," she said, then added in an annoyed whisper, "There's Poi sneaking after us. I'll fasten him to this tree till I come home and keep him tied up till the coast's clear. If he knows where you are, he'll try to trail you and maybe give people a steer to where you're hiding."

When he was fastened with a neck-rope Pam took off her horse, Poi sat looking after them in a disconsolate way. The moonlight was so brilliant that it flooded the hills and hollows with a tremendous white light. Pam and Emily rode silently down the rough lava trail to the sea.

When they reached the coast they dismounted and hurried to two small canoes which were always kept in the coconut grove near the shipping pens. Removing the dry fronds that covered one, they inched it down to the sea. It was heavy and when they finally got the prow into the water they had to rest before packing in the supplies.

"You've enough to eat for ten days," Pam said, looking over the store of canned goods. "Here's an opener. Don't lose it. Paddle down the coast for two miles. The sea's smooth tonight so it won't be hard to land. Here's a long tether rope to tie the canoe to a coconut tree. It's too heavy for you to drag up the beach alone."

"But how will I know when I've gone two miles?" Emily asked. "I'm not smart about those things yet, like you are."

"You'll see a big black cone jutting out from the coast. Turn in there. On one side is an old grass house and some coconut trees. On the other side is a cave and a shallow lagoon and in the lava is a pool of brackish water. I'm not very good at telling lies, so I've told you two places and can't know for sure which you'll be at."

"Oh, Pam," Emily said, her breath catching.

"You won't feel lonely? You won't be scared, Emily?" Pam asked.

"No," Emily replied. "I'll miss you but there's nothing to be scared of in Hawaii. But even if I was afraid, I'd rather do this than be taken away from Kilohana."

"I'll put in some extra green coconuts, in case the brackish pool is too salty for you to drink when your water-gallon is gone." Shinning up a bending tree, Pam cut down a dozen big nuts with her legging knife, while Emily stored them in the canoe.

"Neither bay you're going to can be reached from the land-side," Pam explained. "They're cut off by the old 1801 lava flow from Hualalai, which is too rough to ride over. No one will guess where you are." Breaking off, Pam stared at the water, glittering like moulten silver in the moonlight. "I'll get up extra early tomorrow and ride up Hualalai till milking time. It's going to be tough when Mother asks me if I know where you are. Now give me a hand and we'll push the canoe out."

Stepping inside the out-rigger, Pam took hold of the cross-piece while Emily pushed from behind. It was hard getting the boat started but it finally rushed forward into the warm, limpid sea. For an instant they stood holding it, breathless and a little afraid. Then Emily stepped into the canoe and picked up the paddle.

"Dig deep and pull, then turn your blade like this, to guide." Taking the paddle, Pam illustrated.

Emily imitated the motion a few times. "I think I've got it into my head," she said stoutly. "Don't tell anyone where I am, no matter what," she begged.

"I won't," Pam promised, then she kissed Emily in a quick way and gave the canoe a shove.

"I feel like the old Hawaiians must have felt when they set out across the Pacific to find new islands—which they hoped would be there," Emily said, with a catch in her voice.

Pam had such a lump in her throat that she couldn't answer. She watched until she could no longer see the dark speck on the water following the rough coast, then went back to her horse and retraced her way up the slopes of Hualalai.

When the girls were not at breakfast next morning Aunt Dode flew into a rage. She and Emily were due to leave for Hilo that afternoon about three to catch the Inter-Island boat connecting with the liner which sailed from Honolulu for the mainland in two days.

"Emily had no right to go off this morning. We've got to finish packing," she stormed.

"Probably the girls are only having a last farewell ride together," Grandfather suggested. "They'll be home for lunch."

Lunch came. No girls. Two, three o'clock came. No girls. *Paniolos* were sent out to scour the country for them, *paniolos* who thought it was a fine joke.

"I don't believe those insolent fellows want Emily to go," Aunt Dode declared angrily.

"Of course they don't," Kulani replied. "Nor do any of us. Emily's as much a part of our family now as Pam. Be sensible, Dode. A child's a handicap to you. Emily has shown definitely that she wants to remain here. If you take her away you can never be sure, after this, that you won't wake up some morning and find her gone. Emily's quiet, but she's a determined youngster, if ever there was one. Why not let us adopt her and go back to Boston in peace?"

"It isn't as if your finances were as they were before," Grandfather added his arguments. "You'll be able to travel now, see things you want to, live in comfort. Children complicate matters. You used to have quite a flair for painting. Why don't you take lessons from someone worth while and develop the talent you possess?" Grandfather let the words hang temptingly in the air.

"It's the downright disobedience that makes me angry," Aunt Dode flashed. "The open rebellion."

"When vital things such as happiness and being with the persons you love are at stake, people will go to any lengths," Kulani explained soothingly. "Without Emily to complicate your set-up, you can devote yourself to art and there's no telling where you'll end. You might even make a name for yourself. Then wouldn't we all be proud of you, Emily most of all."

"I'm not going without her." Aunt Dode's mouth snapped shut. "I'll phone and cancel my passage and get bookings on the boat leaving next week." And she flounced off.

"It looks as though there's no budging her," Grandfather remarked as he and Kulani set off for the Office.

"Something may happen yet," Kulani insisted. "I can't picture Kilohana without the dear little tyke."

Four o'clock came.

"It's about time the runaways came in," Grandfather re-marked as he made his slow way with Kulani to the corrals and milking sheds.

Dusk came. No girls. They went back to the house.

"This is a pretty serious business," Kulani remarked in her calm, steady way.

"Dern tootin'," Grandfather agreed, but there was a ghost of a chuckle behind his words. "Most children have run away in their youth. Don't be too severe when they come in Kulani From Heaven. I remember once when I was a kid—"

Paniolos began trailing in, reporting no signs of the run-aways. Aunt Dode came out, wild-eyed. "Something's hap-pened to them," she cried in a high voice.

"Don't be absurd," Kulani said in her calm voice. "They're all right. They've probably taken food with them, planning to hide out overnight."

Na-lua-hine and Nuhi's white teeth flashed in the dark.

"I hate Hawaii," Aunt Dode said hysterically. "I feel inade-quate here, it—it—"

"Dode, go to bed for a bit," Kulani said taking her kindly by the arm. "This had been hard on you. You're worn out. I'll give you a sedative and in the morning, when the girls come home, we'll straighten matters out." And she took her in-doors. Grandfather sat rocking quietly.

Presently they had dinner and then went back to sit on the porch facing the dark mass of Hualalai. They talked and were silent in turns.

"I understand Emily's hunger to stay here and Pam's wish

to keep her," Kulani said after a while. "But I shall have to punish them for this, probably by taking their horses away for a few days."

"I wish we could use some leverage to pry Dode loose from Emily," Grandfather said, "but she's a stubborn New Englander."

Kulani nodded. The sound of footsteps coming down from the corrals through the dark garden sounded. "Pam," Grandfather said.

When she came on to the porch Kulani asked, "Where's Emily?"

"I don't know."

Putting out her hand, Kulani drew Pam to her. "Yes, you do, Pam."

"Not—absolutely," Pam insisted. "Oh, Kulani From Heaven, don't push me. Emily made me promise not to say where she'd gone. It's one of two places. I'm not sure which. We arranged it that way so I wouldn't have to tell you a lie. She's safe. She's—" Pam's voice trembled. "She couldn't bear to go away from us. Aunt Dode's cruel to want to take her to Boston against her will. Oh, do something, Mother, so she won't have to go—" and she burst into tears.

"Don't cry, dear, I don't want to make you break your word, even if it was wrongly given. When Dode—"

"Did she go anyway?" Pam interrupted hopefully.

"No, she's still here, but she's upset about having to miss her boat. She had to cancel her bookings and naturally is very angry."

"But you and Grandfather aren't, are you?" Pam choked.
"*You* understand because you love Kilohana the way Emily
and I do."

"Of course, we understand, Pam, but that doesn't affect the
right and wrong of the matter. Tomorrow you must get Emily
and while you're gone Grandfather and I will give Aunt Dode
some high-powered talk which will persuade her to let Emily
stay here."

Pam looked crestfallen. "Oh, *Mother*—" she began protest-
ingly.

"Pam," Kulani said, "don't you trust me, don't you know
that I usually accomplish what I set out to do?"

"Mostly," Pam quavered.

"Then tomorrow early, you and Na-lua-hine go and fetch
her."

Hearing voices, Aunt Dode came out in her narrow high-
necked wrapper.

"Where's Emily?" she screamed.

Kulani spoke to her and explained.

"You mean she's hidden somewhere—*alone!* Where?"

"I don't know—exactly," Pam said, glaring at her. "She's
somewhere down in the lava flows."

"Lava flows! You mean she prefers lava flows to me and to
Boston?" Aunt Dode raged. "Kulani, tell Pamela to fetch her,"
she ordered in stifled tones. "I won't be made a fool of! Emily's
disloyal and ungrateful!"

"Emily isn't either!" Pam said indignantly. "You simply
don't understand about loving things. Just suppose someone

stronger and bigger than you are told you you *had* to stay in Hawaii and never see Boston again?"

"Don't be absurd."

"But just supposing. Wouldn't you fight to get back there?" Aunt Dode glared at her niece.

"You had better go and get Ah Sam to give you some supper and go to bed, Pam," Kulani suggested, in her quiet way. Pam gave her a quick kiss. "Work on Aunt Dode till she gives in, Mother," she whispered. "And Na-lua-hine and I will get Emily tomorrow."

Next morning Pam set off with Na-lua-hine but they returned about dark with frightened, white faces. "Emily's not at either bay," Pam said, her eyes wild with alarm. "And the canoe's not there."

The ranch was stunned with horror, Na-lua-hine half out of his mind.

"I know she isn't dead," Pam insisted. "I know she didn't drown, even if she wasn't smart about paddling a canoe—"

"How can you know?" Aunt Dode screamed.

"Because I love her so much. I'd know, inside, if anything dreadful had happened to her. She may have gone farther down the coast to hide better, in case I had to tell where she was."

"That's possible," Kulani agreed, but her face was drawn. "This is serious. If anything has happened you're partly responsible, Pam."

"Pam isn't—*I* am," Aunt Dode said in a funny, tight voice. "I drove her to this. There's no use cheating myself about it to spare myself. I'm an adult. Pam and Emily are only children. If Emily's dead it's *my fault!*"

Aunt Dode stood looking at unhappy distances of her own, seeing in her imagination a small girl paddling off in a canoe over the loneliness of the Pacific. Na-lua-hine began crying in the dreadful way Hawaiians do when someone they love has gone from them. Grandfather paced back and forth like a lion trying to escape from a cage. Ah Sam wrung his apron, Tatsu hid her face in the sleeve of her kimono and the other ranch people moved about in a lost way.

Aunt Dode began crying and Kulani went to her. "Oh, Kulani," the poor woman sobbed, "if Emily comes back, if she's found, she can stay here. I was a monster to try and compel her to go. Oh, God, please give her back to us!"

"Steady, Dode, steady," Grandfather urged patting her hand. "We'll phone the police, organize search parties of our own, cover every foot of the island, send canoes out into the channel—"

Kulani remained calm with the terrible calmness that comes in the midst of catastrophe. The garden where they were all collected made little restless rustlings as night began settling down in it. With a worried forehead, old Poi sat looking on from the tree where Pam had kept him tied for the past twenty-four hours. Aunt Dode stood dully staring at nothing and all the life seemed to have gone out of her. Pam rushed to her mother and buried her face against her arm.

"Stop shaking, Pam," Kulani said. "We can't do anything until it's light but I'll start phoning right away and the *paniolos* can set off in different directions about midnight."

Poi gave a low woof then began jumping about, whimpering to get free, his tail wagging wildly. Pam stiffened, stared at the road and went flying off into the dark, screaming "Emily!"

A weary, fagged little figure came out of the dark-leaning trees growing on each side of the avenue. After the hubbub of rejoicing died down, Emily went to her Aunt.

"Aunt Dode—" she began.

"Oh Emily, I thought you were dead. I thought—I thought I'd never see you again." They clung to one another.

"Now tell us what happened," Grandfather said, blowing his nose in a relieved way.

"Just as I was going to get out of the canoe," Emily said, "a big wave came travelling from nowhere, tossed the canoe up and I fell overboard. It was only a little distance from shore and I managed to swim to it. I was frightened because all my food and water was gone, for the canoe drifted out to sea. Then I remembered Pam said there were coconuts growing by the black cone."

Emily swallowed.

"I felt sort of scared till it got light. Then I climbed an old bent tree and pulled off three green nuts. And then I got to thinking about how scared Aunt Dode would be and—" Emily began crying, "and how naughty I'd been."

"Don't cry, dear. Oh, I'm so utterly thankful to have you back safe," Aunt Dode said.

"I only did it because I love Kilohana so—"

"I understand now, Emily. You're going to remain."

"Oh—oh—oh—" Emily gasped in a delirious way.

"Tell us the rest," Aunt Dode went on, suddenly her practical self, now her decision had been made.

"I knew that no one could cross the 1801 Hualalai lava flow on horseback," Emily went on, "so I tied two nuts together by the stems, like Hawaiians do, so I'd have water to drink, and started off across the lava beds. I could see the faint mark of the Government road far above and kept heading for it, but it was awfully rough. Look at my boots. And awfully long, and dreadfully hot. . . ."

"You poor child," Aunt Dode said in a moved way.

"Anyway, I got here—finally," Emily finished. "And I'm sorry I was bad—"

"And I'm sorry I tried to force you to leave Hawaii when it means so much to you," Aunt Dode repeated. "I didn't know how much you meant to me until I thought I might never see you again, that you might be dead—" Aunt Dode's face got all broken and funny. "I want to know beyond everything that you're happy, so—"

Emily hugged her in a glad way.

Na-lua-hine came forward. "Auntie speak Em'ly can stay?" he asked hopefully. "Or my ear no hear right?"

"I'm leaving Emily with you all," Aunt Dode said stiffly.

Na-lua-hine stared at her, then came forward. "*Mahalo nui loa*—much thank you," he said. "I take good care on her. Like she my own kid. And—" his dark eyes went to Aunt Dode's face, "And—" taking up her hand he held it to his forehead silently for an instant, then he let it go and held Emily's hand there.

"What—what does that mean?" Aunt Dode asked in a bewildered voice.

"He's pledging his undying fidelity to you—both," Kulani said. "After the old Hawaiian fashion."

Aunt Dode didn't say anything for a moment, then she blew her nose in a ladylike fashion. "How quaint, how—how beautiful," she stammered.

CHAPTER XIII

SCHOOL

A WEEK OF SO AFTER MR. BANKS, THE FAMILY LAWYER, HAD drawn up Emily's adoption papers, Aunt Dode started for Boston and the family went to Honolulu to see her off on the boat. Cousin Laura's children arrived at the wharf, laden with jasmine *leis* which they piled about her neck. The servants had farewell gifts, according to Island custom. Siziko, the house-girl, had made her a kimono. Oda, the chauffeur who had driven her for six months, presented her with a funny little Japanese teapot with a handle sticking out of one side.

"Japan-style candy inside," he told her importantly. "Hard for get this-kind in Honolulu so my Mama-san make herself for you."

Aunt Dode's eyes misted. Somehow, now that the time had come for her to board the liner, she wasn't so keen about getting away.

Of course, Kane, Na-lua-hine, Tatsu and the family had *leis* and presents as well, so that when Aunt Dode went up the gangway she could hardly see over the flowers piled around her neck and two stewards had to carry the last-minute gifts.

"Upon my word," she called, straining over the rail, "I feel like royalty!" She dabbed at her eyes and blew her nose.

The band began playing *Aloha Oe*. Garlands flew through the air, paper streamers that departing passengers threw to friends they were leaving behind made a sort of rainbow-colored spider web that tried to hold the ship to the shore. Aunt Dode blew her nose again and waved madly.

"Throw away a *lei!*" Pam screamed across the widening strip of water, where broken streamers floated in masses, like colored seaweed.

Aunt Dode obeyed and Pam watched anxiously. The water sucked the bright circle of flowers back to the land.

"See, you'll be back," Pam called.

Aunt Dode dabbed at her eyes with her handkerchief, then called out something that sounded like, "Maybe-I-will-Emily-be-a-good-girl!"

"*Aloha, Aloha!*" the crowd on the wharf called and it sounded like one great voice, the voice of Hawaii calling, "My love to you! My love to you!"

A few days later Pam and the family returned to the ranch.

"Well, that turned out fine—for everyone," Grandfather said in a satisfied way. "Now when we get Kingsley's pie baked to suit, I can settle down to a placid old age."

"You'll never be old, Grandfather, if you live to be a hundred," Pam laughed. "You'll run us ragged hunting for new varieties of land shells and be so busy helping Mother with the ranch and running your plantation between whiles that—"

"That I'll probably be a general nuisance to everyone, including myself?" Grandfather suggested with a chuckle.

"I simply can't realize that I'm here—for keeps," Emily kept repeating as she and Pam made their daily rounds.

She shook her head like an exultant little colt. Gone were the stiff, tight braids. Her hair blew free, like Pam's, catching sunlight in its shining strands. Her cheeks were tanned, her eyes brilliant with happiness and health. Spurs rang at her heels, polished boots caught light each time she stepped and flowers circled the crown of her wide-brimmed *paniolo* hat.

"Isn't it swell to know you don't have to go back to Boston— ever!" Pam declared. "After everything has turned out so fine about you, I know the rest will come out all right, too."

Emily nodded.

A few days later, while Grandfather and the girls were waiting for Kulani to come in for lunch, the telephone rang. Pam answered it. "It's our lawyer in Hilo. He has a radio—from New York." Her voice dropped a little.

"Get a pencil and paper and write down the message as Banks gives it to me," Grandfather said, getting up and going to the telephone.

"All right, Grandfather, go ahead," Pam said when she had the materials.

When the long message was written down, the pencil dropped from Pam's fingers. Grandfather hung up, felt for his chair and sat down heavily. "Boiled down to plain English that mess of legal terms means that beggar Kingsley doesn't want to re-lease or sell."

The girls stood close together, silent and white-faced.

"Pam—Emily—where are you?" Grandfather put out a groping hand. A sharp little pain jabbed through the numbness filling Pam. The gesture told plainer than words that Grandfather suddenly felt lost in the darkness in which he had moved for so long, undaunted and unchained.

"Hi—!" Kulani's cheery hail floated to them as she came briskly down the slope of the garden. "What's up?" she asked, sensing the tenseness of the group on the back veranda.

Grandfather told her. She was as quiet as if she were carved out of stone, then brushed a stray lock back from her valiant forehead. "Well," she said in a matter-of-fact, undisturbed way, "we've got to go into action now." She thought for a minute. "I'm going to New York. Grandfather can run the ranch. I'll put you girls in Punahou School for the time being—"

Pam started to protest, then closed her lips.

"Good girl, Pam," Kulani said, flashing a quick, grateful look at her. "I know what you started to say and—didn't. Thank you. We all must help in the fight! You girls can help me best by keeping out of the way. I'll need all my wits about me while I'm gone. If even a bit of my mind stopped to wonder if you were in mischief here, I might miss some important move. I haven't time to hunt up a reliable manager for Kilohana, so Grandfather will have to take over here, if he will. Though Kingsley doesn't know it, he's going to agree to let us keep Kilohana, before I'm through with him. Pam, call Hilo and get Mr. Banks again. Emily, look in today's paper, it's on the Office desk, and find out what boats are sailing for San Francisco next week."

When Kulani went into action things clicked and clicked, without bustle, noise or confusion. Ten days later the girls found themselves in a big, rather plain room in the Girl's Dormitory at Punahou, breathless and stunned.

They had arrived about four that morning on the Inter-Island steamer. A truck had taken their baggage out to the school—trunks, suitcases and their two saddles, neatly sewed into gunny-sacks. They had breakfasted at the Young Hotel with Kulani, who seemed to do more telephoning than eating. Then there had been a hurried dash to school, a brief interview with the principal and house mother. School had been in session three days and the green, shaded campus was swarming with boys and girls, hurrying to and from classes. Then there had been another dash to the waterfront, where the great liner that was to take Kulani away was getting ready to cast off. . . .

As they ran toward the gangway Kulani had given her last instructions. "Remember, dears, not a word to anyone as to

why I've gone East. . . . What's our business is our business.
. . . Remember . . . for the first time in your lives you're
absolutely *on your own.* . . . There's no Tatsu, Kane, or Na-
lua-hine or Grandfather to fall back on for guidance or advice. . . . Where are the boys with my bags?" She glanced
over her shoulder. "I see them. . . . We're all entered on the
biggest battle of our lives—the battle to keep Kilohana! I'm
counting on you both to give a one hundred per cent perform-
ance while I'm gone. It's hard, I know, being jerked away from
the things you love without much preparation and dumped in
a school. But life's that way sometimes. You're my beloved
daughters—" She kissed them swiftly. "This is a pretty stiff
assignment but I know you'll be Happy Warriors!"

Pam clung to her mother, choking. They had never been
separated for more than a night or so and had always tele-
phoned every day. It did not seem real that there would be
thousands of miles of water and land between them for, she
did not know how long. Tears stung her eyelids. Her mother
released her and a tear splashed down and made a dark spot
on the wharf. Pam stamped upon it angrily and Kulani laughed.

"That's my girl!" she said delightedly.

Emily fought to control her face. Kulani kissed her again,
embraced Pam fiercely and ran up the gangway.

"Keep the flag flying—for Kilohana!" she had called, as the
majestic liner pulled away.

Like a person waking from a dream, Pam looked around
from where she was seated on the narrow bed placed against

the wall. "It *is* a hard assignment, Emily," she remarked in a voice that hardly sounded like her own. "But we won't fail Mother, will we?"

"No, we won't fail—Mother," Emily echoed, her face flushing as if a dawn were rising inside her. Then she said, "I haven't had time to realize Kulani From Heaven *is* my Mother—till now. It makes me feel rich, and sort of solemn."

"As we don't have to attend classes today, we might as well get our stuff unpacked and settled," Pam suggested, looking and sounding absurdly like her mother.

They went at the job with all their might. It seemed odd to Pam not to have Tatsu to hang up her clothes and put underthings away in the bureau drawers. Everything got in a jumble and Emily, who had taken care of her own things until she came to Kilohana, took charge.

"Look, Pam, put all your pyjamas in one pile, stockings in another, shorts in another—like this. You line up our shoes and riding boots in the cupboard, put the boots farthest back because we won't use them every day, just on Saturdays. Put my shoes on one side and yours on the other—"

It took an hour to get the trunks unpacked and the suitcases neatly stored away.

"Now we can have some fun!" Pam said, wiping her hot face. "Fixing up this ugly old room with the things we brought from the ranch is going to be something!" Stepping back, she surveyed the walls.

The ceiling was high, the walls papered with dull brown that would not show dirt easily. The door was tall and narrow, like a long, disapproving face, but two big windows looked out on the campus with its lily-pond, monkey-pod trees and fine buildings.

"Go downstairs, Emily, and get a lot of those red and yellow cannas in the flower bed by the front steps. I'll fill this tin waste basket with water and we'll set it over in the corner to brighten things up. While you're getting them, I'll hammer some nails in the wall and hang up our lassos, bridles and spurs."

Emily had a moment of doubt. She had been in school before, but concluded that in Hawaii it was probably all right to pick flowers anywhere, so scurried off. When she returned with her plunder Pam had transformed the room a lot. A brave array of gear decorated the wall between the two dressers; dark, well-oiled leather and polished bits and spurs hung side by side, flanked by two coiled lassos. On the battered imitation oak table in the center of the room the Free For All cup stood imposingly.

"Doesn't it look better?" Pam asked.

"Yes, it's going to be lovely. Here are the flowers."

"You arrange them, Emily, Tatsu taught you how. I'm going to put our stitched Hawaiian quilts over these funny wrinkled covers on the beds."

The girls rushed to the windows as a bell rang in the nearest building. Students were pouring out of it and hurrying across the green lawns toward other buildings, crossing other streams of persons rushing in the opposite direction.

"They remind me of herds of cattle being shifted from one pasture to another," Pam said. "How will we know where to go, Emily? It looks confusing and crazy."

"It's really quite simple, Pam. I've been in schools before. I'll show you the ropes."

"I'm glad you're here," Pam said rather grimly. "It would be awful alone. I wonder when it's lunch, I'm getting empty."

"A teacher will probably come for us, or one of the girls will take us to the dining room, as it's our first day here."

"Well, let's put up our pictures, Emily," Pam suggested.

Before long the walls were dotted with enlarged snapshots of *paniolos*, race horses, cattle being shipped and other Kilohana activities. Just as the last picture was hung a tap sounded on the door, but before either Pam or Emily could call out, "Come in!" a tall woman entered.

"I'm Mrs. Sheldon, the dormitory mother—" she stopped and her eyes travelled along the wall where the riding gear hung and she gave a faint gasp.

"Those decorations are more appropriate to a tack-room than a bedroom," she remarked with a wry smile.

"We're ranch girls, they're beautiful to us," Pam said in an edged voice.

"I'm accustomed to pennants, movie-stars' pictures and absurd long-legged dolls," Mrs. Sheldon went on. "But, after all, this room is your home for the time being and you're at liberty to arrange it as you wish. What is this gorgeous thing?" She went towards the center table.

"That's the Hawaiian Free For All cup that our race horse, Malolo, won this Fourth of July," Pam told her proudly.

"I've a notion you girls are going to be a great addition to our school family," Mrs. Sheldon said pleasantly, then her eyes lighted on the sheaf of cannas slashing their orange and red against the drab wall. "My dear, where did you get those flowers? They look like the ones we have by the steps."

"They are," Pam announced.

"It's against the rules to pick flowers growing on the school grounds, Pam."

"Why?" she asked. "If you don't cut them they die anyway after a few days."

"If everyone picked bouquets for her room, there'd be no flowers to make the place pretty, Pamela. They're grown for everybody to enjoy."

"I won't do it again. I didn't know."

"I should make you throw them away, but I'll let it pass this time and explain to the girls this evening at dinner that you didn't understand."

An electric bell began ringing shrilly in the hall downstairs.

"That's the lunch bell," Mrs. Sheldon said. "Brush up and come down. I'll be waiting at the dining-room door for you."

Suddenly the big house was roaring with girls, laughing, talking, racing up the stairway. Doors opened and closed. Voices called out. Feet rushed up and down the hall.

"I wish we didn't have to go down, Emily."

"It won't be bad after a day or so. I've never been in a boarding school but day school was much the same. The first time I went I felt lost and sunk, but at the end of the week it was okay."

Lunch was an ordeal to Pam. "It's lucky you're here, Emily,

or I don't think I could stand it," she said as they came away. "Why do they all stare at us so?"

"Because we're new girls. By Monday you won't feel so strange."

The first few days while Pam attended classes she felt like running away. It was an ordeal to have to stand up to reply to questions. Although learning was easy to her, having countless eyes fastened upon her made her ill at ease. However, she speedily discovered that many of her dormitory mates were nice. Most of them were girls from the outlying islands, like herself. The majority lived on sugar plantations, but six or eight came from cattle ranches and liked to talk about horses, *paniolos*, and cattle. After study hour and dinner they collected on the front steps, or in someone's room, and Pam played Kane's guitar and Emily the new accordion that Na-lua-hine had given her.

On Saturdays one of the younger teachers went with Pam and Emily to the Diamond Head polo field. Kulani had arranged with Honolulu polo friends to let her girls help to exercise the ponies once a week. They galloped around the old race track, rode through Kapiolani Park and followed trails winding around Diamond Head. It wasn't like riding on the ranch but better than not being able to smell horses and feel a saddle under them. Several of the horses in the Oahu polo string had been bred and trained at Kilohana and being with them made Pam feel as if she had a bit of the ranch close again.

In the afternoon the same teacher took Pam, Emily and a

dozen or so of the other girls to Waikiki Beach. Bronzed beach boys took them out tandem on their boards to teach them to surf-ride, among great green rollers tossing their white manes in the sunshiny air. Miss Ross, the teacher who always accompanied them on these expeditions, seemed hardly older than the girls in her charge. She was Island-born, an expert horsewoman and a finished surf-board rider, and the girls all adored her.

As if she sensed that Pam was rather volcanic material that needed careful handling, Miss Ross singled her out to instruct and to be friends with.

"I know you can stand up today, Pam," she said one Saturday afternoon as they paddled out toward the reef. "You got to your knees last time we were out—?"

Pam dug her arms deep into the water, pulling herself forward, enjoying the taut feel of her body on the cool *koa* board. "I'll try but I bet I take a header or get slung sky-high," Pam said, eyeing the big rollers. "How are you coming, Emily?"

"Fine," she panted, "but my shoulders get stiff lying flat like this and paddling."

Beach boys were taking out less expert girls, and they called out encouragingly, as they began lining up, watching for the right kind of waves. Some were too slow, others too large for beginners to attempt. It was thrilling sitting on the long polished boards, waiting for the signal to go. Suddenly one of the beach boys shouted;

"Here she come!"

Everyone lay flat and began paddling furiously for land,

glancing back occasionally to watch the great wave overtaking them. Water roared and boiled behind them as the comber began piling up and cresting. It seized the boards; some slewed around because of poor steering, others rushed on. Pam, tense, got cautiously to her knees when she had sufficient impetus, then rose inch by inch until she stood erect. It was glorious! The wave was smoking shoreward with the speed of a railway train, spray stood out on either side of the blunt brown nose of her surfboard, as if it had magically sprouted sheer silver wings that rushed her forward with dizzying speed. Faster, faster they went, while people shouted, laughed and screamed. She glanced back. Emily was crouching on her board, almost up.

"Go on, you can do it," she called, forgot about guiding her board, and over she toppled into acres of creamy foam. Millions of bubbles burst and raced over her, she saw the long dark shapes of boards passing over and dived deep to avoid being struck by them. When her lungs couldn't hold any more air she shot to the surface, shook the water out of her eyes and started swimming back to her board.

On Sundays after church older teachers took the girls to see things of interest: up to the *pali* where Kamehameha's victorious army drove the Oahu warriors over the sheer cliffs in a human waterfall, as they tried to defend their island from him; another time they visited the Aquarium, where fish as highly colored and beautiful as flowers drifted around in glass compartments like under-sea Birds of Paradise.

One Sunday they visited Kawaihao Church, where all the

funerals of Hawaiian Royalty had been held since 1842, when it was dedicated. The structure had an atmosphere of dignity and simple splendor, with sunlight beating on the white coral slabs of which it was built, and tall coconut trees moving like languid *kahalis* * about it.

Another day the girls were taken to the Bishop Museum to see relics of Hawaii's royal past, which private individuals and men of science had collected to preserve for posterity to enjoy. Emily was awed by the splendor of the feather cloaks and helmets which Grandfather had told her about when they rode up to hunt for land shells in the secret forests swathing Hualalai.

At intervals letters came from Kulani. She was to see Kingsley. . . . She had seen him and his lawyer, but Kingsley was proving obdurate about changing his plans, arguing that it was no easy matter to buy large estates in Hawaii any longer. She seemed to be making some headway. . . . She had lost ground. . . . The girls mustn't fret. . . . She'd compel him to see things her way. . . . She wouldn't come home until she had Kilohana safe for them.

Pam grew more and more uneasy. "I won't believe that it'll go out of our hands, Emily," she kept saying when she was sleepless at night. "This school's beginning to get me on the run. I don't like our Math teacher, she picks on me—"

"But we can't go back until Kulani From Heaven comes home."

* Kahali = Ceremonial feather emblems.

"I know!" Pam said, looking around the high-ceilinged, shadowy room. "Let's go out on the balcony, Emily. These walls shut all my feelings in on me."

Emily got up and they tiptoed down the main hall and went on to the big roofless balcony that jutted over the main entrance steps, covering half of them. Leaning her elbows on the balustrade, Pam gazed at tree tops moving like a dark surf against fields of glittering stars.

"Suppose we lose Kilohana," Pam said in a hard, breathless voice. "We're wasting days here that we could be spending at home—" Breaking off, she stared across the campus.

In the starry night the rich history behind the school seemed to quicken to life. Pam knew that the land had been given by Kamehameha III to the missionaries. In the beginning, the school had been built for the education of missionary children, but took in other white girls and boys. Punahou had been the first really good American school west of the Rockies. After the Gold Rush in California in '49, many children were sent from the mainland to be educated at Punahou.

Little by little, Punahou had let down its bars. First a few Hawaiians and part-Hawaiian children, of Christian families, had been enrolled. Now all nationalities attended. East and West met on its friendly campus, worked side by side on the school paper, in plays and pageants, in sports, without the slightest hint of racial superiority or inferiority complexes.

Punahou had entered into all the girls and boys who had ever been there, whether they realized it or not. It had shaped them, moulded them, put its invisible stamp upon them. It

offered sound instruction in conventional subjects and a stirring education in world citizenship. Here blue, gray, and brown
eyes looked into each other without suspicion. The mighty
nations of the world could learn a new working basis for world
friendship and world fellowship from its spirit of *Aloha*, unit-
ing East, West, North and South into a unit.

Pam felt the spell of the place falling on her troubled spirit
and voiced some of the thoughts which had been sifting
through her mind.

"If it weren't for wondering what is happening in New York,
I'd love Punahou a lot," she said to Emily. "Mother was here
for two years before she went to Boston. Grandfather was here
and his grandfather before him. They walked on these old paths
where we walk—" Breaking off, she stared at the constellations
overhead. "It's a sort of family school, isn't it, Emily, for all of
Hawaii? Now we belong to it, too."

Next day Pam's budding loyalty suffered a jar. Her Math
teacher was irritable and impatient and took her to task in class
for some mistake. Pam said nothing but when the bell rang
and her classmates poured down the wide steps, a Maui girl
came over and took hold of her arm.

"Don't feel mad with Miss Scully, Pam. She's in love with
one of the young officers out at Fort Shafter. Maybe they had
a tiff—" the girl giggled.

Pam retorted with a faint snort of disgust. "Miss Scully picks
on me all the time. I hate Math. I get good marks in History,
Literature, and—"

"Well, don't look like a bunch of dynamite about to go off," her friend said, dashing away to her next class.

"After school let's go swimming, so I can cool off," Pam said, linking her arm through Emily's. "I'm shaking inside. I think it's awful for a teacher to tell a person off before fifty others. She could have kept me after class—"

Emily nodded.

All afternoon and evening Pam felt dull anger burning inside her. That night she was sleepless again and stole out on to the balcony.

Going to the railing, she leaned her elbows on it and turned her hot face to the cool wind. From the steps below came the subdued murmur of voices. She looked down. In the dim starlight she recognized Miss Scully, sitting shoulder to shoulder with a young man in uniform. An impish expression flitted over Pam's face. Tiptoeing back to her room, she woke Emily, whispered to her, took her lasso off the wall and two pyjama figures stole carefully back to the balcony.

Taking a careful turn around one of the stout posts in the railing, Pam leaned over, whirled the noose twice and dropped it over the two seated figures. Then she pulled in the slack with lightning swiftness. There was a faint cry, a smothered roar. In their astonishment, the lovers had leaped to their feet and Pam had taken a second swift turn so that their toes barely touched the concrete steps. The fierce efforts of the officer to get free, Miss Scully's frantic, raging commands to "Let us go!" made Pam laugh aloud.

Pam felt eased of the tension by the escapade. She giggled and began letting out slack.

But it was too late. Girls were pouring on to the balcony, roused from their sleep by voices and laughter. Teachers in hastily donned wrappers hurried out. Next day Pam was taken on the mat by the principal and when she came out her face was as white as *kukui* ashes.

"Have you been expelled?" Emily asked in a shaking voice.

"No, but I've been confined to the grounds for a month! I can't ride Saturdays, or surf, or go anywhere. I'm—a prisoner! Miss Scully's leaving for San Francisco tonight. She won't remain here after being made a public laughing stock, she told the principal. I—I tried to explain that I was only having some fun and didn't know it was against the rules to rope a teacher and her beau when they were making love—" Pam's eyes had a far-away expression in them. "Even Mrs. Sheldon, the housemother, is angry with me, a bit. I tried to explain to her that I didn't think of anything but the fun. If it hadn't been for Mrs. Sheldon, though, I would have been expelled, but she explained about Mother being East and how it would worry her when she was occupied with business to have her daughter thrown out of school. Oh, I *wish* that horrible Mr. Kingsley would come to time!"

"He will," Emily insisted.

Pam stood the confinement for a week, then announced to Emily:

"We're going home, tonight. I can't stand this feeling of being a prisoner any longer. The teachers look sad when they pass me and all the girls shake with laughter. They call me *Paniolo Pupule*—crazy cowboy! I'll tell Grandfather everything and he

can write to Kulani From Heaven so she'll understand. Won't
he be surprised when we appear tomorrow!"

"But you'll have to phone from the wharf for the car," Emily protested.

"No. I've got it all figured out so it'll be a real surprise. We'll
get Pili to take us to Kilohana in his mail truck. The *Mauna Kea*
sails for Hawaii tonight about ten. Lights go off at nine. We
can catch a streetcar and get to the wharf in plenty of time."

"But our things—"

"We'll leave them here and write afterwards to have them
sent to us. The only thing I'll take is the Free For All cup."

That night the Captain of the *Mauna Kea*, watching from
the bridge to give the signal to cast off, was astonished when
two small girls came up the companionway leading from the
main deck. One clutched a huge object in a chamois-skin bag.

"Didn't you see the sign saying that passengers aren't allowed on the bridge?" the burly old fellow began.

"Yes," Pam said, and told her story. "I haven't any money,
Captain Riddle, but Mother will pay you for our tickets when
she comes back," she finished.

The old man began shaking with laughter, then his face
sobered.

"I saw you ride on the Fourth of July, Pam, and I took my
hat off to you. You got some bad bumping when you were
running in the mob, and you took it like a trooper, but you
didn't quit in the middle of the race because it hurt—"

"Of course not!" Pam said indignantly.

"But you're quitting in the middle of a school term because

you think you've come a cropper. It doesn't match up." Breaking off, he let it sink in.

Pam stared at him for an instant, then her face grew blank and funny. "I see what you mean," she said slowly. "Garlands don't—quit! We've got to go back, Emily. If we sneak in they'll never know—"

"Good girl," the Captain applauded. "Here's five dollars. Get a taxi and make it snappy. The longer you're gone, the more likely your absence will be discovered. Kilohana'll keep."

Pam's face screwed up, then she shook herself like a colt trying to get rid of a rope binding it. "Come quickly, Emily, or I'll weaken!" she cried, scooting down the companionway.

The front door of the dormitory was locked but they climbed into a tree whose boughs brushed the big balcony. "Luck was with us," Emily whispered when they were safely in their room.

"Yes," Pam agreed. "But I feel like smashing furniture."

Next morning as they were dressing Mrs. Sheldon came to the door.

"The principal wants you in his office at once, Pam."

Her heart stopped. "All right," she said in a tight voice.

"Someone must have seen us climb in," Emily said, when the door closed. "We'll be expelled and Kulani From Heaven —" her chin quivered.

Pam thought for a moment. "They only want me, Emily. If we'd been seen we'd both be called up. Maybe something has happened to Mother! Come with me, Emily."

Scrambling into their clothes, they tore across the campus. The principal was seated in his office, a concerned expression on his face.

"Girls," he said, gently, "your Grandfather has been hurt. His horse fell with him and he broke four ribs. It's not dangerous but he wants you to go home to assist with the running of the ranch. He doesn't wish the news of his accident wired East for fear it might worry Mrs. Garland. He'll have to be in bed for three weeks and will write to your mother as soon as he's better."

"Oh, poor Grandfather," Emily gasped.

"Broken ribs aren't serious," Pam said, "just uncomfortable, specially if you're heavy, like Grandfather is. Oh Emily, we're going—*home!*"

The principal glanced at the youthful pair and smiled in an odd manner. "Your Grandfather wired me money to make reservations for you on the nine-twenty plane. It lands in Kohala at eleven forty-five and a car will be there to meet you. Take what you must have and Mrs. Sheldon will ship the rest of your things by the first boat."

"We'll be home this afternoon!" Pam said in awed tones. "It seems too wonderful to be true!"

"Well, it is true, Pamela," the principal said kindly.

The girls hurried back across the peaceful campus to the big white dormitory thrusting up among monkey-pod trees.

"It pays to play the game, doesn't it, Pam?" Emily remarked. "We didn't run away last night and immediately something happens to make it right for us to go back to Kilohana without being disgraced. Of course, I'm sorry about Grandfather's breaking his ribs, but—"

"He's tough," Pam said cheerily, her gay nature zooming up. "I've a hunch he misses us and this is just a good excuse to get us back. He doesn't really need us. Mother left instructions about work for way ahead. Grandfather will have a good laugh about us going to the ship last night and coming back. I know just what he'll say. 'So—the reward of virtue is my having four ribs broken! Well, I like THAT!'"

CHAPTER XIV

TIED DOWN

WHEN THEY GOT HOME THEY FOUND GRANDFATHER IN BED, propped up on quantities of pillows. A nurse in a crackling white uniform stood in the room. "Careful, young ones, don't jar me," the old man warned as they hurried toward him. "My confounded side hurts like blazes and I have to be absolutely still for eight or ten days. The doctor strapped me with adhesive tape last night—" his strong voice sounded a little tired.

"Oh, Grandfather," the girls said, tiptoeing forward and kissing him on his damp forehead.

"This is Nurse Williams," he told them. "I'm under her

orders for the time being. She's a regular tyrant!" He laughed, then grabbed at his side, but the day, which had been a little heavy, picked up.

After they had talked for a while and Grandfather had given Pam a few instructions about work, the nurse told them they must go and let her patient rest until supper.

"It seems empty and scary, being here without Mother and with Grandfather in bed," Pam confessed to Emily. "I feel small and inadequate, thinking about running the ranch alone, but the *paniolos* will help me. They'll remember Mother's instructions and follow them."

They did remember and because they loved the acres which gave them their living, they rallied about Pam to see that work went forward on oiled wheels.

"Don't bother your Grandfather more than is absolutely necessary for a few days," Miss Williams warned Pam the next evening at dinner. "In a man of his age, with a rib-fracture such as he has, there's a possibility that pneumonia may develop. Once his ribs begin healing, which they should do in eight or ten days, he'll get better fast. Don't look so concerned, Pam, there's no reason to worry. I'm just cautioning you."

"I feel about the size of a peanut, Emily," Pam confessed. "Sleep with me. The ranch is so big, there are so many people and animals on it. With Mother away and Grandfather in bed, if some unexpected emergency came up, I'd have to jump into the breach, be its head—"

"I know you can steer things splendidly," Emily said.

"I'll try my best. There's a big shipment of steers to get off to Honolulu in four days." Jumping out of bed, Pam went into her mother's room. Seeing her things about, just as though she were home, gave Pam comfort and courage.

The shipment went off without a hitch and Pam settled down in the traces. She was up before daylight and worked till dark. She was too level-headed and practical to let her position of authority go to her head. She knew she didn't "know it all" but tried to fill her mother's shoes to the best of her ability.

"You smart like any-kind," the men told her.

"Because you all stand by and help me," she declared. "I'll be glad when Grandfather's up and about again."

"No be scare kid, all fellas work number one hard for you and if us make some-few mistake, Kulani From Heaven fix up for us quick when she come home."

"Sure, sure!" Na-lua-hine agreed cheerily. "But what-for Kulani no come back? No good stop so long in America. Gone more from seven weeks now."

Pam's eyes went over the big, careless figures lounging about the Office, getting supplies, smoking, discussing details of to-morrow's work. Her mother was in the East, fighting to keep Kilohana for them, but she was not at liberty to tell them so. Her job was to hold the fort as best she could and attend to the myriad details of a two hundred thousand-acre estate that supported five thousand head of stock and about sixty persons.

A curious twilight was stealing through the garden, filling it with mystery. Between the slender spears of two Italian cypresses there was a glimpse of the sea. Heavy clouds were piled above the horizon and a jagged crimson crack in the west looked like a long wound across the sky. Pam felt oppressed and haunted by some uneasy presence which would not assert itself.

When the milking was done and the men had dispersed, she closed up the Office. "I feel as restless as an animal before a storm," she confided to Emily as they started toward the house. "Let's talk to Grandfather for a while. The eight days are past and there's no danger of pneumonia."

Breaking off, she stopped walking and stood absolutely still, giving her entire attention to invisible waves she sensed coming through the ether. The silence was so intense, she fancied that she could hear the grass growing. Then a wild peacock screeched from the hill and a dog gave an answering bark. She was intensely aware of the uninhabited spaces about her, forests and ancient lava flows that shut off the rest of the island, and of some current passing stealthily through the evening.

"Why are you so still?" Emily asked uneasily, after a few moments.

"The sky and land and water are trying to tell me something which I can't quite understand," Pam replied.

"How do you know?"

"I know the way Hawaiians know, and animals know," Pam said. "Big things are beginning to move."

Emily shivered violently. "I feel that, too," she admitted reluctantly.

They hurried into the house. Grandfather was sitting up in bed, having supper off a tray. "How did things go today, Pam?" he asked, as they came into his room.

"Okay. Pia shot six wild sheep and two turkeys. He'll salt them down tomorrow. Kimmo put a new hinge on the gate into the Waiho pasture. We shifted seventy head of steers into Kipuka Nui, and Lehua had a fine colt." Pam perched herself on the foot of the big bed. "But I'll be glad when you're up and can help me. When I'm up the mountain alone, looking at the fence lines and water troughs, everything seems bigger than it ever did before."

Grandfather chuckled. "It's only a matter of a day or two before I'm on my feet, Tyrant Williams informs me." He jerked his head roguishly at the nurse.

"We'll have to have Doctor MacFarlaine's approval on that before you start trying to get caught up with yourself, Mr. Storm," the nurse said, taking away his empty soup bowl and replacing it with a dish of curry.

"I've known Mac since he was a sprout," Grandfather said, "and I won't take any back talk from him just because he grew up and became a medico." Miss Williams went out and he beckoned the girls closer. "There's encouraging news from New York, girls. Banks phoned from Hilo this afternoon. He had a long letter and for the first time Kulani feels it's only a question of staying put and Kingsley will come around to our way of seeing things."

"Oh, Grandfather, how swell!" the girls chorused.

"Isn't it?" he agreed. "I'm glad now I didn't write and tell her about my accident. It would have worried her and she might have felt that she ought to come home. After I'm up and about I can mention it and explain why I sent for you both. In the meantime, no matter what happens, we've got to keep our end of things up until Kulani has accomplished what she set out to do. It's probably only a matter of two or three weeks more."

"I feel better," Pam announced. "Coming down from the Office I felt sort of stampeded inside, Grandfather—"

"Why?" the old man asked.

"I feel things in the air, as you do before a big storm."

"Probably you've been working too hard. Go to bed right after dinner and you'll wake up feeling tiptop."

She did wake up feeling that way, but the strange premonition of mighty happenings in the offing came back and stayed with her while she worked and made her rounds of the ranch. It was whispering to her, trying to tell her things. Sky, water and earth were united in one message that her ears could not quite hear and her mind just missed understanding.

She watched the *paniolos* covertly, for she knew that Hawaiians were quick to grasp whispered warnings in the atmosphere. But they appeared their usual gay selves. Maybe they were play-acting to keep her spirits up; maybe she was more aware, for the time being, because in a way she was responsible for Kilohana and the things they all loved.

When they all rode home and went into the Office, she was as taut as a violin string wound to breaking point. Sounds seemed unnaturally loud: the echo of the distant sea, the hearty slap of men's hands on sweat-caked haunches as tired horses were sent out to pasture. While she busied herself handing out supplies and putting them down in the ledger, she noticed old

Kane standing in the doorway and his body was intent and aware. "Some big-kind coming," he remarked, as if to himself. The other men nodded.

Pam's heart missed a stroke. "Will you run down to the house, Emily," she asked, "and see if Grandfather has had some word from Mother?"

Emily glanced at Pam. Her face looked tired and strained. She hurried through the garden and returned as fast as possible. "Everything's fine, Pam. Mr. Banks had a wire today and Grandfather got an air-mail from Mother at noon. Mr. Kingsley's beginning to weaken."

Pam felt momentarily relieved but at dinner her uneasiness returned. It seemed nice to have Grandfather back at table with them but even his presence, softly shaded candles spilling their light on flowers, and the beautiful white cloth could not entirely dispel the feeling created by the darkness, the feeling Kane's words had confirmed, of an enormous, menacing curtain hiding preparations of violence.

Then suddenly the island moved sharply beneath them, as if it winced at some deep-hidden pang. Windows rattled, pictures flapped against the wall. Emily stifled the scream that leaped to her lips. Miss Williams turned white. From the dark hillside where the *paniolos'* cottages were came a long, drawn-out cry "Oni-oni!" Then everything was still.

"Oh, how swell!" Pam cried. "We're going to have an eruption. Mauna Loa's long overdue. That explains why I've felt so stifled the last few days."

Another jerk came and subtly, in the movement of the

island, they were all conscious of big doings deep in the earth. Miss Williams, recently from the mainland, leaped to her feet. Emily sat in a small huddle.

"There's nothing to be scared of," Grandfather assured them. "If it's going to be a big eruption, we'll have earthquakes for several days. The shocks get harder and harder, until fissures are torn open in the mountain and the lava can come through—"

Another earthquake came, longer and more violent. Some mighty force seemed to be shaking the four thousand square miles of the island, as if it were nothing. Dogs howled, birds rose shrieking out of the trees, stock began stampeding about the pastures. The house lurched like a ship hit by a great sea, then came to a shuddering stop.

"That was a pretty hefty shake," Grandfather commented. "Guess the old mountain's going to put on a real show this time. It's almost six years since it last erupted. Listen—" he broke off. "There's another one coming!"

The house tilted sharply, then began swinging savagely back and forth. Bookcases went over, furniture danced about absurdly and from the kitchen came the sound of rowdy avalanches of saucepans being flung off the stove and the crashing of crockery hurled from shelves to the floor. Finally the ground came to a quivering stop but little shudders continued to run through the earth, like breezes ruffling the smooth surface of a lake.

Pam's heart was thumping so hard that it shook her whole body.

"Maybe we'd better all sleep in the garden tonight," Grandfather suggested.

"I'll call the *paniolos* to take out a bed for you," Pam said, leaping up.

But before she reached the door the men came running through the garden, frightened women and children behind them. "Help Grandfather outside," Pam directed, "but move him carefully. Be quick about it, though, before another *oni-oni* comes. Kane, take out blankets and wrap Grandfather up till we can get his bed made. He mustn't take cold."

Miss Williams, her face livid, tried her legs. "I'll take charge of my patient," she said unsteadily.

"Fine," Pam said. Terrified *wahines*, clutching their littlest babies, were crowding into the house. "Go outside," Pam ordered. "You'll be hurt by the furniture if another shake comes harder than the last one. Where's Emily—"

"Already Na-lua-hine take outside," one of the Japanese yardboys said.

"Ah Sam, put the fire in the stove out—"

"Aledy put water on top," the old man said without emotion.

"Good. Now let's take the pictures down and put what vases haven't already been broken on sofas. Wrap the big ones in blankets. I don't want all Mother's pretty things smashed."

Willing hands went to work. Japanese and Hawaiians scurried about, collecting bric-a-brac. The array of silver racing cups which had been hurled off the grand piano and scattered over the floor were picked up and put in a place of safety. *Paniolos* removed china from cabinets and wrapped it in towels and blankets that the house-boy brought in. While they worked, two or three sharp jars hit the island but did not last as long as the big tremblor which had preceded them.

"There," Pam looked around, "I guess that's about all we can do. Probably Mauna Loa will be in full eruption tomorrow and then the earthquakes will stop."

The telephone rang and Pam ran to answer it. "Is that you, Aunt Mag? Yes, we've had several big shocks. Do I want you to come over? There's no need. I'm not scared. Grandfather's here. The house is all which-way, but we've taken what care we can of Mother's valuables. I think I hear another big shake coming. When it's over I'll call you—"

Everyone had run into the garden except Kane, who stood close beside her. "Better us go outside quick—" he said, but before the words were out of his mouth the house suddenly and savagely humped upwards, as if it had been kicked by a Titan from below. Then it began wrenching and jerking back and forth, as if it had gone mad. With a deafening crash, the chimney fell on the roof. Instinctively Pam started for the garden but Kane grabbed her back, just as avalanches of bricks slid over the gutter, smashing on the concrete walk. Pam looked at them in a dazed way and realized that only her *paniolo's* presence of mind had prevented her from being crushed. A second chimney went down with a roar. . . .

The world was filled with noise, water hissing as it was tossed about in great tanks, the extraordinary sound of trees lashing about without wind to shake them. Wild geese screamed overhead, women wailed, stock raced around, dogs howled. Pam's face was white but even in the terrific confusion her mind was registering and recording every detail in her shaken world.

The house staggered to a stop. Cries diminished, sounds grew muffled, gradually everything was still. Kane looked at Pam, his old face was tense, but unafraid. "Come, us go outside now—*quick!*"

They darted into the garden.

"Whew, that was a whopper and no fooling!" Grandfather said, when some sort of order had been brought out of the confusion. Two of the *paniolos* lighted a big bonfire, so the electric lighting plant could be switched off. Figures wrapped in blankets crowded into the circle of light. Ah Sam, with some of the men helping, made coffee and served it. Emily sat pressed up against Na-lua-hine, looking like a small, frightened ghost.

"That ought to have opened up the fissures," Grandfather remarked in a satisfied way, as he nursed a cup of hot coffee between his hands.

"I hope we don't have any more like that one," Pam said. "Or the big water tanks below the barns will be flung off their foundations. I think I'll get a lantern and see if they're all right."

Three or four *paniolos* jumped up to go with her.

"Keep well away from them in case another shake should come and fling them over," Grandfather called. "Undoubtedly their under-pinnings have been weakened."

"I'll be careful," Pam promised.

"The tanks will have to be braced tomorrow, Grandfather,"

she informed him when she returned. "The stone walls are all down around here. I hope they've held up on the mountain."

"There'll be mischief to pay if the stock all gets mixed up," Grandfather agreed.

"Now I'm going to the stable to see if Malolo and the rest of the thoroughbreds are all right," Pam said. Emily struggled to her feet. "My legs feel like wet macaroni, Pam," she said, "but I'll go with you." Pam nodded and with their escort of *paniolos* they went off.

"We might as well try to get some rest while we can," Grandfather said when the tour of inspection was ended. "There will probably be a couple of more busters before morning." And he settled himself matter-of-factly into bed. Miss Williams drew up the covers and tucked them about him.

"Stay close to me, Na-lua-hine," Emily begged. "Lie down, Poi." And she poked the old dog under her blanket.

"Sure I sit by you, I no sleepy," Na-lua-hine said cheerfully. "Sure lava come out tomorrow and the *onis-onis* finish."

But the terrible shaking had only begun. For three days the island struggled, writhed and fought to rid itself of the lava ripping out its vitals. Five of the fifteen tanks on the ranch were flung over. In spite of the risk of running short, Pam ordered the men to let out half the water in those that were left standing, then had them solidly braced. Every stone wall on the place was flat, Holsteins, Herefords and Guernseys roamed together, restless and ill at ease.

The garden looked like a refugee camp. Ah Sam and the yardboys built outdoor cooking stoves with cemented bricks and sheets of corrugated iron. The ranch women assisted with the preparing of meals. Grandfather sat like an old chief, directing operations and consulting when Pam and Emily and the *paniolos* came in from their hourly rounds. Milking had to go on, tanks had to be braced and re-braced, stock had to be driven in, watered, and watched. . . .

Pam looked grim. "I wish old Mauna Loa would erupt and be done with it. It drives me crazy to see everything in such a mess. It'll take months and months to rebuild all the miles and miles of stone walls and cost a frightful lot of money. It'll take ages to straighten out the stock. The house has some bad cracks, the grand piano has almost broken through one wall, the stone walks in the garden are all scattered—"

"Don't get so boiled up, Pam. It's all in a lifetime," Grandfather consoled. "You've done fine. You haven't lost your head and have kept functioning on all twelve cylinders. If your mother had been here, she couldn't have done much more than you have."

"Oh, Grandfather!" She rushed to him. "Do you mean that?"

"Of course I do. You've been a trump all the way through. This has been a mean mess of shakes, more severe than anything I remember and I've lived in Hawaii seventy years. Things have been noticeably quieter these past few days. I guess it's a false alarm and Mauna Loa isn't going to erupt after all."

Three more days went by. The earth was still. People stopped watching the mountain and returned to their homes. *Paniolos* and servants restored the big house to order. Over-turned tanks were hoisted up and replaced on their foundations.

"Nothing can be done with the stock until the stone walls are rebuilt," Grandfather said. "Phone Geyer in Kona and tell him to send fifty workmen over, a hundred if he has them. You'll have to arrange to feed them, Pam. They'll have their own tents. I was on the verge of wiring Kulani about ten days ago, but as long as things have quieted down, I'm glad I didn't. Actually there wasn't anything she could do that we haven't. Even Kulani can't stop Mauna Loa from shaking or force it to erupt," he concluded with a chuckle. "And she seems to be accomplishing things with Kingsley."

"But she doesn't say when she'll be home," Pam sighed. "It seems years and years since she went and it's only three months."

"From her last letter I imagine things will be settled any day now. I'm on deck once more, thank God."

"Tomorrow the *paniolos* and I are going up Hualalai," Pam broke in. "All the wild cattle have moved to lower levels to escape the extra shaking that takes place the higher you get up the mountains. Three wild bulls are rampaging with the tame bulls. We've got to get them. Our best Hereford bull is badly gored. We had to bring him in last night. We'll catch the bulls and kill them for the stone-wall gang. You've never seen wild cattle roped, Emily—do you want to go with us?"

"Yes," Emily replied, rather dubiously.

In spite of her apprehension at going closer to Mauna Loa, Emily was stirred when she got up at two the next morning for her first night ride. The dark silhouettes of riders against stars, the spurt of lighted matches, the fragrance of cigarette smoke drifting back over men's shoulders, horses blowing out their nostrils and reaching for their bits, brewed an atmosphere of excitement.

Riding along, Na-lua-hine explained that the stock they were after were the descendants of the original Long-horns brought from California by Lord Vancouver in 1793. Owing to the roughness of the mountain tops and the denseness of the forests, many of the original herd could not be collected when they were rounded up after the twenty year taboo had expired. Each generation had become wilder and fiercer and whenever ranch work was slack *paniolos* tried to rope as many of the animals as possible because they ate up good pasturage without profit and menaced the purity of registered herds.

While Emily listened she tried to keep the cold wind blowing down from the high mountains from freezing her hands. Finally, after they had ridden high up Hualalai, everyone dismounted. Kane lighted a *kawao* bush and they all crowded about it to thaw out. Clouds of dense white smoke poured upward and little red tongues of flame licked the resinous branches greedily. The men began going over three-yard lengths of *manila* rope, finished with a swivel at one end. Each rider carried three or four, tied to his saddle.

"What are they used for?" Emily asked.

"To tie up wild bulls after they've been caught, so the men can use their lassos again," Pam explained.

Dawn began breaking with deliberate majesty in the east, lighting the huge waste land lying between the three monster volcanoes forming the bulk of the island. Emily looked at the awesome terrain. Miles upon miles of black lava flows which had once poured in molten scarlet streams from the mountains. Here and there half-hearted forests tried to grow in ash and cinders, but mostly it was devoid of life and vegetation. Silence, mystery and violence brooded over everything, intensified by the memory of the earthquakes which had recently shaken the island. Emily shivered and tried not to think of Mauna Loa erupting. She simply couldn't imagine a mountain really spouting fire!

The *paniolos* began riding off in pairs, posting themselves on commanding ridges. Emily noticed that each man had tied his lasso-end fast to his pommel before he recoiled it and arranged it afresh so it would be handy when wanted. Na-lua-hine explained that in Hawaii, for a man to lose his rope, or cast off from an animal once he had caught it, was a supreme disgrace. Every *paniolo* with a real pride in his calling rode "Tied to Death," to translate an old Spanish term.

Na-lua-hine warned Emily to keep her eyes open when they began chasing the wild cattle. The mountain tops were pocked with lava holes, some only a foot or so deep but sufficient to throw a horse running at full speed, while others were death traps, forty or fifty feet in depth.

"Plenty fella and horse broke-neck in this kind," Na-lua-hine concluded cheerfully. "More better you ride close behind me, I smart for see these *pukas*."

Emily gritted her teeth to keep them from chattering with fright.

She sensed that men and horses were tense and alert. The hour was approaching when the wild cattle would be working back from the rich pastures they were robbing under cover of night, to seek the safety of their own waste lands until dark came again. A warning shout floated through the air from another hilltop: *"Pipi ahiu makai—*wild cattle below us!"

Na-lua-hine pointed at a band of about forty huge beasts making their way warily across a grassy opening. From their actions it was obvious that they were reluctant to leave the protection of the forests, but keen to get back to the lava beds, where horses could not follow them. A bull with horns like arms lifted for a wicked embrace, halted, snuffed the air and began pawing up dust and tossing it over his shoulder. While he pawed he bellowed dully and lashed his sides with his tail.

The horses began trembling with excitement and Emily could hardly breathe. Na-lua-hine reminded her that if she should happen to get in the way of a wild bull to race her horse uphill, never down. Wild cattle could outrun horses downhill, but not up; besides when a bull charged from above he had the pitch of the land added to the weight of his body, to give more impetus.

"I'll remember," Emily promised shakily.

The wild cattle began working across the grassy flat cautiously. Instinct warned them that hidden enemies were near. Suddenly the hidden riders swooped in on them. The quiet mountain top echoed with a commotion of life: bulls bellowing, men shouting, the thud of horses' hoofs, the whine of swinging lassos. Nooses whanged shut about great horns, bulls went head over heels, leaped up. *Paniolos* dodged about expertly, inviting them to charge and when they had maneuvered the enraged beasts into the right position dodged around a tree, snapping the great lowered heads and deadly horns against the stout trunks. The horses were as expert as the riders, and as keen. In less than ten minutes eight great beasts were secured, while the rest of the wild band streamed on toward the lava wastes and safety.

Pam was elated. Two of the bulls which had attacked the Hereford "Lord of the Herd" had been secured. The third was still at large.

"Too late for get him today," Kane insisted, squinting at the sun. "All wild cattle gone up mountains by now. Better us come back tomorrow and try again."

Pam was reluctant to go home. She had roped a yearling bull. Its horns were only three inches long but it was her first and the thrill of the achievement was still stinging in her veins. However, she knew Kane was wise in the ways of wild stock and said "Okay."

"What are you going to do with the wild bulls, now you've got them?" Emily asked, watching the great beasts raging and trying to break free from the trees to which they had been tied.

"We'll leave them where they are for a couple of days. By that time their necks are so sore from fighting the rope that they're easy to lead. A couple of the *paniolos* will come up with old oxen, tie the bulls to them, and the oxen will drag them home. Sometimes it takes a day or so before they come in but they never fail to bring in their prisoners."

"Why don't you kill them here?"

"For several reasons. It's much easier to slaughter them properly at the ranch with the right equipment, so they might as well carry their own meat in, instead of having to send men and pack horses after it."

"Oh," Emily said. "I hadn't thought of that. But I thought bull meat was strong—"

"It is, usually, but Hawaiians and Japanese like it. These cattle will be for the fence gangs that are going to rebuild the walls. I hate to have to go home to that mess of broken fences and tanks but we do a little each day and things are beginning to look a bit more shipshape. I'd hate Mother to come home and see the place looking the way it is. You old rascal!" Pam stared at the long slopes of Mauna Loa. "Raising all that rumpus—for nothing!" She started down the trail.

For a while they rode along slowly, then Pam challenged Nuhi to play lasso-tag. "I feel so full of bubbles I can't bear to ride slowly. Bet you can't rope me between here and home!" And she dashed down the mountain at full speed.

Nuhi unfastened his lasso, whipped out a noose and took off in pursuit. Emily watched, envying Pam her superb horsemanship, then consoled herself with the thought that each day she was getting to be a better rider. In another year, maybe, she would be able to play lasso-tag with Na-lua-hine. The racing figures vanished over a rise and she surrendered herself to the pleasure of jogging along with the *paniolos*, who were full of glee over their morning's work.

They dropped over the brow of the hill, then Kane gave a

long, dreadful cry. There, below them, Nuhi was off his horse, bending over Pam's prostrate form! They raced down the steep slope. Nuhi's brown eyes were spilling tears. Pam's horse had put his foot through the crust of a lava bubble, which had broken through, flinging the animal head over heels. As far as he could tell, no bones were broken, but Pam was unconscious.

CHAPTER XV

KULANI RETURNS

I<small>T WAS A SAD PARTY THAT HEADED FOR HOME</small>. N<small>UHI'S BIG</small> brown eyes kept spilling slow tears, Emily and the other *paniolos* were stunned, and old Kane simply beside himself with grief. From the moment he reached Pam he would allow no one else to touch her. His hands went feverishly over her body, along her limbs. . . . She was his child. . . . She had walked into his heart with her first toddling steps. . . . He had carried her before his saddle on a pillow. . . . Her little bronze head had rested on his arm when she dozed. . . . Kulani had given her into his safekeeping for as long as he lived . . . And now, when she was away, this awful thing had happened!

"Maybe it isn't so bad, maybe she's just been knocked senseless," Emily suggested, trying to fortify herself and ease the old fellow's despair.

"Maybe-so-yes," the other men chorused. "Pam tough like any-kind, plenty times before fall down with horse. . . . No need be scare. . . . Sure tomorrow all right again. . . ." So they talked as Kane rode home slowly, with Pam's limp form before him.

"Better you go tell Kaiko, Emily," Kimmo said. "But tell him easy. He old man—"

Emily nodded and scooted for the house. Grandfather was seated on the back veranda, listening to the radio. She slid off her horse and dropped the reins, then thought, "I mustn't run to him, or he'll know something has happened. I must walk."

She started toward the house slowly, with unsteady legs. The sound of her footsteps brought Grandfather to his feet with a jerk. "Something has happened, Emily! Tell me quickly—"

"It's Pam." She fought to keep her voice from trembling. "Her horse turned a somersault. Kane's bringing her in—"

"Is she—" Grandfather could not get any farther.

"She's alive but unconscious—"

"Tell Tatsu to get her bed ready; phone Doctor Mac; get hold of Miss Williams, if you can. How soon will they be in?"

"They're coming down past the Office now. I'll attend to everything, Grandfather."

He hurried off through the garden.

Emily wondered how she could be so calm, all at once. She found Tatsu, told her not to cry, explained what had happened to Ah Sam, who went running out of the house as if a demon were after him. She instructed one of the yardboys to bring the Packard around, in case it might be needed, then rushed to the phone. The doctor's line was busy but she got hold of Miss Williams.

"I'm just off a case, Emily, but I'll hire a car and come over as fast as I can."

While she was trying the doctor again, Emily caught glimpses of the *paniolos* carrying Pam through a side door to her room. Grandfather suddenly looked tired, old, and unsure of his movements. Emily fought a wild surge of tears, and mastered them. Then she heard the doctor's voice, instructing her, and realized that she'd been talking to him while she thought she was only watching sad people trailing through the big, flower-filled house.

"Don't have her moved more than is absolutely necessary, Emily, until I can get over and see what injuries she has sustained. If she regains consciousness, keep her absolutely still. I'll be with you in an hour and fifteen minutes, at the latest—" The phone clicked and Emily hung up her receiver, feeling suddenly limp.

The whole ranch, even the gardens and pastures, seemed to stop breathing until the doctor's car came tearing up the road. Emily and Grandfather sat beside Pam's bed, gripping hands. Tatsu stood at her other side, her face wooden and dead. As the car pulled to a stop, *paniolos* and their wives, yardboys and scared-eyed children swarmed about it for an instant. The doctor spoke in a kind, reassuring way, then hurried in. Women wiped their eyes on folds of their voluminous *holokus*, men dug tears away with the backs of their brawny brown wrists and Ah Sam wrung his apron silently.

"She has sustained a concussion and, as far as I can tell yet, has some sort of injury to her spine," Doctor Mac said when he had finished his examination. "It may be a week before she recovers consciousness, or only a matter of a few hours. She'll need a nurse—"

"I phoned Miss Williams. She's on her way," Emily said.

"Good girl." The doctor patted her rigid shoulder. "Her mother must be radioed for at once."

"Shall I attend to it for you, Grandfather?" Emily asked.

"Thanks, Emily. Phone Mr. Banks and he'll get word to her. Mac—you don't think—" Grandfather moved restlessly.

"It's impossible to predict anything yet. She'll recover, but it may be a long time before she's up and around again. She'll have to be kept here for the present. You're seventy-six miles from the nearest hospital and it would be too risky to take her over such rough roads when there's a spine injury. I'll wait here, of course, until Miss Williams arrives."

Emily hurried to the phone and when she went out on the back veranda the people waiting in the garden came up like a troubled tide to ask for details. Emily gave them the doctor's report and exhausted relief came into their faces.

"I think you'd better all go to your work and homes," Emily

suggested gently, after she had talked to the lawyer. "There's nothing that anyone can do."

"Sure, sure, us go," the men chorused. "Little more time for milk."

"When Pam come-to, you tell her no worry, us all work hard and take good care of every kind," Nuhi said briskly.

"Send radio for Kulani to come home?" Kimmo asked. Emily nodded.

"How many day before she get here?" Pili inquired.

"Let's see. . . . She'll fly. Four or five days at the most."

"Swell!" everyone cried. "Swell!"

Emily swallowed a lump that kept pushing into her throat. How devoted and loyal they all were. Their love spilled into the day, making it overflow with invisible gold. They began going away in groups, talking in lowered voices, to milk, to care for horses, to help themselves to food, which someone who could write would put down and try to keep track of. . . . She stood still, thinking, then saw a desolate figure seated on the grass. Kane. . . . His eyes came to hers, asking a question. . . .

"Come Kane," she said softly. "Your place is beside her."

Rising, he came forward, picked up her hand and kissed it. The gesture, so reverent, so simple and touching, untied something inside Emily and she began crying wildly.

"No cry, Em'ly, no cry," the gentle old fellow begged, patting her awkwardly.

"Oh, Kane," she choked, clinging to him. "I know she'll get well but it seems so funny to see her so still in bed during the daytime. I mustn't go to pieces. Grandfather needs me—"

It was three days before Pam regained consciousness. During that time Kane sat like a graven image in the corner of the bedroom, never taking his eyes off the bright head on the pillow. Occasionally he tiptoed out for the food Ah Sam served him in the kitchen but he was never gone for more than a few minutes. Tatsu kept vigil with him and when meals were served and the kitchen spotless, Ah Sam stole in quietly and took his place, too. Grandfather had his big chair brought in and Emily sat in a small rocker beside him. Night and morning *paniolos* and their families came to inquire how Pam was progressing and left gorgeous *leis*, which Miss Williams draped over the foot of the big bed.

Then one afternoon Pam opened her eyes, smiled faintly, and closed them again, but recognition was there, instead of the glazed, feverish stare. After a bit, she turned her head slightly and began looking around her in a dazed way. She saw Kane, Tatsu, Grandfather, Emily, old Ah Sam, and opened her lips to speak, but Miss Williams signed quickly for her to be still.

"Don't try to talk, Pam. You had a fall with your horse."

"I remember," she murmured and dropped back to sleep.

Doctor Mac came twice a day to see her. "After her mother gets here and she's completely conscious, I'd like to have a consultation about her spine injury. X-rays will have to be taken as soon as it's safe to move her."

"Kulani will be here tomorrow," Grandfather said. "I just had a radio from San Francisco. She's catching the Clipper at two, will arrive in Honolulu early tomorrow morning and I've chartered a plane to bring her right over."

Relief went silently through the house, which had been so hushed—a rustle of gladness, as if it were rousing itself from its stupor to welcome Kulani. Emily stole out of the room. Tatsu would not leave her beloved Baby-san, nor Kane his *"keiki."* Grandfather could not see. It rested upon her to get fresh flowers and make the house beautiful for tomorrow.

Going into the garden, she picked armfuls of blossoms and brought them into the end of the *lanai* which stretched its sunny windows along the front of the house. The house-boys scurried about gladly, filling vases with water for her to arrange.

As she worked, a sort of peaceful happiness filtered through her. She realized that she had never really grasped the fact that this was her home. She was no longer an orphan; she had a sister and a mother! The old house put protection about her.

"Keep Kilohana safe, God," she prayed silently. "Don't let it be taken from us. Something would die in this house if all these people who love it, and have worked to keep it beautiful, went away."

"Orr, too much fine, too much nice," the house-boys approved, when she had finished placing the flowers around. "Kulani too much glad come back and look all this pritty."

"When Tatsu see how nice you fix flowers this time, it knock out her eye," Nishi remarked, as he gathered up the litter of stems and leaves that had been snipped off.

Emily looked at her handiwork with deep satisfaction. It seemed marvelous, and unreal, that Kulani From Heaven would be here this time tomorrow. A warm rush of happiness went

through her that made the day brighter, the island more beautiful, and the sea a prouder blue. . . .

When she and Grandfather sat down to dinner, she tried to
grasp the fact that next day at lunch time Kulani would be at
the head of the table again.

"Isn't it lucky there are airplanes nowadays?" she said. "Else
it would be weeks before Mother could get here."

"Yes, isn't it?" Grandfather agreed. "These past four days
have seemed like endless years." Turning his head, he drew a
deep breath. "Fresh flowers! Did you arrange them, Emily?"

"Yes."

"You're grand. I believe in giving bouquets to people as they
earn them. I don't know what I would have done without you.
You've stood by like a soldier, kept your head, and been more
comfort to me and the ranch than you'll ever know."

"Oh, Grandfather," she said softly, "it's a funny time to
feel as happy as I do now. But this afternoon, while I was ar-
ranging the flowers, it sank into me that Kilohana is my home
and that I belong to you all."

"It's difficult for me to realize that you haven't always been
with us, Emily. You're part of this place—"

Emily was so happy that she couldn't speak. After they had
eaten, they went to be with Pam, so Miss Williams could have
her dinner. Pam was awake, old Kane sitting holding her hand
and Tatsu was fanning her, as the evening was warm.

"Okay, I'm better," she said, smiling weakly.

Bending over, Grandfather kissed her forehead and a tear
splashed down.

"Grandfather, are you crying?"

"Just a stray tear, Pam, I'm so happy. Kulani gets back tomorrow."

"Oh, Grandfather! Is everything all right? Did Mr. Kingsley—"

"Hush, Pam, you've talked enough," Miss Williams warned from the doorway. "You'll have plenty of time tomorrow to get caught up on lost news. Promise, dear—no more talking, or I'll have to sit here and go without my dinner."

"Promise," Pam murmured. Her eyes went slowly and happily over the room, rested on the *leis* draping the foot of her bed, lingered on faces she loved, gathered about her. The thought was plain in her eyes: "Everything's fixed up, or Mother wouldn't be coming home."

New life was injected into the ranch when the car bringing Kulani came smoking up the driveway next morning. Everyone had collected on the lawn to greet her. There were cries of *Aloha, Aloha*, happy tears, and laughter—which had been strangely absent for the past five days in gardens which usually echoed with it.

Nuhi, who had taken the car over to Kohala to meet the plane, swaggered about importantly, as if he were entirely responsible for the return of Kulani From Heaven. His eyes danced and his white teeth flashed like white surf in the brownness of his face as he snatched up Kulani's suitcases and started for the house.

Kulani lingered for a moment with her brown and yellow children who had never quite grown up in their hearts, but whose devotion had enriched the days and years of her life.

"People of Kilohana," she said in Hawaiian. "Your love has been proved to me in a thousand ways. We've shared work, laughter and happiness. Now we share sorrow, and the bond draws us closer. We must stand closer together than ever, now that dark days are upon us. We must believe, though clouds hide the sun, that it still shines for us. *Aloha!*"

"*Aloha*, Kulani, *Aloha!*" they chorused in one great voice that sounded as though it rose from the depths of the soil they all loved. Na-lua-hine stepped forward. He was no longer the wag and clown of the ranch, but a figure of heroic dignity.

"Kulani, as the oldest man here, I am spokesman for my people. We stand with you always. In the words of the woman Ruth to Naomi, written in the Bible, we say, 'Whither Thou goest we will go. Thy people are our people. Thy gods are our gods. *Aloha!*' "

Kulani made a quick, expressive gesture to signify that feelings too deep for words had hold of her throat, then walked swiftly into the house.

CHAPTER XVI

INVALID

WITH THANKFUL RELIEF THE RANCH SETTLED BACK INTO ITS
accustomed routine. Kulani From Heaven was back, her hand
was on the helm, steering their ship forward. It was only a
question of time before their joyous comrade, Pam, would once
more take her place in their ranks.

Pam's eyes cleared, faint color crept back into her cheeks,
but from the waist down her body, which had been a dynamo
of energy, remained limp and inert. Specialists were flown over
from Honolulu. Consultations were held. When her condition
warranted it, she was flown to Honolulu and X-rayed, but the
root of the trouble could not be isolated. Treatments were
suggested and tried, without results. . . .

"You mustn't give up hope, Mrs. Garland," the serious-eyed, kind-faced men in white told her. "She has youth, amazing strength and vitality. She must be kept cheerful and the belief instilled into her that she'll get well. Science isn't infallible. Miracles still occur in the medical world. Take her home, where she's happiest. MacFarlaine is competent to handle this phase of her trouble. You can count upon him to leave no stone unturned and keep us in constant touch with her case history. If she has made no noticeable improvement in two months, fly her back here for more X-rays. In the meantime, we'll try out—" They went off into a bewildering maze of medical terms. Kulani listened calmly, but her eyes were unnaturally dilated, her body taut and movements a trifle unsteady.

When the doctors were done, she went to Pam's room and told her she was to go home. "Oh, Mother! Oh, *Mother!*" she cried. "I won't mind being in bed there so much. I can hear ranch things going on, talk to our people and have fun till I'm up and around again. Do you think I'll be up by Thanksgiving?"

"It's impossible to predict anything, yet, Pam. You may get well very slowly, or whatever's wrong may clear up practically overnight. In the meantime, they're going to try—" She outlined the new treatment.

"I don't care what they do as long as it makes me better. When can we go back to Kilohana? Tomorrow?"

"Yes, dear."

"Mother, your voice sounds funny. Is everything all right? I mean about the ranch and Mr. Kingsley—"

"He hadn't given in entirely when I was called home, but I'm working on him from long distance." Kulani made her tired voice light and gay. "Your main job, Pam, for the time being, is not to concern yourself about anything except getting well."

"Okay, Kulani From Heaven," Pam promised, her face radiant with the knowledge that she was leaving the hospital to go home.

Back at Kilohana, Pam was patience itself, uncomplaining, interesting herself in everything, second-hand. Her room became a sort of camp-ground where people came and went all day long. She lay in bed with *leis* around her neck listening to horses going by, dogs barking, cattle calling in the hills and men shouting and singing as they went about their work.

Kane and Tatsu were never out of her room very long. When Ah Sam's kitchen was clean, he stole in to chat. Grandfather's big chair squeaked like a cheerful cricket as he rocked back and forth all day. Emily dashed in and out and read aloud in the afternoon when Miss Williams took her nap. In the evening Kulani was there, keeping Pam abreast of each detail of the work.

"The tanks are all up again and the stone-wall gang is getting on well with the fences. . . . Tomorrow we're shipping fifty steers to Honolulu. . . . The feed in the pastures up the mountain is coming along fine after the last rain."

Pam listened avidly. Though her body was a prisoner, her mind was free to wander over the acres she loved. Land smells, tree smells, and the great clean smell of the sea came in through the open windows. The lawn was gilded with sunset light, pheasants crowed from the hill, turkeys gobbled, cows lowed for their calves. A flock of wild Hawaiian geese swooped onto the lawn and walked across it, stretching out their long sinuous necks, then rose again and settled about a water trough at the foot of the hill.

A wistful expression flitted over Pam's face. "It'll be Thanksgiving in a few days," she remarked, and her words hung in the room.

"We won't be able to go to Aunt Jolly's valley this year," Kulani said. "Shall I ask her to come here and spend it with us?"

Pam's face brightened. "Oh, Mother, that would be fun!"

"I think she'd enjoy it, Pam. She has had us every year and it seems about time for us to return her hospitality."

"I love Thanksgiving, Mother, and Christmas. . . . Do you think I'll be able to get up for Christmas?"

Kulani moved slightly, as though her chair were uncomfortable. "It's difficult to say, Pam, but if you can't, we'll have the tree here, so we can all be together as usual."

"Your voice sounds tired, Kulani From Heaven."

"I am a little tired. There has been so much extra work, because of the earthquakes, and having my right hand laid up puts extra burdens on my shoulders. I miss you a thousand times a day. Emily's grand but she's not *kama-aina* about ranch work yet. Well, let's plan for Thanksgiving and I'll write Aunt Jolly."

Pam was full of suggestions. "It might be more fun for Aunt Jolly if we had an American Thanksgiving, instead of a Hawaiian one. Could we have the table in here with a monstrous turkey, pumpkin pies and all the trimmings?"

"Of course, darling. We'll make it an extra-special occasion because we've lots to be thankful for, even if you're still in bed."

Aunt Jolly arrived a few days later. She was of Chief stock and stood fully six feet. A voluminous black silk *holoku* failed to conceal her noble figure, as sumptuous as the land. She had heavily lashed, curiously young eyes, a proud, merry mouth, and carried herself imperiously. When she laughed she seemed to put out her arms and exultantly hug all the joy of the world to her heart.

She came sweeping into Pam's room like a high, clean wind and, bending down, showered kisses on her forehead. "This mighty swell of you, Pam, asking me here. I like fine to try one American-style Thanksgiving. Bad shame you still in bed, but not can help, so us have fun anyhow," she announced philosophically. "Next year you come my valley again and us make up for lost time."

Magically, she made Pam's illness appear a dividend instead of a tragedy. Seating herself in a rocker, she kept looking about her like a delighted child.

"Now whoever thinking that old style Hawaiian womans like me coming to swell place like this! Might be I make some small mistakes-and-errors but us all good friends, so who care?" She tossed her head blithely and her bell-like laughter floated out of the windows.

Pam gazed at her adoringly. She knew the noble heart that

lodged in her big, careless body, the great up-well of kindness springing from her royal soul, her joy in living, her delight in little pleasures and her gift of making simple things adventures. Just having Aunt Jolly in the room seemed to transport Pam to the lost valley, where the Chieftess lived with a happy handful of her people who had foresworn the influence of whites to cling to the old ways of their forefathers.

Thanksgiving night, when the family gathered about the lavishly laden table set up in Pam's bedroom, Aunt Jolly looked like a queen. A *Mamo* feather *lei* sat on her high-piled, wavy hair, like a lustrous halo of pale golden sunlight. Her eyes were shining and under the oyster-colored lace *holoku* you sensed her proud strength.

When the family was seated and Grandfather had said Grace, she looked about her, then her eyes misted with happy tears.

"You the only white fellas I ever ask to come into my valley," she said. "But when people love, like we all do, us all the same color in our hearts. Kaiko here," she gestured at Grandfather, "is my brother, Kulani is my girl, and Pam and Emily are my little *moopunas*—grandchildren. Swell for us to be together every year. No matter if here, or in my valley. We eat food together and give thanks for all the rich things we got. And now," she turned to Pam, "because you sick and not having good fun—"

"But I am!" Pam cried. "It's always fun when you're around, Aunt Jolly."

"I old, I fat, I not got much education but I know some few

things! God never meant mans to be unhappy." Rising, she walked to Pam's bed. "So, I want you to be happy like anything tonight." Reaching up, she removed the precious feather-*lei* from her head and placed it on Pam's bronze curls. "For you, Pam—a *Mamo lei!* Kulani been telling me how fine you take your sick. Grandfather tell to me how swell you are when the earthquakes come so hard. I think you the only American girl who will ever have a *Mamo lei.* It has been worn in honor all the way down. It is a symbol of Chiefs who walked in might and guarded their people. *Aloha.* I know you will wear it the same way!"

"Oh, Aunt Jolly! *Aunt Jolly!*" Pam was crying, hysterical with happiness, while she pressed the priceless *lei* against her face. "I never thought, I never dreamed, I'd have a *Mamo lei!* I bet," she laughed unsteadily, "that I'll wake up and find out it's just a dream!"

Kulani wiped her eyes, Grandfather blew his nose, Emily swallowed, but a golden glow came down into the room and stayed there.

"Make a *kahuna*, Aunt Jolly," Pam said next day when she left, "that when I wear my *lei* at Thanksgiving next year it will be in your valley."

"No need make *kahunas.* If doctor not nuff smart for cure you, God will—in some way. You see!" And when she went out richness and peace lay over Pam like a blanket. She knew, she knew that some day she would wake up whole again!

Autumn began sliding into the thrilling winter of the subtropics. *Kona* storms roared up from the Equator, convulsing the atmosphere for forty-eight or seventy-two hours. First came a louder note in the surf, then electrical wind, then clouds black with thunder and savage rain. When the atmosphere cleared Mauna Kea and Mauna Loa were covered with glittering capes of snow, in contrast to the palm-fringed, sun-baked beaches at their feet. Between the royal upheavals of the atmosphere, days crept over land and sea which were so utterly beautiful that it seemed as though if a person breathed too loudly he would shatter the fragile loveliness of earth, water, and sky. The island, soaked and rich with moisture, stretched out contentedly, generating new power for growth. Mystery tingled in the light vagrant air, which replaced the steady Trade Wind blowing for seven months of the year.

Above everything Pam loved the autumn of Hawaii. This was the time of growth and gathering up of forces for the future. One afternoon, while Miss Williams was resting and Emily was seated by her bed, she turned and said:

"Emily!" in a tight voice.

"What is it?" Emily asked, taking her hand.

"Emily, what if I never get well? What if I can never ride again, never swim in Lua-hine-wai, never see places in the mountains and forests that I love? I couldn't bear it—" she finished wildly, tears rolling down her cheeks.

"Oh, Pam, of course you'll get well!" Emily choked.

"Kane's made *kahunas*, Ah Sam and Tatsu have burned punks to Budda, Mother's paid hundreds and hundreds of dollars to doctors and I'm still—here!" She pounded the bed with

her small fist. "I've tried to be a Happy Warrior, to believe as
Mother said people must, when there seems nothing to believe
in, but my legs won't move yet. Not even one toe! I want to
feel a horse between my knees, bridle-reins in my fingers, to
swing a lasso. I want to get my hands on Malolo again, to rub
my cheek against his soft nose—" Breaking off, she stared out
of the windows in a lost way.

Clean, rich scents crept into the room. The blue day leaned
over the world, stilling it to peace. Shadows on the sides of
Hualalai took on strange significance; clouds waited; a skylark
shot upward from the land, singing as it went. There were minute rustlings and whisperings of vegetation moving in the sun,
like the voice of the great Force behind everything, directing
the universe. A sort of calmness climbed over the panic and re-
volt which had suddenly filled Pam.

"Don't tell Kulani From Heaven about this, Emily," Pam
said. "I don't want her to know how I'm exploding with longing to be outside, doing things I love. Don't tell her that I'm
getting scared that maybe I'll always be like this." Her voice
was hard and breathless, but under control. "I keep wondering
and thinking . . . about things as I lie here. You are the only
person I can let go to. Mother has so much to do, so many
things to worry her—besides me. Grandfather's too old to
make sad. Tatsu and Kane," she moved restively, "look at me
with such sad eyes that I have to joke to make them jolly."

"Oh, Pam, if only I could help you," Emily said in the desolate, frozen way people do when they are powerless to do anything for someone they love who is greatly troubled.

"People can't help thinking when they have to be still," Pam went on. "I try not to. Get me my *Mamo lei* so I can hold it and remember what it stands for. What if Mr. Kingsley won't sell Kilohana to us. I'm lying here and missing the last of it!"

"But he can't, he couldn't take it away *now!*" Emily protested, looking outraged.

"What do you mean—*now?*" Pam asked.

"Would you send a girl away from a place she loved, if she were injured, like you are?"

Pam weighed her words, then her eyes lighted. "Oh, Emily, I never thought of that!" she gasped. "Maybe I had to be hurt so I could keep the ranch *for all of us!* I don't care now if I have to be like this always if it means we can stay here. Does Mother—"

"I don't believe Kulani From Heaven has thought of it, she's always wiring and writing East."

"How smart you are, Emily. I'm sure you're right. Go and tell Kulani quickly to write to Mr. Kingsley. Then she won't have to worry any more." Pam let out a great sigh, like a person who has accomplished a seemingly impossible task.

Emily scampered off, found Tatsu, then headed for the Office, where she knew Kulani would be. Every day now she and Grandfather went through books and papers. When Emily had asked rather timorously why she spent so much time with accounts now, Kulani had replied that it was the end of the year and accounts must be brought up to date and audited. But Emily had wondered if, maybe, she was getting things in order for another person to take over. . . .

Grandfather was seated on a grain bag near the door. Words quivered in the air that Emily's approaching footsteps had silenced. With a rush she told them her thought. Neither spoke for a moment after she finished. Emily looked from Kulani's face to Grandfather's.

"But would *you?*" she asked.

"Of course not, dear. You've given us another weapon to try on him—" Kulani said.

"You mean—" Emily could not finish.

"Exactly that. For some reason Mr. Kingsley has made up his mind all of a sudden that he isn't to be bought off. Probably because of having lots of money, he's accustomed to having his own way and doesn't like to be crossed. It goes against the grain to resort to appealing to his sympathies, but I'll do *anything* to keep Kilohana for us all. Grandfather and I were just debating whether or not we should tell everyone that probably this would be the last Christmas we'll spend here—"

"Oh Kulani From Heaven!" Emily cried, as if someone had struck her. "It's my *first* one here. I couldn't bear it if it was my last, too!"

"It's eight months since we first got word of this thing." Kulani's voice shook ever so little. "Ten months are left before our lease runs out. Now—" she swept Emily to her. "Now we'll use this brain-storm of yours as a new leverage to pry him loose!"

"He'd be an ogre if he made us go now!" Emily declared hotly.

"Exactly right!" Grandfather agreed heartily. "This may

solve the great puzzle Kulani and I have been wrestling with!
How did we ever get on without you?" he demanded.

"Like I got on without all of you, Grandfather. Badly,"
Emily suggested with a flash of fun.

"Dern tootin!" Grandfather said. "I feel as if tons had rolled
off my shoulders. For the first time in my life I was actually
dreading Christmas. Now—" his face glowed. "Well, it's only
ten days until December twenty-fourth. We'll have to make
this communication a letter and can hardly expect a reply before Christmas is over. People are always rushed during the
holiday season and our friend in New York will doubtless have
to give the matter profound thought—" His voice was a little
mocking.

Kulani tapped the desk with her pencil. "I've never asked
quarter from anyone," she said slowly. "I've never traded on
men's sympathies, just because I'm a woman in a man's game.
But this time not only our immediate happiness is at stake, but
that of the entire personnel of the ranch."

Getting up, she walked to the door and gazed at the acres
to which she had dedicated her youth, strength and effort.
When she turned, her face held a special light. "If we get it
through Pam being crippled, I still won't believe that she'll be
that way always. In the meantime, Emily, you've given us a
ray of hope to keep Christmas the beautiful thing it has always
been on the ranch."

A golden radiance filled the dusty Office that made canned
goods on shelves and sacks of flour and coffee on the floor dear
and beautiful. Grandfather got to his feet and his figure didn't

sag any more. It looked vital and full of strength, courage and hope.

"I'm happy again!" he exulted. "Happy as we all used to be before that blighter Kingsley's letter came and Pam was hurt. It's a fine thing, happiness. It makes you feel like a god. Rich and boundless, and you want to pour your abundance over the earth and your fellows."

Kulani's eyes brimmed, and spilled over.

"Oh, Mother—" Emily gasped.

"It's fine! Don't mind me. As the Hawaiian say in moments of great joy, 'My happy too big for me to hold!' " Her voice shook.

"We should do some very special thing to celebrate!" Grandfather boomed. "Come Inspiration-Emily, what'll it be?"

"I know one thing that'll make Pam happy," Emily spoke so fast the words tumbled over each other. "She's aching to see Malolo, to get her hands on him. Would it be very bad to take her into the garden?"

"She mustn't be moved more than is absolutely necessary but we can take the horse in to her, right now!" Kulani cried excitedly.

"Into the house?" Emily asked, as if she were not hearing right.

"Why not? Malolo's been taken onto ships, into trucks. It'll be a bit tricky. Why haven't we thought of this before? Run and tell Pam to freshen up, as she's going to have a very special caller. Only don't give away who—"

"I wouldn't for anything!" Emily cried.

"But who is it?" Pam kept asking, as Emily helped Miss Williams to comb out her curls and put a fresh *lei* around her neck.

"You'd never guess if you tried for a year!" Emily retorted, her cheeks a fiery-rose with excitement.

Hoofs sounded on the grass at the side door, there was a slight commotion, soothing voices. The door opened and Malolo, his eyes almost bulging out of his head, stood quivering and snuffing at strange objects he had never seen—chairs, bureaus, a towering bed. Opiopio had hold of one ring of his snaffle, Kulani grasped the other. No one breathed as they gently led the great, shining horse to the bed. Pam tried to speak but emotion choked her then she managed to whisper in a small, ghostly voice, "Malolo!"

The horse's ears, keener than human ones, heard and pricked up eagerly. He snuffed, caught her familiar scent, and reached out his head. Hungrily, her little fingers, starved for contact with the glorious animal she loved, went over the beautiful sweep of his jaw, slid down his velvety muzzle.

Miss Williams walked to the window, Tatsu, Kane, Ah Sam and Grandfather, who were crowded in the doorway, wiped wet eyes. Pam made soft, loving sounds and the magnificent thoroughbred nickered softly.

"Oh, Mother, how did you know I wanted to see him so badly?" Pam asked, after Malolo was, finally, led away.

"Emily told me."

Pam's eyes jumped to Emily's with a wild question in their depths. Emily shook her head, just enough so that Pam and no one else saw. "I didn't tell the rest," her eyes said, and Pam relaxed happily.

"Can he come in every day?" she asked dreamily.

"Of course."

"I'm brimful of happiness, Mother!"

"Me, too," Grandfather boomed. "And I have more good news that'll make us brimmer-ful of joy. While you were getting Malolo ready to bring in here, Kulani, Doctor Clemens wired from Honolulu. Doctor Van Dyke, the foremost spine specialist in America, arrives by Clipper from the mainland in a few days. He's coming to Hawaii for a rest but we'll have him over here if I have to shanghai him."

"Oh, *Father!*" Kulani cried. "If he won't come, we'll take Pam to him, even if it means foregoing Christmas."

"I've a better idea than that," Grandfather announced. "Let's invite the great man over here to sample a real Hawaiian Christmas, the kind that's only held on the outside Islands. He can rest, see something the average tourist never gets a chance to, and study Pam's case at the same time."

"Splendid!" Kulani agreed, her face like a rose. "I'll write him immediately."

"But Mother," Pam protested, "if he cures me, Mr. Kingsley—"

"Darling, your health comes before everything and as your Mother it's my duty not to let this opportunity slip through my hands."

Pam said no more but her eyes stole to Emily's, commanding her to remain after the others had gone. When the room was empty, Pam beckoned her over, a great resolution in her young face.

"You'll have to help to fix things, Emily, so I can talk to Dr. Van Dyke *alone!* Isn't it funny how quickly things change? A while ago I'd have been wild with hope that I could be cured. Now I'm terrified that I will be!"

CHAPTER XVII

CHRISTMAS

"Emily should be here with the mail. It's almost one."
Kulani tried to control the slight unsteadiness in her voice.

"Pili's probably been visiting his friends all along the line."
Getting up from the grain bags which he loved to sit on,
Grandfather went over to the desk and laid his hand on Kulani's

shoulder. "I know we'll hear from Van Dyke today, dear. A man of his caliber, even on a holiday, has a deep sense of responsibility toward his profession, which would make it impossible for him to refuse to give medical aid where it's needed. Moreover, cases that baffle other doctors are always a challenge to someone who is tops in some specific line." Grandfather's voice shook slightly and he cleared his throat impatiently.

"I'm hoping he'll agree to come here for Christmas, instead of having to take Pam to Honolulu," Kulani said. "If he wants us to do that it will mean we will have to forego our usual celebration, which would be a tragedy, since it may be our last."

"My dear, keep a high heart," Grandfather said. "I know what you're thinking—"

"It can't, it shan't be!" Kulani said fiercely. "Oh, Father, it's all such a tangle again. For an hour, before Doctor Clements' radio came, I felt confident that we had something that would put Kingsley on the run. No man except an ogre, as Emily expressed it, could send a sick child from the home she adores. But no mother, who's a real mother, can leave any stone unturned when her child's health and future are at stake—as Pam's is."

Grandfather nodded.

"I feel like a squirrel trapped in a cage," Kulani said. "Spinning madly around on a wheel that gets nowhere. For months the same thoughts, the same problems have whirled through my mind. In the beginning the problem was simple—how to hold this place. Now it's worse. My daughter's interests—or my people's. If Pam's cured—"

"We lose our main weapon to hold Kilohana," Grandfather finished, when Kulani did not go on.

Kulani nodded. A ray of sunlight slanted through the Office window, lighting her tense profile. She was the spirit of the acres she loved as she sat there, in her riding breeches and saddle-worn boots.

Bending down, Grandfather kissed her valiant forehead. "I think, my dear, the time has come for us to stop trying to manage this situation and hand it over to God to work out for us—"

The words hung in the air.

"You're right, Father," Kulani agreed.

"That doesn't mean sitting down on the job. We must listen with our mind for guidance, so to speak, then obey orders without question." The old man's voice rang with wisdom gathered from seventy years of living.

Kulani gripped his hand. Walking to the door, they stood shoulder to shoulder gazing at the beauty of the universe: the sun moving across the azure arch of the sky, the splendid, fruitful island, and the sea forever ebbing and flowing with unvarying rhythm, obeying the command which set it in motion when the world began. . . . The courage and faith which had almost slipped from them returned and the love they had shared all their lives wrapped them like a glittering cloak dropped over them by some invisible hand.

Grandfather turned his head slightly. "Emily's coming," he announced.

Kulani listened. She heard nothing, but did not question,

for she knew how keen blind people's ears are. The turmoil which had filled her for so long, vanished, and was replaced by a deep peace.

"There's a letter from Doctor Van Dyke," Emily called when she rode up, and she whirled the leather mail bag around her head.

When Kulani had read it, she looked up. "He's coming over, Father," she said breathlessly. "He says he's enchanted at having the opportunity to experience an Island Christmas, and after seeing Pam's case history, which Doctor Clements gave him, he feels convinced that something can be done to cure her! Oh, Father—"

"When will he get here?" Grandfather asked.

"He's resting for a week and will arrive the morning of December twenty-fourth."

"We'd better start getting things in shape for Christmas at once then! It's just eight days away."

"Shall I tell Pam, or would you rather, Kulani From Heaven?" Emily asked excitedly.

"I will, darling."

When Pam heard the news she smiled in a quiet fashion. Kulani told her what Grandfather had said about handing over their problems to a mightier Mind than human ones. Pam nodded but the expression in her eyes did not change.

"You don't seem to understand, Mother," she said. "I wouldn't mind staying like this if it means we can keep Kilohana. But, of course, if I could have both, be well, and stay here—"

"That's the point, exactly. Both can be, *if* we have enough faith. Life's like a great Persian rug. Sometimes the pattern's so intricate you can't see the design, until it's all finished. The millions of knots and colors that are woven into the rug seem confusing and crazy, but the weaver knows what he's about. If a thread tangles, he stops and straightens it out, then goes on his way serenely. Two of the threads in our beautiful set-up here are knotted, but that doesn't mean they have to *stay that way!*"

"Oh, Kulani From Heaven, I see what you mean!"

"Then let's make up our minds that this will be the happiest and loveliest Christmas we've ever had, one that will stand out all our lives."

"Bet-you-my-life, Mother," Pam cried in ringing tones, but a wistful expression crept into her eyes. Last year she had ridden up Hualalai to select the Christmas tree. . . . Last year she had gone with the *paniolos* to shoot wild hogs and turkeys. . . . Then her little face set in resolute lines. She mustn't spoil other people's happiness just because she could not take her usual active part in the Christmas preparations.

That evening when the *paniolos* came home, Kulani told them that Doctor Van Dyke was coming, and explained who he was and what he hoped to do. Japanese *Banzied-ed*, Hawaiians threw their hats into the air and yelled, "*Welakahao!*" Then in a body they hurried to Pam's room.

"Ha! Soon you be well again—and sassy like before," Na-lua-hine announced.

Nuhi walked around the room on his hands, kicking absurdly

with his big legs, sending everyone into gales of laughter.

"Well, better us all go finish up the work and tomorrow start to make hot-style *Kalikamaka!*" Kimmo said.

"What's that funny word?" Emily asked, from where she perched on the edge of Pam's bed.

"It's Hawaiian for Christmas."

"Hey, Em'ly, you say!" Kane ordered, his eyes twinkling for the first time for months.

She said it without a stumble.

"Joke on *you* this time, Kane," the men chorused.

"Bet-you-my-life!" the old man agreed. "Emily smart for speak Hawaiian now!"

Next morning the ranch had a new air of bustle and expectancy. Japanese began concocting *Mochi*, a kind of rice cake only eaten during the holiday week of the year. Emily watched them putting rice kernels in a big hollowed-out tree trunk; then in turn men and women beat them with great wooden flails until they had a powder-fine flour. When at last this reached the right consistency, it was moistened with water and patted into balls that looked like round, pale cakes of soap. Next a finger deftly inserted into the center of each one a black, sticky bean paste. Then the cakes were stacked in tin washtubs, covered with clean cloths and put away to heat on Christmas morning.

Emily wished she were triplets, instead of one person, there were so many exciting things going on at once. The two Portuguese teamsters' wives were baking huge round yellow loaves of bread, a yard across, with whole hard-boiled eggs inside them. Then they made black pork sausage, like policemen's clubs, out of wild boar meat.

Ah Sam was mixing up plum puddings and Christmas cakes. Hawaiian women were mixing *kulolo* and *hau-pai*. *Hau-pai*, made from a starchy root and sweetened with coconut cream, had the consistency of gelatine when it was finished, and tasted like divinity fudge crossed with coconut! *Kulolo*, made from sweet potatoes and shredded coconut, baked underground, looked like great yellowish-brown plum puddings and tasted vaguely like caramels.

Enticing smells filled the air; spurred men rode off with strings of pack animals and returned with the plunder of the forest: wild turkeys, sheep and hogs. Fun, the bustle of preparation, filled the atmosphere from dawn long into the night.

Relatives and friends of the *paniolos* began to arrive. White-haired *Tutus*—Grandparents, with eyes as bright and eager as children's set in their wrinkled faces. Large, kindly women and deliberate, nobly built men, moving like slow bronze gods. Slim young girls, graceful as fawns; lusty young boys, who strummed guitars all day long; and children who went skittering around, their legs looking mischievous and gay.

Then the Japanese contingent began appearing; neat Mama-sans in spotless kimonos, with their littlest babies strapped on their backs. Papa-sans in uncomfortable store suits and straw hats. Boy-sans and girl-sans, with black hair cut straight across their foreheads and bright, slanted eyes. When they met relatives and friends there were endless bows, inhalings of breath and polite exchanges of greetings in Japanese.

"But, Kulani From Heaven, are *all* these people going to be here for the tree?" Emily asked, amazed. "There must be over a hundred—counting ourselves!"

"About a hundred and seventy are here every year, Emily, including the dozen or so relatives who come to Kilohana, too."

"Whew!" Emily gasped. "Christmas in Boston was never like this!"

"Nor anywhere else in the world—quite," Kulani smiled. "Wait till you see the whole thing to the end. It's—something!" Her voice rang with happy pride.

"What are you going to do with all the food these people have brought you? It's piled in the Office, on the porch, and in the garden. There are bunches and bunches of bananas, heaps of coconuts, gunny-sacks of *kulolo*, pigs, chickens, rice cakes and who knows what else. Everyone came loaded. Wait till you see!"

Kulani tousled Emily's hair. "Yes, everyone brings the best he has. And everything will be eaten, honey. The tree is held Christmas Eve and on Christmas Day there's a *luau*. How would you like to ride up the mountain with me tomorrow to get a sandalwood log to burn in the fire Christmas Eve?"

"A sandalwood log!" Emily cried. "My Hawaiian history says that all the sandalwood trees were cut down in the early 1800's—"

"There are a few scattered groves left still, which are cherished and guarded by people lucky enough to have them on their land."

Next morning Kulani, Emily and three of the *paniolos* set off to collect the Hawaiian "yule-log." The quiet forests rang with the laughter of Nuhi, Pia and Na-lua-hine. With the bringing down of the sandalwood log, the Christmas season was formally ushered in. Emily was intrigued because without the snow and the roaring fires that she had always known at this time of year, the atmosphere was so charged with the spirit of Christmas. It was in the air, in people's faces, singing in their hearts. . . . "If only Pam was with us it would be super-perfect," Emily said. "Sure!" the *paniolos* agreed. "But next year she come, too."

A short distance below the summit of Hualalai, Kulani halted in a small grove of the precious, fragrant trees, overlooked by the men who had robbed the Hawaiian forests long ago. A log about three feet long and ten inches in diameter was cut from a fallen tree and placed in the cross-pieces of a pack-saddle. After it was lashed on, they started down the mountain. Lower, on the forested slopes, the men halted and wove green wreaths of fragrant *maile* leaves, then draped the sandalwood log with them. Remounting their horses, they rode homeward, singing hulas that drifted away to become part of the beauty of the day.

Next morning, two fat heifers were killed and divided equally among the workmen's families. Pack trains of mules, which had been sent off to distant valleys, returned with additional supplies of *poi* and sweet potatoes. Each family must have all it could possibly eat between December twenty-fourth and January first, to insure abundance during the coming year.

The day before Christmas Eve, a small ox-wagon, drawn by six yoke of sturdy oxen, went bumping up the mountain for the Christmas tree. At the seven thousand foot level, where frost cracked the ground and occasional snow fell, Kulani had planted a grove of fir and spruce trees. Each year one was cut down and another planted to replace it.

Emily watched the tree fall, but it seemed to feel no sorrow as it laid its green head against the earth. When it was set up in Pam's room the next day the final splash of splendor seemed to spring into life. Brawny *paniolos* carried it in reverently, and placed it in a corner. With great arguments, punctured by explosions of laughter, they finally agreed upon the exact position. Green branches stood out like graceful arms and its tip just touched the ceiling.

"There, how you tink that look?" Na-lua-hine asked, turning to Pam, watching from her bed.

"It's beautiful. I don't believe we've ever had a prettier tree," Pam said gallantly, but tears lay like ghosts behind the words, as she silently wondered if she would ever ride up the mountain again to see a Christmas tree cut down.

"S'pose you tink Okay I go call Kulani for start, then Ah Sam and us fellas and Tatsu finish and put on everykind," Nuhi suggested. "This year Kulani tell to us she no can fix because she and Kaiko go Kohala for meet the *Kauka-Akamai*—Smart Doctor. Bet he have his eye knock-out when he see this tree tonight!"

"Bet he will, Nuhi," Pam said.

Kulani came in, climbed up a ladder two of the men held for her, and Grandfather handed her a silver star, which she placed on the highest tip. To the left she hung a colored picture of the Three Wise Men and to the right a picture of the Holy Child in His manger. Then she climbed down, kissed Pam good-bye and she and Grandfather left for Kohala to meet the plane bringing Doctor Van Dyke.

Ah Sam, Tatsu, Emily, and a half dozen *paniolos* who were not busy with outdoor preparations, finished the decorating. Glittering yards of tinsel, bright ornaments, transparent bags of hard candy were hung in the boughs and gifts stacked for yards around the base. House and gardens spilled over with activity. Hawaiians swarmed in carrying yards and yards of fragrant green *maile* vines to drape door, rafters and windows. Ranch workers and their visiting relatives poured in, looking pleased and important as they added their gifts to those already heaped about the base of the tree. Hawaiian girls trouped in, with arms laden with carnation *leis* like red feather boas to add the last rich, exotic touch to its beauty. House-boys scurried around, placing bowls of shiny red apples, bananas and nuts on convenient tables, throughout the house. The fire was laid, the sandalwood log placed carefully upon it. Suddenly the house, the island, the whole world smelled of Christmas. . . .

As the afternoon wore on the atmosphere of wonder-in-waiting mounted steadily. Rich aromas drifted from the kitchen, turkeys and pheasants roasting, plum puddings boiling noisily. Tatsu and the house-boys spread the table with the finest linen, silver and glass. Flowers were heaped in the center and a *lei* draped on each chair for the guests to put on when they sat down. Emily kept scooting in and out of Pam's room, dithery with excitement. "If only you were up, it would be perfect!" she cried.

"I know it all by heart, Emily. Each sound and smell tells me what's happening," Pam said, trying to make her voice bright.

Kane came in, carrying a transparent strip of banana bark, like a cool, green cylinder. Inside lay a twelve-strand *lei* of jasmine flowers, like carved ivory and pearls. "For you, my *keiki*," he said solemnly. "I make for you with my own hands."

"Oh, Kane!" Pam cried. "How beautiful!"

"Soon you ride again with me, Pam," the old man said, wiping happy tears from his eyes. "Swell, this doctor coming—"

There was a sound of wheels driving into the garden. "Put on your *lei*," Kane ordered. "When he see you I-bet-you-my-life this doctor guy thinking, 'Never I see one small girl nice like this Pam,' and he fix you up quick."

Gently he helped her to put on the flowers, then stepped back to get the effect. "Your face beautiful like *Wanaao*—The Ghost Dawn—when it come out of the darkness into the sky."

Pam put out her hand. "Stay with me, Kane. I want you around when the doctor comes."

"You scare maybe too much hurt before you getting well?" Kane asked in concern, noting an odd inflection in her voice.

"No, but I like to have you near when big things are on their way toward me."

Kane kissed her hand gratefully. "That sound swell to my heart." Smile wrinkles gathered up the outer corners of his eyes. "Even when you got fifty year, you still my baby," he said, and drawing up a chair, seated himself by the bed.

The door opened and Kulani entered, followed by a very tall man in an expensive gray flannel suit. He was graceful, in spite of his length of limb. His movements were deliberate, as though he possessed all eternity to use, but people felt instinctively that his leisurely manner was not laziness but an immense, untroubled serenity. His fine, intelligent face seemed longer than it actually was, because of a becoming baldness and when he smiled it was as though the inner man lighted up with a warm impulse of liking for his fellows.

An amazed and delighted expression flitted over his face when he saw the old brown man seated beside a small girl in bed, whose face was framed with flowers.

"Before anything else," Doctor Van Dyke remarked in a low, deep-toned voice, "I want to thank you, Pam, for giving me this chance to come to such a beautiful place. Hawaii, Kilohana—it that how you pronounce it? It's simply—incredible."

Pam beamed. "*Aloha*—my love to you, Doctor Van Dyke," she said.

"*Aloha*—my love to you," Kane echoed, stepping back, as though effacing himself.

"What a beautiful way to greet a stranger," the doctor remarked, glancing over his shoulder at Kulani. "How different from the casual 'Hello' of America or the formal 'How do you do?' "

"Doctor, this is Kane—my *paniolo*," Pam said, gesturing at Kane.

The doctor smiled at the lovable old fellow but his eyes had a slightly puzzled expression. Kulani explained and Doctor

Van Dyke murmured. "Beautiful, and somehow in keeping with everything else here."

He looked at the Christmas tree, glanced out at the gardens seething with people, listened to gusts of music coming from the corrals, then he breathed deeply. "Christmas is in the air—with a spirit. Christmas—in Paradise! I never dreamed I'd sample it—on earth!"

He had the magical gift of making people love him instantly, of making them feel richer and happier simply because he was there. Pam put out her hand shyly and he took it with his long, expressive fingers, fingers which were expert in driving out pain and steadying fear. Fingers that matched the mind that worked unceasingly for the betterment of mankind.

"Thank you for coming," Pam said. "If you hadn't, Mother would have had to take me to Honolulu and it would have spoiled Christmas for us and our people." She motioned toward the knots of adults and children drifting happily across the lawn.

"If I had missed this experience, I would have felt cheated all my life," Doctor Van Dyke said. "But I'm a fortunate person and it was on the books that I couldn't."

Kane glanced at him and murmured something in Hawaiian. Doctor Van Dyke looked at Kulani.

"Pam's *paniolo* is giving you a wish in Hawaiian, the richest one in the language of his people. He says 'May ripe breadfruit load the trees lining all the roads you travel.' In other words 'May abundance be the lot of your days.' "

"Thank you, Kane," the doctor said, his brown eyes lighting

up. "Tomorrow we'll come down to earth, Pam, and get acquainted and see what's to be done so you can get back the fullness of your life. Tonight let's just enjoy—Christmas."

"Oh, Doctor, how did you know I wanted it that way?" Pam asked, her cheeks glowing.

"A fairy told me, maybe, or because I want it that way, too."

Christmas seemed to bound joyously into the air, like a colt overflowing with life and glee. The happy shouts of children chasing each other in the garden came through the windows; singing, laughter and the ancient, un-ending song of the sea.

"I think," Kulani suggested, "it's time we all dressed for dinner. The sooner it's over the sooner the real fun begins for everyone."

When she went off to show the doctor his room, Pam turned to Kane, but before she could speak, he did. "*Keiki*—Child, never I see one fella more swell from this guy. He no a man, he a great *Alii*—Chief." He could not go on.

Pam nodded. She had the same impression. He wasn't just a person but a mighty personage from some distant planet who was temporarily visiting the earth. His presence lent Christmas an added flavor, placed it above all the other Christmases which had high-lighted the happy years which had marched over Kilohana. . . .

Dinner was just another rung up the ladder of fun. As soon as it was over, everyone came into Pam's room to drink coffee. Kulani, in a beautiful evening gown of frost-blue satin with a *lei* of shell-pink carnations about her neck, looked impossibly lovely. Grandfather, in evening dress, resembled a visiting duke.

Emily, in ruffled organdie, was an old-fashioned cameo-girl, with a quaint little face rising above a circle of white gardenias and the tall doctor was a visiting celebrity from some far-off shining place. . . .

Doctor Van seated himself in the chair beside Pam, facing the tree. Pam waited with held breath for the moment when Christmas would spring full-fledged into the night. Suddenly she heard the sound she longed for: spurs ringing, horses' hoofs, men singing. The great shouting Kilohana hula was bursting from strong brown throats as the *paniolos*, mounted on their best horses, rode up under the windows, pledging their love and allegiance to the family, and to the great mountain on which they all lived.

When the stirring song died away, Kulani walked to the door. "*Aloha*, Merry Christmas!" she called and was answered with the same words.

The men tied up their horses and came in, hugging great brown guitars. On their heels came their womenfolk, carrying the newest, little babies. After them came grandfathers, grandmothers, grandchildren and all the betweens. Japanese, Hawaiian, Portuguese, Chinese and all the criss-crossings. . . . Kulani, Grandfather, and Emily greeted each in turn; then they found chairs or couches, and the overflow sat down cross-legged on the floor.

Ah Sam, his mummy-face cracked by a grin, came in importantly with a lighted candle tied to the end of a long bamboo pole. Gravely and in silence, he lighted the tree. Kulani went to a small piano and struck the opening chords of "Little

Town of Bethlehem." The old, moving words were sung by everyone and went floating away into the deep blue night like the music from a great organ. The house-boys lighted the living-room fire and the fragrance of sandalwood floated in, mingling with the smell of burning candles. When the last verse of the song ended, everyone shouted again. "*Aloha, Aloha*—Merry Christmas!"

Then Kulani, Emily, old Ah Sam and Tatsu began handing out presents, interspersed with speeches, chants and hulas. *Paniolos* exulted over bolts of sturdy dungaree which their wives would later make into riding breeches. Women squealed over yards of bright material for future *holokus*. Young girls slipped on shining bracelets and ear-rings for their admirers to exclaim over. Young bloods exhibited gay bandanas and noisy neckties. Children played excitedly with new toys, rolled oranges across the floor. Babies slept happily on grandmothers' laps, under the shelter of new shawls provided to keep old shoulders warm, and grandfathers sucked on new pipes and admired their glossy beauty.

When the last gift was given out, the house-boys began making rounds with refreshments: cake, candy, lemonade, nuts, fruit. Then the night caught its breath again. More hoofs approaching, more ringing spurs and singing. The first group of visiting serenaders from neighboring ranches was arriving to swell the steadily increasing richness of the evening. After they had been welcomed, competitive singing began.

Pam watched from her bed, and Doctor Van sat looking on as if he were trying to remember for always every shade and incident of the evening.

After the singing was over, dancing began. Japanese Mama-sans unstrapped sleeping babies from their backs and laid them in the nearest arms. Then going on to the floor, they did the stiff, butterfly-dances of their land. Hawaiian girls did hulas, as graceful as bamboo trees swaying in the wind. All difference of color, station and race was wiped out. The garland-draped roof sheltered members of the great human family, gathered into a unit to celebrate a day holy to all mankind.

Emily came over and stood beside Pam's bed, near the watchful doctor whose eyes missed nothing. "Oh, Pam," Emily said, "I'll never forget my first Christmas in Hawaii!"

"In Hawaii, child?" Doctor Van smiled gently. "This is Christmas in *Paradise*. The first *real* Christmas I've ever known in my life."

When dawn broke families began assembling, calling out "*Aloha, Aloha*—my love to you. Merry Christmas! See you at the *luau*—"

Paniolos gathered up their instruments, took their leave and the Birthday of all birthdays was carried to a triumphant dawning by singing horsemen riding off into the light pouring its splendor out of the east.

CHAPTER XVIII

A LAST EFFORT

DOCTOR VAN NOT ONLY STAYED FOR CHRISTMAS BUT RE-
mained over New Year. For the first time in his life he had
run into something which absorbed him as deeply as his profession. He spent hours with Pam every day, talking to her and
getting to know her, and through her, Hawaii. When he was
not at her bedside, he wandered about the grounds, fascinated
by the mighty ebb and flow of ranch life.

"After being here, I realize how badly you must want to be in the thick of it again, Pam," he said one afternoon. "This is like a mighty drama, with different races for actors playing their parts. Your wonderful mother is the heroine—"

Pam nodded.

"Getting you well may be a long business, Pam. First you'll have to go with me to Honolulu for more X-rays, consultations. . . . You know the routine?"

Pam nodded.

"And then," Doctor Van's eyes grew thoughtful, "if the cause of your paralysis can't be located, I'll have to take you East with me for further study and treatments. It may take a year, or two, or it may only be a matter of a few weeks or months."

Pam made no reply. Her eyes hung on the doctor's, as though she were turning some matter over and over in her mind, then her hand stole out and found his.

"Doctor Van, would it make much difference in my getting well—if it was put off for a bit? Eight months or a year?"

"That's impossible to tell until the new X-rays have been taken. As well, I have to leave in three weeks. Being a doctor with a big practice, I have many responsibilities that I can't shirk. My life's not my own, it belongs to the people who have trusted their lives and health to me—"

"I understand," Pam broke in. "It may sound silly, but in a way I'm in the same fix. You see—"

She told him about Kingsley and he listened without comment to the end. "So that's it," he remarked. "That's why you don't want to be cured until you know you have Kilohana safe for the people who live on it and love it."

"Oh," Pam exclaimed, with a rush of gratitude, "I was afraid you might think I was crazy, but you do understand!"

"If I hadn't visited here, I would have thought it a fantastic gesture for a child of your years to feel as you do. As it is, I understand perfectly how you feel. Here it isn't the individual that matters, it's the whole. Suppose we leave it this way. You come to Honolulu with me and we'll try to locate the cause of your trouble. When we have, it will be time enough to decide whether it's imperative to have immediate treatments, such as can only be given with the equipment I have in the East, or if we can let things ride until you have your beloved acres safe."

"Doctor Van, would you count me as a special friend?" Pam asked.

"I'm honored that you want me to be," the great man said. "From all accounts and personal observations you're a rare little person." Pam flushed with pleasure. He patted her hand. "As long as I live I'll never forget my feelings when I saw you for the first time."

"Why?"

"I'd never seen anyone wearing garlands around her neck— in bed!" Doctor Van chuckled. "And your *paniolo*-nurse— simply slew me!" His nice face wrinkled up with fun. "It was so incongruous. His spurs, his faded riding clothes, his lasso lying on the floor. It was—epic! The picture is inked indelibly on my mind."

Pam smiled and they chatted for a while. When Kulani came in Doctor Van rose. "It's all settled, Kulani From Heaven," he said in his low, resonant voice. "You and Pam will go to Honolulu with me in two days. We'll plan from there whether Pam remains in Honolulu for treatments, goes East with me, or returns here."

Kulani glanced at him in an odd way.

"You see, Pam told me how things stand with the ranch at present and she's agreed to let me decide which course to follow—"

"Oh, Pam," Kulani said in a quick way, "you—"

"Mother, Doctor Van's part of our family now," she protested. "Don't you feel it?"

"Yes," she agreed.

"Even when I'm thousands of miles from here, a part of me will remain at Kilohana," Doctor Van announced. "It has sunk in deep, the ranch—all of you. Ah Sam, Tatsu, the *paniolos*. . . . Your way of living is so very different from my life in the East that it will seem as if it were all some gorgeous dream that couldn't be real. But I'll know it *is* real. That it actually exists. When life, and people, behave outrageously, or sickeningly, as they often do, my spirit will slip away to Kilohana to be comforted."

Two days later they flew to Honolulu, leaving Grandfather and Emily in charge of the ranch. The old routine began again, rounds of X-rays, consultations, examinations, tests. . . . One evening Doctor Van came to visit in Pam's room, after dinner and when it was time for visitors to leave, Doctor Van offered to drive Kulani home.

"How did you know I wanted it?" she asked, as the car rolled out toward Waikiki, where she was staying with relatives.

"Because I wanted it, too, perhaps," he smiled. "The sterilized atmosphere of a hospital has a way of reducing life to a sort of medical formula that leaves the main issues out in the cold."

"Have you found any clue as to what's wrong?"

"No, Pam's is as baffling a case as I've ever run into. I leave for New York in three days and want to decide with you whether or not you feel Pam should go with me now, or if you would prefer to follow with her later."

Kulani looked at the purple ocean sleeping under the stars, then she gripped Doctor Van Dyke's arm.

"Van," she said, "the ranch is to all purposes—gone. Kingsley has written saying he will be here in September to take possession."

"In spite of knowing—" Doctor Van began indignantly.

"Yes, in spite of knowing how Pam is. He points out the fact that he is in no way responsible for her being crippled and not obligated to alter the course of his life when we can, as easily, alter ours. His decision is final. Now the question is—what about Pam? Should she be told? Would it be better to send her East without knowing? Oh, Van—" She broke off and took a hurried breath. "You see, I'll have to be present when he takes possession. My poor people! How can I break the news to them! Oh, my poor little girl—"

Her eyes were dry and unnaturally brilliant but there were ghostly tears behind her words.

Doctor Van stopped the car beside a beach. "Kulani From Heaven," he said, as quietly as he could, "there's no immediate reason for Pam to go East. Having sampled Kilohana, if she were my child, I'd take her back and let her have all of it she can, while it lasts. Keep her from knowing what's in the wind until the time is ripe for her and the ranch to be told. It will be an awful blow—for everyone. I can't picture the place with some cold trout of a millionaire in possession and all of you colorful, splendid people gone!"

Kulani stared out to sea.

"Probably you're thinking I'm an odd sort of fellow to be a spine-specialist. My brother professionals think I'm a bit odd! But I see more than the face of things only. I've met so-called great people with poor, mangy little souls, and I've met humble persons who had a splash of splendor in them. It isn't what a man has done, but what he *is*, that matters—"

Kulani gave a quick assenting nod.

"You embody the name the Hawaiians gave you, From Heaven. The world may never hear of you in a big way. But life will remember you when you've gone. You've never let it down and I don't believe it will let you down. I may sound foolish when I say this but I know some miracle will keep Kilohana for you."

"Oh, Van, you're such a comfort. I know you wouldn't suggest my taking Pam home if you felt it might be risky—"

"Of course not. Hers is an arrested case—of some sort. Similar to that of the blind Anzac soldier, known to everyone some years ago. He came out of some battle, unwounded, but stone blind. Apparently there was no reason for his being the way he was. Doctors in most of the leading countries of the world studied his case, trying to discover the cause of his blindness, without success. Then one day he tripped going down a flight of steps and the slight jar gave him back his sight instantly. Some unforeseen trifle may do the trick for Pam. If no improvement takes place by the time you leave Kilohana, bring her to me. I've a friend in Baltimore whom I've worked with before. I'll get him on the job with me—"

"Thank you for the hope, Van. Thank you for—everything. I can never repay you for what you've done, and been, to all of us. I can never tell you, never prove, how deeply we all love you—"

"Kulani From Heaven, one of these days I shall retire from the active field of medicine to do research work. If you're still free, if you still feel the way you do now—" He broke off, then said. "Look in my eyes."

"I see what you're trying to tell me, Van. I'll be waiting. Always. All of us . . . wherever we are."

When Kulani and Pam returned to Kilohana, life resumed its old course. Days came and went swiftly. The stirring winter of the subtropics travelled its appointed course, storms and rains alternating with periods of dazzling splendor. Spring leaped into life upon the hills and the days were musical with the cry of new-born calves and the thin whinnying of colts. The

Trade Wind returned, tempering nights and days to an even warmth. Each day, for two hours in the afternoon, Kane wheeled Pam around the gardens, corrals and up to the Office. Although the ranch people were disappointed because she had not returned from Honolulu completely cured, having her among them, even the way she was, gave the impression that she was progressing.

"Make me mad like any-kind you get well so slow," Nuhi remarked one afternoon, "but I bet-you-my-life when Christmas come again you be riding with us."

"It makes me wild, knowing I can't ride in the races this Fourth of July," Pam said. "It's only three weeks away."

"Kulani say no send any horses from Kilohana to Maui this year, no fun for enny man if you no can go."

"But we'll lose the Free For All cup!"

"So what? Sure us win again next year. If no have for little time, more fun when us get again," Nuhi insisted.

"Maybe you're right, but the piano will look queer without it!" Pam protested.

That night, after the household had retired, Kulani and Grandfather sat up talking. "I've got to tell them before much longer, Father. Kingsley's due to arrive about the first of September. That's only three months away—"

Getting up, Grandfather walked to the door and looked across the island whose shape was printed on his memory. It seemed empty of life, in spite of the teeming life about him, and still as some dead, splendid star. Taking a fortifying breath, he turned back to where Kulani sat like a graven image in a deep chair.

"Suppose," Grandfather suggested, "that we let things ride until the first of August. That will give six more weeks of happiness and leave enough time for adjustment to the new order of life. I'm wondering if Kingsley is wise in wanting to stay here before we go. He's within his rights and the laws of decency make it impossible for us to refuse to have him here to 'learn the ropes of ranching,' as he expresses it. But I'd hate to be in his shoes, enduring the dislike he'll be held in by everyone here."

Kulani gripped the arms of her chair. "I shall feel like an executioner when I tell them. As Abraham must have felt when he was commanded by the Lord to kill his son—"

"But just as he was lifting his hand," Grandfather reminded her, "he saw the Lamb and the Burning Bush."

Kulani rose and walked over to her father. "You shame me with your faith," she said. "And at the same time give me strength to do what I have to—when the time comes."

The six weeks slid by with staggering rapidity. "I shall tell them today," Kulani said to Grandfather. "It's Saturday and they all will be in to get their wages."

Grandfather shivered, recoiling unhappily from the mental picture. When he could command his voice, he said, "When a thing must be done—it must be done!"

As usual on Saturday afternoons, the ranch workers gathered in and around the Office, laughing, overflowing with good nature and fun. Pam sat in her wheelchair, the center of everything. Nuhi clowned and Na-lua-hine exchanged rib-nudging jokes with everyone. When the last man had been paid, Kulani held up her hand. "I have something to tell you all, today—"

Pam darted a quick look at her mother's face, but it told her nothing. Emily, who had been playing with Poi, put him out of her lap. For an instant Kulani was afraid that her courage would fail her completely, then she felt the great up-well of strength that comes flowing into people in times of stress.

"People of Kilohana, I have a difficult task to do and I am counting on you to help me—"

"Sure, sure, Kulani," everyone agreed cheerily. Then for some reason a solemn hush fell.

In a steady, even voice, Kulani told them. When she finished the afternoon crashed to a stop. Appalled expressions flitted over faces, men gestured in an overstrung, outraged way. Pam sat shaking in her chair and Emily hid her face in her hands. Then a great angry muttering broke out.

"No can do this kind! No can make this kind! This *haole lapuwale*—trashy whiteman—if that guy come here I rope and drag him behind my horse till he run away and never come back enny more!" Nuhi bellowed.

"You never get chance, I rope him first," Pili roared.

Kulani sighed commandingly. "You cannot do those things!" she cried in ringing tones. "Else you will shame me and yourselves forever in Hawaii. If the song of Kilohana is sung—let it be beautiful and majestic to the end!"

There was a stunned silence, then troubled mutterings. Finally Na-lua-hine stepped forward. "Kulani, you are right.

But *Auwe*—woe is me," his voice rose into the great cry of despair of his people, then he angrily shook the tears from his eyes. "*Auwe*—that Kilohana go from us who love it! But Kilohana *not lose yet! I* got hot-style idea!" His eyes glittered. "Maybe if all us mans get together and write this *haole* letters, make shame-his-eye and he break down and change his mind—"

"Yes—yes—us all write," the men cried.

"I've written hundreds of letters. He won't be moved," Kulani said in an overstrung way.

"No matter. Us try, too. Pam help us!"

Pam's face looked like a small white wedge. She tried to speak but couldn't, so signed that she was with them.

"Too bad this no like olden times. Before mans fight and kill fellas who try to take their land," old Kane said with unexpected and almost shocking violence. His gentle face was stern and savage, his eyes glittering. "Now—just give up. What-for that guy like come here? What-for he like us go away? He no got Kilohana in his heart. What he do if us all just sit down and no go away?"

"He'd import the law to remove us," Kulani said flatly.

Na-lua-hine consulted with his mates in undertones and Kulani waited. When the hurried council ended the some-time clown of Kilohana assumed the role of spokesman again. "Us fellas think best, Kulani, we do like I saying. Write plenty letters for save this place. Tonight us write, and Pam help us. Tomorrow, when all letters finish, I bring to you and Kaiko." He gestured at Grandfather. "After you read, send quick by Clipper before that guy leave New York—"

"All right," Kulani agreed.

Next day Nuhi brought in a pile of pencil-scrawled sheets.

"More from fifty letters," he announced with pride and he placed them on the Office desk before Kulani. "Sure that guy fall down when he get so many fan-mail letters at one time. Never he get so many before, I bet. Make him feel good, like proud movie star—"

Despite herself, Kulani smiled. "I'm sure, Nuhi, Mr. Kingsley has never had a mail like this one. Nor ever will again," she added, glancing at the sheets of yellow Office paper under Nuhi's brown hand.

With the inborn reluctance of Polynesians to intrude on others in momentous passages of life, Nuhi tiptoed out to re-join his fellows sitting on the lawn around the ashes of a bon-fire they'd kept up during the night for the council and letter writing.

Kulani straightened her sagging shoulders and Grandfather shifted his position and waited. Kulani scanned the communi-cations before her then made a slight sound, between sobbing and laughter.

"Father, listen. The dears, they've tried every trick . . . ca-jolery, bribery. . . . Anyone with an ounce of sentiment would capitulate. My children, my brown and yellow chil-dren—" She broke off, cleared her throat and said again, "Father, listen:

"Mr. Kingsley:
Why for you make this humbugger kind? Little more fifty

years I cook at Kilohana, but if you kick out Kulani I go away
quick with her.

Ah Sam.

Mr. Kingsley:

Shame my eye hearing all this bad-kind things peoples talking on you. I tink sure gossip-lie. Swell guy like you with
planty money never stealing away land from under feet of
lone womans and two small girls.

Your friend in hopes.
Nuhi.

Mr. Kingsley:

Mite you wanting sum few hundred more $ for boost price
offered you for Kilohana. This natural kinds and us guys on
the ranch—Hawaiians, Japanese, Chinese and two Portugee,
have big discussion on this matters. Long time us talk las
nite, and cum to conclusion us all wote the same ticket—like
Politicks mans say. Every fella agree give you half his pay for
two years. That add up meny more hundred $. Us glad for
do same. This help Kulani and us to keep this place and giv
you som ectra cash so you can *Letta-Go-Your-Blouse* and
make hot-style Whoopee in New York.

Aloha.
Your old fren
Na-lua-hine.

Grandfather was shaking with helpless laughter. "Kulani,"
he boomed, "you can't make me believe that right won't tri-
umph—yet! I'd like to keep those letters on file to make me
laugh when I feel low. Send 'em off by Clipper! That's the
modern note to a fidelity that belongs to another day!"

CHAPTER XIX

THANKSGIVING

BUT MR. KINGSLEY ARRIVED ON THE DATE HE SPECIFIED. HE was a tall, gaunt man with cold eyes. Ill health had carved deep lines into his face and the way he spoke and moved attested to the way he had lived. The millions he had wrung from life, ruthlessly, had given him no happiness, peace or particular pleasure, except an icy satisfaction and consciousness of power.

The ranch people acted as if he did not exist. They passed him silently, with averted eyes. Pam's cold animosity, behind her restrained behavior, would have disconcerted any normal person. She watched him from her wheelchair in a calculating way, far too old for her years. Emily shunned him and a sort of horror filled her face when she had to sit down at meals with him that made any sort of conversation difficult.

"Of course, Mrs. Garland," Mr. Kingsley said in his chilled way, one day when he and his two secretaries were going through the books, "it's quite obvious that you all regard my taking possession of Kilohana as a major catastrophe."

Kulani made no reply.

"My reception here smacks of a cheap melodrama. Enter— the villain!" His tone mocked her.

"My people—"

"Your people?" Mr. Kingsley interrupted. "You mean these Hawaiians and Japanese?" His voice threw the words from him.

"Yes," Kulani answered with simple dignity. "I doubt, in spite of your millions, whether sixty people of assorted nationalities would get up in a body and follow you if you left a place, determined to share your future—whatever it might be."

Fred Blake, one of Mr. Kingsley's secretaries, a personable young man, darted an amazed look at her. "You mean," he asked in incredulous tones, "that all the laborers will go away when you do?"

"Yes."

"Why?" Mr. Kingsley demanded. "I'll pay them the same wages you do, more if their work warrants it. I intend to modernize this ranch, make it a show-place in Hawaii. These obsolete buildings will be torn down, the house remodelled—"

"Answering the first part of your remark," Kulani went on firmly, "my people will go because they love me as I love them."

"Love, Mrs. Garland, is a much over-rated emotion," Mr. Kingsley observed, his voice tinged with scorn.

"That is what *you* believe," Kulani retorted. Her steady eyes held his. "What, actually, do you know of—love?"

Mr. Kingsley studied her with a masked expression.

"Suppose we leave that. I'm interested in your statement that all the men will go when you do and intend to put it to the test."

"Why don't you? They'll all be in about sunset for tomorrow's orders. You propose to offer them higher pay, I take it?"

"Precisely."

Her laughter filled the Office. "Go ahead. You'll see—and perhaps learn something from the experience."

When long shadows began slanting across the lawn and mystery started walking across the sea, the *paniolos* began trailing in. Kane appeared, pushing Pam. Taking the chair by the wheels, Pia and Kimmo swung it up the steps and the old man thanked them with a nod of his grizzled head and guided it to Pam's accustomed place beside her mother's desk. Pam stared through Mr. Kingsley and he moved irritably.

When supplies had been handed out and orders issued for the next day's work, Kulani looked at her men. "Mr. Kingsley has some words to say to you," she announced.

No one stirred.

"Perhaps if you tell them in Hawaiian, Mrs. Garland, they'll understand better," he suggested. "Tell them that any man who remains here with me will be paid twice what he's getting, after I take possession."

"They understand English as well as I do," Kulani said. "You heard what he said?" she asked, looking around the room.

"Our ear no hear enny kind he say," Nuhi announced truculently.

"Then I will speak to you for him. Mr. Kingsley wished to tell you all that any of you who choose to stay after he takes possession will get paid double what you're earning now."

Nuhi snorted with indignation. His eyes blazed and, flinging around, he stalked out. The other men looked at Mr. Kingsley with smouldering, hostile stares and followed him.

"You see," Kulani said. "It might also interest you to know that if I hadn't stressed the fact that you must not be harmed in any way, long before this one of the *paniolos* would have roped and dragged you behind his horse until you were convinced that Hawaii was not a healthy place for you to be."

"I would have had the law in!" Kingsley almost shouted.

Kulani looked at him with unmoved eyes.

"Tomorrow I want a man to ride up the mountain with me, so I can look the higher pastures over," Mr. Kingsley announced in his frozen way.

"I wouldn't advise it, unless I went along with you," Kulani's words were charged.

"Why?"

"In the eyes of the *paniolos*, you're a monster driving us away from the thing we love best. More than one person has been lost on Hualalai and no trace of them has ever been found. There are lava pits of unknown depth—"

Mr. Kingsley sprang to his feet. "This is outrageous! Are

you threatening me?"

"On the contrary, I'm *warning* you, for your own safety." Kulani signed to Kane to wheel Pam after her and walked off into the deepening twilight.

"Mother, are you trying to scare him so he'll leave?" Pam asked hopefully, as they went toward the house.

"Far from it, Pam, but," she shivered involuntarily, "I feel violence in the air. It's all around us. I feel as if enemies were behind every bush, waiting to pounce upon us—"

"Mother, you've given me an idea," Pam said excitedly.

"What is it?" Kulani asked in a tired voice.

"I'll tell you later, if you don't mind."

"Has it anything to do with Mr. Kingsley?"

"Of course—"

"Then you've got to tell me. I don't quite trust you, for the first time in my life. You're changed, like the *paniolos*. Under their sorrow at leaving, they're boiling like volcanoes ready to erupt."

"Kulani From Heaven, I'm only going to do a little plain-and-fancy haunting to see if I can't wear him down till he goes away."

"Don't waste your time, Pam," Kulani said curtly. "At heart Mr. Kingsley's just an—adding machine!"

"Well, I'm going to try. It'll give me something to do till, oh Mother—" her voice slid up several notes, "where'll we all go?"

"To stay with Grandfather for the present."

"But the horses and cattle, they're ours—"

"The cattle will have to stay, Pam, but the horses will go with us."

"Oh, Kulani From Heaven," Pam's words were a cry. "I can't—I won't—"

"Nor will I, until the moment is on us!"

Pam started her "plain-and-fancy haunting" the next day. When Mr. Kingsley came on to the back veranda before breakfast, she was waiting in her wheelchair.

"Who's going up Hualalai with you today?" she asked.

"I've decided to postpone it. Your mother's occupied with other matters."

"If I could ride, I'd go along and look out for you."

He glanced at her.

"Have you a little girl, Mr. Kingsley?"

"I'm not married."

"Then you must be lonely. I'll give you one of my *leis*—" She started to remove it.

"*Men*," he stressed the word, "where I come from don't wear flowers!"

"Then they've missed lots of fun. When you're riding, as I used to before my accident, the smell kept coming over the edge of my hat—"

He appeared not to hear.

"Why do you want Kilohana so much?"

He stalked away.

But Pam kept it up. Kept it up until Mr. Kingsley was half crazy. Emily relayed her, when Mr. Kingsley went places where Pam and Kane could not follow.

"If you had children you wouldn't be so hard-hearted as to send a little crippled girl away from the place she loves," Emily announced, "Do you enjoy being a cruel man?"

Mr. Kingsley glared at her.

"I don't see how you expect to be happy here when you're making so many people unhappy by sending them away."

"They all don't have to go."

"Yes, they do," Emily insisted. "When people love each other and are in trouble they have to stick together. I bet sometimes when you're here alone, in your mind you'll hear the *paniolos* singing."

"Singing?"

"Oh," Emily recollected herself. "That's right, they haven't sung since you came."

"Why did they sing before?"

"Because they were so happy."

"Oh, *happy!*" Mr. Kingsley exclaimed, a strange emotion in his frozen eyes.

"Don't you like to be happy, Mr. Kingsley?"

"Happy—" He walked off.

And then it was only a few days before November first. A dreadful deadness descended on everyone when they all realized, fully, that there wasn't any more hoping to do. Grandfather sat all day on the back veranda, staring at the great green hill he could not see, that he would never face again from this favorite spot. Kingsley's two secretaries, Mr. Blake and Mr. Bradley, prowled about the grounds restlessly, when they were not busy.

"This is like a funeral," Mr. Blake remarked.

"The funeral of an era—which has almost passed," Mr. Bradley agreed. "This must have been a jolly place, from all accounts, before *we* came into the picture. I'd like to have heard those beggars singing the way Pam described it to me the other day. What a remarkable little thing she is. Did she show you the array of racing cups on the piano? She won four of them, before she was hurt."

"Pretty tough on her, on all of them, being ousted in this way. The place means so much to them. I wouldn't be in Kingsley's boots, for all his millions. He gets nothing out of life!"

That night the two young men, who shared the blue guest room which Emily and Aunt Dode had occupied, woke up suddenly. From the star-lighted garden singing came, such singing as they'd never heard before or ever wanted to hear again. Beauty was in it, and disaster, and the despairing crying of a race dying before its time.

"Listen!" Mr. Blake said.

"Gosh, it stirs the marrow in my bones. Do you suppose someone has died?" Bradley asked.

"There's a light in the garden, like a bonfire—"

Leaping from their beds, they rushed to the windows. On the sloped lawn under the orange trees, shadowy figures were collected about leaping flames. Voices deep as the sea rose, fell, swelled to a crescendo, fell, rose again. . . .

"Let's go out and see what's up—" Mr. Bradley suggested.

"Maybe we'd better not," Mr. Blake remarked.

"Let's sneak out and take a look-see from the back veranda. We needn't switch on the lights."

"What on earth—" Mr. Blake began.

"Maybe they're making some sort of voodoo spell—"

They tiptoed through the big living room, filled with packing cases, and crept on to the back veranda.

"Gosh, I wish they'd stop," Mr. Blake said in a whisper, after a few minutes. "It sends chills along my spine."

Mr. Bradley nodded. "It makes me feel as if all the sorrows, despairs and longings in life were loose in the night."

A door opened somewhere in the house, a light was switched on. Mr. Kingsley in a bathrobe came stalking down the hall. His sparse gray hair was rumpled and standing on end like a wild hog's bristles. His eyes were hot and angry and the lines in his gaunt face looked like scars. Seeing his secretaries, he halted.

"Go stop that caterwauling!" he burst out. "How a man's expected to sleep—"

"Perhaps it wouldn't be wise, Mr. Kingsley," Mr. Bradley suggested. "We aren't technically in possession for three days and haven't the right to interfere."

"Then get hold of Mrs. Garland—"

"I can't very well go to her room and wake her up when she works so hard—"

Mr. Kingsley grew white about the nostrils with anger. He glared at the circle of light with shadowy singing figures crouched around it, then exclaimed in shocked tones, "The child's there! Pam—and that other one, Emily—"

Footsteps sounded in the hall and the three on the veranda turned. Grandfather and Kulani were coming through the house. Kulani's face was expressionless but tears were falling silently down her cheeks. When they came out Mr. Kingsley said in smothered tones, "Stop them, can't you, stop them! I can't stand it. What are they—*doing?*"

"You'll *have* to stand it, Mr. Kingsley," Kulani said. "They're composing a farewell chant to Kilohana. Since time immemorial it has been a Polynesian custom to commemorate victories and disasters with chants. The history of the Pacific was not written, it was sung from the hearts of its people and handed down in musical form from generation to generation."

Mr. Kingsley ran a distracted hand through his hair. Blake and Bradley moved unhappily, as people will when they've intruded unintentionally into a situation where they don't belong. The music rose again in a heart-piercing wail. Kingsley recoiled from the sound as though he had been struck.

Grandfather and Kulani stood silently, with locked arms, listening to the chanting, like persons lost in a deep dream from which there is no awakening. Miss Williams stole out and stood beside them, for during the months she had cared for Pam she had become a part of the family.

"What—what are they *saying?*" Mr. Kingsley asked through clenched teeth, when he could endure the singing no longer.

"Do you really want to know, do you really want me to translate?" Kulani asked.

"Yes," he said violently.

"Very well." She listened intently, until she had established

the words and rhythm in her mind, then she sang with her
people—under her breath.

> We, who must go from Thee,
>   Kilohana,
> Leave our hearts buried here!
>   É. É. *Auwe!*
>   Kilohana É.

> As our voyaging Fathers sung
>   before us,
> When they launched their canoes
>   on the trackless sea,
> 'This is the road my body goes—
> But my heart stays here, remembering!'
>   É! É! *Auwe*
>   Kilohana É!

Mr. Kingsley stared at her with blank, terrible eyes, then fled
to his room.

Next morning, while they were at breakfast, a sharp earthquake hit the house. Mr. Kingsley, who had hardly spoken,
raised haunted eyes and froze in his seat. His secretaries grew
pale. Before anyone could speak, another violent trembling
shook the mountain.

"Well, maybe the long-delayed eruption from Mauna Loa
is really going to come to a head at last," Grandfather remarked.
"It's a year overdue. It should be a big one."

"Are eruptions frequent in Hawaii?" Mr. Kingsley asked in

a strained voice, after the ground stopped shaking.

Grandfather nodded. "More frequent than in any other spot on earth, if you discount the sputterings of Vesuvius. Once all three of these mountains were active. Now the lava exit is centered in Mauna Loa. Perhaps because Mauna Loa is so large, it has two craters. Kilauea, the tourist crater, is on its flank about 4060 feet above sea-level. Mokuaweoweo," he rolled out the awesome word, "at the summit, puts on the real show. Every five to seven years, sometimes more often, it erupts in a big way. Geologically, Mauna Loa is the largest individual mountain mass in the world. It rises 18,000 feet from ocean bottom to sea-level and over 13,000 feet above the sea. When the summit crater becomes active, business of all sorts in Hawaii is virtually at a standstill. Everyone who can possibly arrange to get off rushes by plane and boat to watch the spectacle."

Another angry shudder ran through the island.

"Some people," Mr. Kingsley remarked in frigid tones, "have queer ideas of pleasure. Personally, I've no wish to see a mountain erupt."

"If you plan to live in Hawaii, you'll be compelled to do so whether or not you want it," Grandfather boomed. "An eruption is something that beggars description. The great red glare in the sky, the roar of escaping gasses, the grinding of red lava streams pouring down the dark sides of the mountain. When the stream hits the sea, the whole world seems to recoil and a steam-jet, like a white plume, springs up and the ocean boils for miles."

Pam watched the tense lines of Kingsley's face and nudged Emily gleefully.

When the grown-ups went off, she gripped her adopted sister's hand.

"I hope earthquakes come, flocks of them that'll scare the wits out of him. Then, maybe, he'll go away."

Emily jumped up and down, her face radiant.

Around noon a series of major jolts shook the island. Rebuilt stone walls were shaken down, two of the water tanks pitched over. Mr. Kingsley prowled around restlessly, like a trapped beast, and Pam and the *paniolos* watched hopefully, the same thought in every heart.

"I tink sure if plenty big *oni-onis* come and lava come out that *haole-kapulu*—trashy whiteman—run away," Nuhi chuckled and turned a hand-spring or two.

As the afternoon wore on the earthquakes grew more violent and frequent. They were accompanied by thudding jolts, as lava thumped against the crust of the earth, trying to break through. In the spells of silence between the shocks, the hissing sound of molten rock and gasses surging through underground fissures, deep in the earth, was plainly audible.

"Well, everyone will have to sleep in the garden tonight," Kulani announced, when she came down from the milking. "The foundations of the house have not been properly braced since the last series of quakes we had a few months ago. Eruptions are a costly business, Mr. Kingsley. Damages from the last lot of earthquakes totalled in the neighborhood of sixty thousand dollars." She watched Mr. Kingsley as she talked.

His face looked as though it had been hewed from marble with an ax. Another shock jiggled the four thousand square miles of the island. Mr. Kingsley tensed.

"Don't you like earthquakes?" Pam asked.

"Like them!"

"They're exciting—" Pam insisted.

"Exciting!" And he stalked off.

Then, after forty-eight hours, the threatened eruption took on a menacing note. Even when the ground was apparently quiet, a person was conscious of the island toiling on. Angry shudderings, savage jolts followed each other in rapid succession and the underground roaring was louder. Mr. Kingsley was like a half-crazy person and his secretaries, although interested, were obviously ill at ease.

The second evening, while they were dining under the orange trees, the phone rang and Kulani went to answer it. When she returned there was a curious, concerned expression on her face.

"It seems as though we're in for an eruption out of the usual line. That was Doctor Arlen, the scientist at the Kilauea Observatory. Three days ago he had seismographs set up at various points of the island, trying to locate the center of greatest tension in the earth's crust, so he can tell where the lava is most likely to break through."

Everyone's eyes were fastened on her still face. She glanced at a slip of paper in her hand on which she had hurriedly scribbled.

"He read me his report, which goes to the Department of Geology in Washington. I'll give you the gist of it. The seismographs set up at the north, south, east and west points of Hawaii registered a total of 2095 individual quakes, small and great, in five days—"

Mr. Kingsley stiffened as if someone had run a spear through him.

"Listen Father," Kulani went on, and read hurriedly.

"In the quality of growing to a maximum from tremors to bumping shocks and from bumping shocks to oscillations of longer periods this seismic crisis is unlike anything experienced to date. Therefore it seems probable that the present Hawaiian crisis marks the shift of magma from the Mauna Loa center toward—Hualalai!"

Grandfather started imperceptibly in his chair.

"The fact is," Kulani said in a controlled tone, "Doctor Arlen's rechecking of his seismographs shows that the main Epicenter," she glanced at the mainlanders, "the spot of greatest tension," she explained, "is some miles above us, on Hualalai, where there's an old fault. He advises us to get out of here as fast as possible."

Kingsley tore out of his chair, his secretaries were livid.

"Don't get in a panic," Kulani said. "I'll organize things as quickly as possible, then order the cars."

"Get things *organized!*" Kingsley shouted. "What things? Let's clear out of here before we're blown up!"

"Have you no sense of responsibility?" Kulani asked. "There are sixty-seven people, besides ourselves, to be taken care of. Gates have to be opened for the stock and horses turned out of the stables before we go."

Grandfather got to his feet and his broad figure bulked huge and solid in the glow of the lanterns Ah Sam had strung through the orange trees. Standing there, he was kin to the island beneath his feet, one of the tie-ribs of Kulani's world, shaken, but undaunted.

"Kulani, what can I do to help you?" he asked.

"Stay with Pam. People mustn't be frightened. Possibly there's no immediate danger and the lava will come out of its usual vent. However, Doctor Arlen's a scientist and knows his facts and if he urges us to leave, we must. I can't risk staying when I'm responsible for the safety of so many lives. Emily dear, run up the hill and tell the *paniolos* I want them—*wiki-wiki*—at once!"

Emily was shaking so she could hardly move but forced her legs to support her. "Okay, Mother," she said in a small, dry voice and sped off.

"*GET ME A CAR!*" Mr. Kingsley's voice rose to a hoarse scream, "*I'M GETTING OUT OF HERE.* Only madmen would want to live in such a place! You can—*HAVE YOUR BLASTED RANCH!*"

Kulani's face, which had been intent and thoughtful, changed, suddenly. "You mean—" she began, as if she could not believe what her ears had heard.

"Exactly that! You can have Kilohana! Wild horses couldn't compel me to stay here—after this experience. *GET ME A CAR!*" His voice rose to a hysterical note again.

"I'll get you one—in nothing flat!" Kulani half sobbed and started running toward the big barn where the cars and trucks were garaged, as if she intended establishing a marathon record for the whole world.

But she did not get there. . . . An earthquake seized the island that made all which had preceded it seem like nothing. The island humped upward, arched its back, and shook about as if it had gone insane. Gardens and buildings were plunged into darkness as the lanterns were switched off the trees. Great hollow thuds jarred the night, as tank after tank was flung over. Four thousand miles of solid earth strained, pulled. Roars of avalanches ripping out the forested slopes of the green hill rent the atmosphere. Stock careened about the pastures. Trees lashed about. People called to each other. And behind all the nearer noises was the terrible sound of solid old lava beds splitting like melting ice floes, and grinding against each other. Stifled screams, the doleful howling of dogs, sounded behind the greater noises of the night. People lay flat on the ground, gripping the grass.

Then, with long, exhausted shudderings, the island abandoned its futile efforts. The earth steadied but the crashing of splintered forest trees and the rattle of boulders slithering down gashed hillsides continued. Dogs' howls dropped to whimpers, as they crawled closer to their masters for comfort, and birds shrieked as they circled overhead, reluctant to settle down in still-trembling boughs.

"Anyone hurt?" Kulani called, sitting up.

"I'm all right, Mother. I'm over here," Pam called back in a rather shaky voice. "My chair got knocked over." Then she gave a little wild, half-strangled cry. "Oh Kulani From Heaven,

I'm—I'm crawling to you. I feel like a weak bug," she laughed hysterically, "but my legs—move!"

Kulani lunged in the direction of her voice. "Pam! Oh dear God thank you for—everything! My child, the ranch—" But behind the tears in her voice was the sound of angels chanting.

She found Pam and they clung to one another, but only for a completely happy moment. Then Kulani's mind snapped into line.

"Now we must get out. Quickly! A shock of that magnitude will tear anything loose!"

Suddenly the dark was filled with running figures, women, children, men. Kulani was engulfed in a seething mass of appalled humanity. "Be quiet!" she commanded. "I'm here. I'll take care of you! Are you not my people?"

Voices subsided, babies and children were hushed. Ah Sam and the *paniolos* scattered to get extra supplies of flashlights and lanterns, always kept ready for earthquake times.

"Pia, Kimmo, Pili, get the trucks. Nuhi, take the Packard and get Mr. Kingsley and his secretaries away. Women and children go next. Opiopio and Mahiai loose the thoroughbreds, if the stable isn't down and they're loose already. Kane and Na-lua-hine stay with Emily and Pam. Eole and Pilipo open the gates so the stock—no the stone walls are all flat so they're gone." Kulani spoke a little breathlessly but her words rang out like the commanding notes of a bugle.

Pam looked at her mother in the lantern-light. She was thinking for all of them, strong, steady, even in the face of threatened destruction. She was a great Chief, she was Kulani From

Heaven! Pam moved her foot a little and gladness ran through her like a silver wire. Soon she'd be riding again, soon she could help her mother, be her right hand once more!

Men were streaking off to obey Kulani's commands but Nuhi did not move. "Hurry, Nuhi, get these *haoles* out—"

"I no like take him!" Nuhi said belligerently.

"Take him! He's leaving—for good!"

"*Welakahao!*" Nuhi shouted, charging for the barn.

Engines roared, cars and trucks rolled out. Mr. Kingsley sprinted for the Packard, his flying legs looking like an ungainly grasshopper's in the light of moving lanterns. Women and children piled into the trucks, dogs whined and looked up, eager to go.

Kulani oversaw the loading. Nuhi rolled off. Just as the third truck was ready to pull for safety, Nuhi came running back on foot.

"No can take car out!" he cried in a terrible voice. "Landslide from the big hill wipe out the road!"

Kulani's face turned pale. "Where are Mr. Kingsley and the young men?"

"Come back but no can run quick like me. I speak us get horses—"

"They're running loose everywhere," Kulani gasped.

"Hard for catch 'em in the dark, they so scare from all the *oni-onis*," Nuhi agreed, glancing involuntarily in the direction of Hualalai.

"No matter, us try. Some old fellas no run very far," Pili broke in and half a dozen men rushed toward the corrals for ropes. Others found saddles and opened the gates leading to the horse pasture. Pam and Emily sat by their *paniolos*.

"No scare, no scare," Kane soothed. "Kulani never let any bad-kind come to us. Soon get horses and then all man go. Maybe lava no come out till tomorrow."

"Of course it won't," Pam said. "Look Kane, look at me move my foot! I don't know how it happened, but when I fell—"

"No matter, okay now," Kane beamed through tears that spilled unashamedly down his cheeks. "Swell, swell! I too happy."

Mr. Kingsley came panting up. "Get me a horse, get me out of here," he said in a voice all out of shape from horror and shattered nerves.

"Get hold of yourself," Kulani ordered shortly. "We're doing the best we can. The first horse that's caught, you can have—"

Then the heavy darkness, lighted only by the feeble rays of lanterns and the long beams of flashlights, lifted suddenly as a terrific roar sounded. The night staggered and recoiled. Everyone wheeled and faced Hualalai. Behind its dark, gigantic shape, far to the south, there was a red glare in the sky and a titanic smoke column was poking and thrusting higher and higher toward the stars. The reflection from it changed the world to a bowl of bronze and threw a dull and frightful shadow across the sea.

There was a paralyzed silence, then the Hawaiians began calling in relieved voices, "Mauna Loa! Mauna Loa!"

"Get-me-out-of-here! Get-me-out-of-here!" Mr. Kingsley kept shouting hoarsely.

"The lava has found its right exit," Kulani told him. "We're perfectly safe here—"

"*I won't stay!*" Mr. Kingsley yelled.

"Okay, okay, I catch one horse and take you away my own self." Nuhi gloated, starting for the pasture.

"Get horses for his secretaries, too." Kulani called after him. "Then we'll all go up the hill and watch Mauna Loa."

"It seems odd, after what we've just experienced," Fred Blake remarked, "but I'd give my eye-teeth to stay with you and see the eruption."

"You'll be able to see it tomorrow night from Hilo, while Mr. Kingsley waits for the steamer," Kulani said.

"I'm chartering a plane to take me to Honolulu. I won't stay on this terrible island an instant longer than I have to," Mr. Kingsley choked.

When Nuhi came with the horses, Kulani gave him a few instructions, then signed to Mr. Kingsley and his secretaries to mount.

"We'll think of you sometimes in this awesomely beautiful place that you love so much," Mr. Bradley said as he shook hands with Kulani. "I'm glad things turned out the way they have for you, and for all of these people," he gestured at the groups of Hawaiians, Japanese and whites standing on the lawn.

"Thank you," Kulani said smiling. "Kilohana is very dear to us all." Then she turned to Mr. Kingsley. "Where shall I have your things sent?"

"The Royal Hawaiian will reach us for a few days," Kingsley snapped. "We'll be taking the first Clipper back to the main-land."

"One arrives from the Orient in three days," Kulani told him. "If I can't get your stuff out of here by then, I'll ship it to New York."

"That'll do, anything'll do, let's get going!" Kingsley mut-tered.

"Good riddance!" Pam remarked to Emily, watching Nuhi and the other three riders going off into the red glare of the night. Emily giggled.

Kimmo swaggered over. "I the bull of Kilohana, Pam," he announced, tensing his biceps proudly and displaying his brawn. "I carry you up the hill for look at Mauna Loa."

"Okay, Kimmo," Pam agreed jubilantly. Once more she was one of them, sharing life with them, instead of being a chained invalid. Her limbs were weak and wobbly, but they had feeling in them. "Oh, Kulani From Heaven," she sang out. "I'm so happy I could burst."

"Aren't we all?" Grandfather cried in ringing tones.

"Well, now that all our real *pilikeas*—troubles—are over, except for the matter of most of our water tanks being down again, the house badly damaged, stock mixed up," Kulani laughed gaily, "let's go up and pay our respects to old Mauna Loa. She may have raised havoc around here but her antics drove Kingsley away and kept Kilohana for us."

"Sure, sure," everyone chorused, "swell us all go up and look

Mauna Loa."

When they were seated in the dip between the green hill and rough Hualalai, now strangely still, the full glory of the spectacle burst on them and fears of the past hours were forgotten in the majesty of what they saw.

From the summit of Mauna Loa a smoke column reared some twenty thousand feet into the sky, transforming the heavens into a red-hot oven. Two lava flows were already making their way down the sides of the mountain, sending out livid red tentacles to gather up forests and grasslands and swallow them. Behind the gigantic rivers of fire a series of new cones which had broken through the crust, were shooting out white-hot, incandescent boulders, while streams of liquid lava played back and forth like giant fire hoses moved by invisible hands.

"Isn't it—beautiful?" Emily gasped in astonishment. "I thought it would be terrible."

"Mauna Loa in full eruption is one of the most marvelous sights on earth," Kulani announced, staring at the big mountain in the south.

Occasionally deep roarings and shattering noises reached them, like charges of distant artillery.

"I didn't realize volcanoes made so much noise," Emily remarked in a slightly awed voice.

Grandfather chuckled. "Old Mauna Loa has a lot to say about matters when she Letta-goes-her-blouse."

For a while everyone was silent, watching. One flow was moving slowly forward toward the huge waste land between the three mountains, the other was making its way toward the sea. Forests smoked at their edges, sending up bluish, twisted vapors, while splendid green, pink and lavender lightings tore the smoke column into twisted shapes. When they ceased it re-assembled itself and went on poking upward, as if it intended to reach the stars.

"Too much land lose when lava come out," old Ah Sam, remarked, his eyes on the red serpents writhing down the mountain.

"Lava not bad," old Kane insisted, "it make Hawaii."

Then he lifted his hand and signed at the *paniolos*. Taking a deep breath he began a solemn chant, which after a moment, his comrades took up.

> Big Mountain—Mauna Loa!
> Great Dome of Fire,
> Grant us this, our heart's desire,
> Spare us from the warmth within you,
> Mauna Loa.
> O hear our prayer!
>
> For all the day-time
> We'll spend in play-time
> With songs and laughter
> We'll pass the golden hours away.
> O Mauna Loa,
> Hear our prayer!

Pam sat beside Emily, between Grandfather and Kulani,

gazing across the violently lighted miles at the volcano exploding into the sky. Her little face looked like a white star in the red light. In her eyes was deep contentment. She looked at the ranch people clustered on the slope of the hill, then reaching out took Kulani's hand. Kulani flashed a quick happy smile at her, then they listened to the solemn words the *paniolos* were singing, which sounded like muffled drums echoing down the ages. When the last line of the hula ended, old Kane stood up and saluted the volcano.

"Thank you, mighty Dome of Fire," he called out in Hawaiian. "Your fury drove our enemy away. Kilohana is ours forever. You gave your children back their Paradise! Thank you, Mauna Loa!"